T0245488

BY CAITLIN SCHNEIDERHAN
Stranger Things: Flight of Icarus
Medici Heist

FLIGHT OF ICARUS

FLIGHT OF
ICARUS

CAITLIN
SCHNEIDERHAN

RANDOM HOUSE

WORLDS

NEW YORK

Published in the United States by Random House Worlds,
an imprint of Random House, a division of
Penguin Random House LLC, New York.

RANDOM HOUSE is a registered trademark,
and RANDOM HOUSE WORLDS and colophon
are trademarks of Penguin Random House LLC.

Hardback ISBN 978-0-593-72324-1
International edition ISBN 978-0-593-72467-5
Ebook ISBN 978-0-593-72325-8

Printed in the United States of America on acid-free paper

randomhousebooks.com

2 4 6 8 9 7 5 3 1

First Edition

Book design by Elizabeth A. D. Eno

*For all the little lost sheep
and the people who give them
a place to belong*

FLIGHT OF ICARUS

Chapter One

"**W**ell. You're dead."

The kid gapes at me across the table, really showing off his sparkly orthodontic hardware. "No, I'm not."

"You took on a kraken by yourself. You're fucking dead, man."

Stan kicks me in the shin. "Can you cut him a break? He's a freshman."

"He's been playing for almost a year now. Hey, freshman—"

"Gareth," mumbles Gareth from somewhere beneath his plume of puffy, wavy hair.

"How many hit points you got?"

He mutters something I can't make out, but I'm pretty sure it rhymes with *Nero.*

"That's what I thought. So let me walk you through the next part." I lean forward, one hand on either side of my DM screen. "It's the final swipe of the monster's tentacles that does you in.

Agony crashes through you, overwhelming your willpower. And your lungs pay the price."

Ronnie throws an eraser at my head. "Jesus Christ, Eddie," she says, but I can hear the laughter in her voice.

"On instinct, you try to draw breath. But you're two dozen feet beneath the surface of the Solnor Ocean, and the rest of your party is all the way back on shore. Which means there is no one to save you as the sea fills your throat."

"That's sick," says Dougie, watching me with wide, awe-struck eyes.

"And there is no one to watch as your body twitches one final time and sinks, lifeless, into the black depths of the unknown. So ends the tale of Illian the Unvanquished, half-elf paladin and Champion of the Lost Lands."

Applause springs up around the table, a respectable smattering from my players. Ronnie and Dougie are the most enthusiastic, Dougie even surging to his feet in a much appreciated display of approval. Gareth, in contrast, sinks low in his chair, poking at his D20 with a dejected finger.

"This is bullshit," he says.

"What is up your *ass*, Gareth?" Dougie demands. "You got a crazy Munson death monologue. That's, like, worth its weight in gold."

Gareth's skinny shoulders are up around his ears, but he still turns an impressive glare on Dougie. "Am I supposed to be happy? He killed me!"

"You're not special, he's trying to kill all of us!"

"*Okay.*" I hold up both hands, trying to fend off whatever explosion is brewing here. "As your humble dungeon master, would you gentlemen allow me the pleasure of your shutting the hell up?"

They shut the hell up. Which gives me just enough time to meet each of my players' eyes in turn . . . while I scramble around, figuring out what the hell I'm gonna do next.

Hellfire membership isn't exactly bursting at the seams; counting myself, there're only six of us. Ronnie and I have both been members since we walked in the door together the first week of ninth grade, and even though Dougie had resisted "joining nerd club," a bare month of listening to us recite inside jokes from our Hellfire sessions had him almost *begging* for a seat at the table.

Stan, a junior, had come along the following year, though his attendance is . . . hit-or-miss. His family's got it in their brains that D & D comes straight from Satan himself, and that even *touching* dice with more than six sides would be enough to send their precious baby boy straight into the flames of eternal damnation. Stan tries his best to get around this by spinning stories about weekly algebra tutoring and by giving Ronnie all his Hellfire shit to keep at her place so his snooping mom can't find it. But even with all this cloak-and-dagger maneuvering, Stan winds up missing one game out of three.

Sophomore Jeff has been part of Hellfire for two years now, but it feels like longer. He'd been playing with his older brothers before he started at Hawkins High, and he knows almost as much about the game as I do. He definitely knows more about playing bass than I do, which is why he'd been a welcome addition to Corroded Coffin, rounding out the sound in a way that Ronnie, Dougie, and I hadn't been able to on our own.

And then there's little freshman Gareth, who's glaring at the laminated chart of U.S. presidents on the wall like he wants to start using it for target practice.

He better not. We can't afford to land on the shit list of another teacher, not when so many of them already refuse to share space with "that Satanic cult." As it stands, every Monday, I start the process of wheeling and dealing with the small handful of teachers with the smallest slice of sympathy to our cause, bargaining for the right to roll a couple of dice in their classrooms once the final bell rings at 2:50 on Wednesday afternoon. And every Monday, as I go through the motions of asking about Mrs. Debbs's upcoming retirement and cleaning chalkboards in Mr. Vick's lab, I ask myself the same question.

Why am I doing this?

I've never been able to answer it. But I'm still here, week after week. Isn't that the definition of insanity?

"Maybe you *should* be happy, freshman," I say. "You learned a valuable lesson today."

I can feel Ronnie watching me. She's twirling a pencil between her fingers, so fast that it blurs. I don't look over at her.

Gareth snorts. "How valuable can it be if I won't be around to use it?"

Some of Gareth's angst slams into focus. But it's not something I can deal with here, in front of all these watching eyes. "Well, boys and girls," I say, straightening up, "I think that just about wraps up our session here today." There's a chorus of groans, mostly from Stan and Dougie. "We'll regroup next week, as our surviving adventurers journey deep into the labyrinth of . . . *Ralishaz the Mad.*"

Gareth is packed almost as soon as I finish speaking, throwing all his shit into his backpack as fast as he can. He shoves his chair back with an ungodly squeal of aluminum legs on linoleum and stomps to the door, throwing it open with a crash that rattles the wall.

Dougie sucks his teeth, watching the door swing shut behind Gareth. "This kid *sucks.*"

"Shut up, Dougie," Ronnie comments calmly. She raises an eyebrow at me in silent question, but I'm already on my feet and sidling around the table.

"Same time," I lecture the room over my shoulder as I stalk out the door. "If you're late, you get the Illian treatment. *Comprende?*" A chorus of *sure*s and *whatever*s sweeps me into the hallway.

Gareth is already a sea of lockers away and moving fast. "Hey! Freshman!"

For a second, I think the kid isn't going to stop. But then he does, turning to face me with an eye roll and a sigh. "What."

"You got somewhere to be?"

"My mom's picking me up in like minus-two minutes, so yeah." He glowers up at me, adjusting his backpack on his shoulder. As he does it, the hem of his shirt catches on the strap, pulling just enough for me to catch sight of something purple and painful spreading across his side. "You already kicked me out of your club. What else do you want from me?"

"Whoa whoa whoa, who said anything about kicking you out?"

"You did. When you *killed me.*"

"So?" I ask.

"So . . ." Gareth is starting to look more uncertain now, shifting from foot to foot. "So Illian's gone. So I'm gone."

"So you make a new character."

Gareth blinks at me, like he honestly never considered that possibility before. "I do?"

"You think I'm gonna let someone crazy enough to tangle with a kraken walk away from this party? No way." I lean in closer, conspiratorial. "Those other assholes won't last one millisecond in Ralishaz's labyrinth without your guts."

"Is it gonna be bad?"

"It's gonna be the *worst,*" I say, and laugh at Gareth's aluminum grin. "We just gotta get you set up with another character. You free tomorrow after school?"

"I have to ask my mom," Gareth says, but the force of his nodding makes it clear that, mom's approval or not, he'll be there.

There's a distant *honk* of a car horn from the direction of the school parking lot. Someone's losing their patience. "Shit," Gareth says. "I gotta—"

"Absolutely, dude."

The kid takes a few running steps down the hall, and then stops, like he can't help himself. "You're sure, right?" he falters. "I can come back?"

"As long as you wanna be in Hellfire, you can be in Hellfire."

He nods, gaze turned inside, like he's making himself memorize those words. "Okay," he says, and then he's scurrying toward the school's front entrance. I watch after him until he's out of sight.

"Wow. And I left my Kleenex at home."

Ronnie is behind me, arms wrapped around an overstuffed Trapper Keeper. She pretends to dab her eyes as I walk over and lets out a laughing yell as I shoulder-check her off-balance.

"Careful!" She shoves me back. "Stan's gonna be such a dick if I drop this thing."

"You got something to say, Ecker?"

"The only thing I would even *dream* of saying is 'can I get a ride?'"

I roll my eyes. "This is the last time."

"Last time," Ronnie promises, following me toward the parking lot.

It's not the last time and we both know it, but Ronnie's and my little script is the foundation of our friendship. She bums tiny favors off me; I get to pretend like I'm responsible; we both benefit. It's been that way since I semi-inherited Dad's van at the beginning of junior year. It's been that way since the day we first met.

"*What are you doing?*" she'd asked. Even at eight, she'd been taller than I was, looming over my shoulder in her beaten-in overalls like the ghost of a tiny farmer.

What I'd been doing was feeling sorry for myself. A call from an old drinking buddy had had my dad running out the door with a couple half-finished promises about "back before you know it," and "you know how to work the stove, right?" I'd spent the night watching the drive for him, waiting, waiting, waiting, until I'd fallen asleep where I sat, slumped against the window.

It had been the first time he'd fallen off the face of the planet—first in a long string of next times. But I hadn't realized that then. Instead, I'd just scraped around the empty house for two days, living off stale peanut butter sandwiches and flat pop, until my uncle Wayne had realized what was up and came to get me, swooping me back to live with him at his trailer "*'til Al gets his head out of his ass and turns up.*"

I'd hated it at the trailer park, mostly because it meant that Dad wouldn't know where to find me when he *did* come back. But Wayne would not believe me when I stubbornly insisted that a third grader was more than capable of taking care of himself, and so I was stuck in this dusty old lot with nothing to do except dig holes in the nearby woods.

And then this other kid had turned up.

Ronnie, it turned out, had just moved into the trailer park too. She was living with her granny because her dad was dead and her mom had gotten sick and started talking to the walls. She had brown hair and brown eyes, and people thought we were siblings when they saw us together. And when I told her I was digging a hole to China, she asked if she could help me out because she didn't have anything else to do.

Later I found out this was a lie, and that she'd passed up watching *M*A*S*H* with Granny Ecker in order to hang out with me. But in the moment I was too busy having a friend for the first time in a billion years to suspect anything. And even when my dad had rolled back into Hawkins, telling stories about some asshole in Kentucky who owed him money and taking me back to the house, Ronnie and I stayed close.

Everyone else at Hellfire has moms picking them up after school and framed family photos hanging over their fireplaces. It helps to have someone around whose life wasn't stamped from a picture-perfect suburban cookie cutter.

"Home?" I ask as I start the van. These days, Ronnie's tall enough that her head nearly scrapes the roof, and the brim of her corduroy ball cap fills in those last few centimeters for her.

She nods, stowing the Trapper Keeper in the footwell. "Granny wants me around for dinner."

"But you're still coming tonight, right?"

The punch she lands on my arm is hard enough to bruise. "You worry too much."

We keep bickering as the van chugs down the road toward the outskirts of Hawkins. It's comfortable, a routine back-and-forth we've done a million times. Once, when we were thirteen, I'd thought for a second that this meant we were maybe dating—having a friend who knew me so well had felt like it had to be special in that way. After sitting on this revelation for a sweaty few weeks, I'd decided that the only option was to make a move, to plant one on Ronnie, to make it official.

I hadn't been prepared for the way she'd yelped and scrambled away from me as I'd leaned in. *"What the hell is wrong with you, Munson?!"* she'd squawked, and all I'd been able to do was stammer and flush and run away like a coward. But a few days later, once everything had calmed down and we'd both felt a little less like the world was ending, Ronnie had explained to me that it wasn't just me she didn't like that way. She didn't think she'd ever have a crush on anybody, and was that okay with me?

I'd considered it for a moment. *"Does that mean we can still be friends?"*

She'd punched my arm in the same place she always did. *"Don't be an idiot."*

Now I just groan as Ronnie plants her feet up on my dashboard. "Are you serious?"

"I don't want to step on Stan's thingie. And it's not my fault that your van is too small."

"My van is not the problem. You've just got freakish legs."

"Let me tell you a secret about these freakish legs," Ronnie says. She still hasn't put her feet down, and I know a losing battle when I see one, so I don't say anything. "In four months? They are gonna be walking into their new apartment in *New. York. City.*"

I almost slam the brakes. "No."

"Yep."

"You got the scholarship?"

Ronnie grins. "NYU class of '88, baby. *Full. Ride.*"

Now I do slam on the brakes, fishtailing the car to the side of the road. "Holy shit. Holy shit! When—"

"Last night."

"Last night?! Why didn't you tell me earlier?"

"I'm telling you now."

I know why she didn't tell me earlier. "Hey. You know I'm happy for you, right?"

Ronnie just shrugs. "I know," she says, but I'm not buying it.

Because Ronnie and I are supersimilar, right? Same broken homes, same secondhand clothes, same haircut. Same trailer park. But there is one major difference between us. There always has been.

Veronica Ecker is going places. She's headed to college, she's headed to law school, she's getting the hell out of Indiana.

Eddie Munson? He's gonna die in this stupid town.

It's not her fault. Obviously, it's not Ronnie's fault. But she's always had a knack for—school, learning, all that bullshit. I've never really seen the point of it. To me, Hawkins High is just the place where I waste eight hours a day before, if I'm charming enough about Mrs. Debbs's grandbaby, escaping into a pad of graph paper and twenty-sided dice for a few hours. Ronnie's got straight A's and a deep bench of teachers lining up to write her glowing recommendations. And I've got the last name—

"Munson."

It would be generous to call the sound from the driver's window a tap. It's more of a hammering, loud enough that I'm briefly worried for the glass. Ronnie and I both whip around in our seats to look.

My heart sinks. I'd been so wrapped up in Ronnie's news and my own bullshit reaction to it that I hadn't noticed the police car pulling up behind me. Now there's a cop standing outside, giving me a shit-eating grin as he gestures for me to roll down my window.

"Again?" Ronnie mutters.

"Always," I mutter back, cranking the window down. "Officer Moore. How can I help you on this fine spring afternoon?"

Moore's blond buzz cut and square jaw give him some Superman-level All-American looks, but no amount of ironing his uniform and polishing his shoes can combat his growing midforties beer gut. He's been a shining star of the Hawkins police force since before I was born, a town hero. Or so I've been told. I can't count the number of times he's hassled me, and it's gotten only worse since I turned eighteen. If I didn't know any better, I'd say he was gunning for me.

He shakes his head, oozing fake disappointment. "I thought that was you, Munson. How many times do we have to have this conversation?"

"That's a question you'll have to ask yourself, Officer. You're the one who's always filling up my dance card."

"That was some erratic driving," Moore tuts. "Started drinking a little early today?"

"Nope."

"We just came from school," Ronnie supplies. She's trying to help me out, but I can tell her right now it's not going to work.

"If I search the car, am I gonna find any illicit substances?"

"You never do."

Moore's expression darkens. He opens his mouth, probably to order me to unlock the back, and I brace myself to lose an hour as Moore tears apart the van like he always does.

But the radio back in his squad car gives a crackle. "Officer Moore, we got a ten-sixteen over on Fleming—"

Moore gives a huff of exasperation. If this traffic stop had any real merit, he'd tell dispatch that he was occupied, but since it doesn't . . .

"I've got my eye on you," he says.

"Promise?" I bat my eyelashes at him and don't wince when Ronnie elbows me in the side.

He snorts. "Get your laughs now. Not even your dad could joke in a jail cell. And that's where all you Munsons wind up, sooner or later."

We're quiet as Moore ambles back to his car. He kicks on the lights and speeds past us, tearing down the road. I watch him go and try to relax my white-knuckled grip on the steering wheel.

"Eddie," Ronnie starts, but I can't hear it right now. Not from someone who got their Golden Ticket—someone the world thinks is worth investing in.

"Put your feet down," I say. She puts her feet down without argument. "You don't want to be late for dinner." And I hammer the gas.

If I'm going nowhere, at least I'll get there as fast as I can.

Chapter Two

The Hideout is the most accurately named building in Indiana. Its location is convenient for precisely nobody; it skulks somewhere between an abandoned steelworks and a fallow cornfield. And while this neighborhood might have been the kiss of death for any other business, it's practically a requirement for a dive bar that's heavy on the dive, the kind of place people go when they can't stand the sight of daylight. The windows have been bricked up since forever, because it's harder to throw someone through a solid wall, the carpeted floors have never been cleaned or vacuumed, and the countertops are so sticky they've pretty much developed their own ecosystem.

So what does it say about me that this shithole is one of the bright spots of my life?

"Junior! PBR!"

Bev has been the proud owner of this fine establishment

ever since her "stray dog of a husband" (her words) died under mysterious circumstances ten years ago. She's got dyed-maroon hair, a permanent squint, and she always yells like there's music blasting, like this place is crammed with people. But the Hideout isn't where you go to party. It's where you go to lurk, and lurking is a quiet activity.

Which just means that Bev's shouts startle the hell out of me every time. "Jesus *Christ*," I mutter, nearly dropping my tub of discarded glasses on Drunk Sam's head. The old man just mutters something incoherent and slugs down his rotgut whiskey.

"She's still calling you Junior?" Ronnie asks. She, Jeff, and Dougie are all clustered around a high-top, taking turns sipping on the single bottle of Coors that their pooled loose change managed to buy them. Jeff keeps throwing nervous glances back toward Bev, like tonight's the night she's going to start giving a shit about the fact that he's barely sixteen, but the Hideout has never demanded an I.D. before, and it's not about to start now. "I thought you told her to stop."

"I'm gonna. I gotta—" I wave my hand and drift toward the bar before Ronnie can demand an end to that sentence.

Bev is already glaring at me by the time I set down my tub with a clatter. "I don't pay you to chitchat with your friends," she says.

"You barely pay me at all," I say. "Speaking of . . . it's ten."

Bev rolls her eyes. "You'd take any excuse not to work."

She's just trying to goad me. I put on my best puppy dog face instead of rising to the bait. Finally, Bev relents. "Fine. Go on. And don't drag it out this time."

"Wouldn't dream of it," I say, giving my hands a quick wipe with a dishrag. Across the room, I catch Ronnie's eye, and give her a nod. *Showtime.*

The Hideout stage barely earns the name. It's just a riser

that Bev's stray dog husband had cobbled together out of two-by-fours and shoved against the wall. It creaks ominously with every step, and I am absolutely certain that one day it will give way underneath me and I'll probably break an ankle.

But it's a stage. And most importantly, it is a stage that will let Corroded Coffin perform (in exchange for me busting my ass on barback duty four nights a week). And that has to be enough.

It doesn't take long for Ronnie, Jeff, and Dougie to get set up—they're pretty much done by the time I grab my guitar from the back. Ronnie had turned up early to load her drums out of the back of my van, and Jeff and Dougie just have to plug their guitar and bass into the threadbare amps Bev never puts away. I hop up next to Jeff, ignoring the creak of the boards, and sling my guitar strap around my neck.

"Killer crowd tonight," Dougie deadpans.

Jeff shrugs, ever hopeful. "Drunk Sam's still awake. That's something."

"Screw all that," I say. "We're here to play."

Ronnie spins a drumstick in her fingers. "So let's give them hell."

She's grinning at me like a devil, and I grin right back. Then, with as big a flourish as this tiny stage allows, I face our tiny audience and—

There's this thing that happens sometimes, when Corroded Coffin plays. If we're locked in, if we're in the pocket, then it's like we're summoning a gale-force wind or a tornado or a fucking *hurricane*. Something massive and primal, a force of nature. But all that terrifying power doesn't overwhelm us. It picks us up, carries us, and we ride it until the final note dies into silence. Swept along in the whirlwind of the music, we *fly*.

And tonight—tonight's a hurricane night. I can sense it from the first crash of Ronnie's drums, marching us into the jaws of "Whiplash," and as the guitars come in, I lose myself for a while. Ronnie's at my back, beating out a rhythm that drives me forward, and Jeff and Dougie keep me centered, bouncing back and forth between them, harmony, melody, harmony—

When I come back to myself, I'm panting and I'm sweaty and the air is still buzzing with feedback from the amps. I wipe a few strands of hair out of my face. My fingers are humming. "We are Corroded Coffin!" I declare to a room of people who do not care. "This next one is—"

My voice stutters on the song title, so suddenly that Jeff actually plays the first bars of "Electric Eye" before he realizes that I'm not with him. "Sorry," I mutter, and the next time I try the intro it goes off without a hitch. We're off into the song, driving through it—

But there're no unstoppable storms this time. I don't lose myself. Because my attention has snagged on something, and I can't seem to tear it away.

There's somebody *new* in the Hideout.

She's at the bar, a short glass of something brown and probably awful in front of her. Her ankles are hooked around the legs of her rickety barstool, and even though I can't make out much of her face through the dim light, I can see how her knee is jigging along with the beat.

Everyone else in this bar is just gritting their teeth and biding their time until we go away. This girl—she's *listening.* Maybe for the first time in my life, I've got an audience who *wants to hear me.*

It's intoxicating. I can feel it seeping into my bones, my skin, my fingers. I'm going liquid under this girl's attention—not liquid like water but liquid like mercury, like quicksilver. "Electric Eye" is coming to an end, and I do something I've never done before—I lead us straight into the next song. No break, just one chord into another, until we're *flying.*

It can't last. Bev is glowering at me from behind the bar,

tapping her watch. But I'm not ready for it to be over, not yet. So as the last strains of Ozzy fade, I throw my hand into the air.

"Thanks for being such a great audience," I shout, loud enough to give Bev a run for her money. I might be losing my mind, but deep in the answering silence, I think I see the girl *wink*. "We've got one more treat for you tonight—"

"Junior—" Bev snaps, but I'm already turning back to my bandmates.

"What the hell, Eddie?" Dougie demands.

"'Fire Shroud,'" I say. "Let's try it."

"We've only ever played that in practice," Jeff protests.

"First time for everything!"

Dougie's eyes are bugging out of his skull. "You're crazy. These people barely want to hear our covers. They *definitely* don't care about our own shit."

I ignore him. "Ronnie?"

But Ronnie's looking past me, out toward the bar—toward the girl. "'Fire Shroud' . . ." she says, and her eyes flick back to me, sparking with laughter. She knows exactly which direction my thoughts are working right now, and she thinks it's hilarious. "You know? That's a *great* idea."

And Dougie can't even protest, because she's slamming her drumsticks down, driving us all into the opening of "Fire Shroud." Jeff and Dougie scramble to catch up, but soon we're all on the same page, and—

We're playing our own music for an audience. I'm wailing out the words to a song I wrote myself. It's not perfect—I stumble over the lyrics once or twice, Jeff forgets the chorus—but also it *is*, it's fucking *perfect*. And at the bar, that girl's knee is still jumping, still keeping in time with the beat—keeping in time with the beat of *my song*.

I've only barely backed off the last note when the amps give an ear-splitting squeal. I flinch, and then flinch again when I spot Bev's face. She's standing next to the stage, the amp's power cord clenched in her fist, and she looks nail-spitting mad.

"Don't push it," she hisses, dropping the cord like a rattlesnake. "You're giving me a migraine."

"That was awesome," Jeff gushes, sliding his bass into the case. Dougie is doing the same, a little quieter—he won't forgive me throwing him in the deep end so easily. "That was *awesome.*"

Ronnie pokes me in the back with her sticks. "Good job," she tells me, sliding her drumsticks into her belt.

"You want a drink?" I ask her. "It's on the house. I owe you, for backing me up."

She just grins. "Tell you what. You pay me back by packing up my drums. Because if you waste what we just did by drinking with *me,* I will never forgive you."

The nod she sends toward the girl is not subtle, and I flush all the way to the tips of my ears. *"Ronnie."*

"Have fun!" she singsongs, hopping off the stage.

"You're a dick," I hiss. But Ronnie just shoots me a backward wave, shoulders shaking with laughter—and a moment later, the front door is slamming shut behind her.

Chapter Three

Bev has disappeared out the back, muttering about her headache the way she does after every single one of our sets, and digging a pack of cigarettes out from beneath the register. Jeff and Dougie are gone too, all excuses about homework and curfews. Family shit. Student shit. Normal shit.

The girl, though—she's still here, still posted up at the bar like a regular, like Drunk Sam. In a staggering display of self-discipline, I give the Hideout two entire sweeps for stray glasses before I let myself circle back in her direction. The whole time, I'm *scary*-aware of her presence, of the swing of her heels against her stool, of the melting ice clinking in her glass. Of her eyes boring a hole between my shoulder blades.

She doesn't look at me as I finally approach, not even when I plunk five dirty glasses onto the counter by her elbow. I take a breath. *Do I keep my mouth shut? Do I say something? What do I say? "What did you think?" "You're the only person who's ever listened to us—did you like it?"*

"Did you like me?"

"Not bad."

But she's the one who speaks first. Her voice is low, a little smoky—but maybe that's just the fact that the air inside the Hideout is 95 percent cigarette fumes. She leans back onto the bar with both elbows, which, as the person in charge of cleaning the counters, I consider a brave decision. Her eyes are huge and dark in the dim light, staring straight ahead across the bar like there's some treasure hidden in Bev's shitty flickering neon sign.

"The drink or the music?"

"Definitely not the drink." Her mouth is twisted in a tiny crooked smile. I wonder what color her lipstick is. It's hard to tell in this light. "I ordered a Jack and Coke. Not sure what this is."

"All Bev's mixers fell off the back of a truck somewhere," I say. "That's our finest Croak-a Cola. More than two'll turn you blind."

She laughs. It's such a bright sound that I find myself blinking. "I'm Paige," she says, holding out a hand. She's turned to face me now, finally, and I get my first look at her face. *Freckles*, is my dumbass first thought, just one word like a total Neanderthal. But it's not exactly my fault because she's got a ton of them, splashed across her nose and cheeks and framed by her chin-length rumpled dark hair.

"Eddie," I say. There's a squeak somewhere around the first syllable, and I totally space on holding out my hand in return.

"Munson, right?"

I fight back a grimace. Game over. She knows who I am, which means there's no way in hell she's sticking around for another Jack and Croak. "Yeah?" I say. It comes out way too defensive, but I know what's coming. Better run up the drawbridge sooner rather than later.

But she just smiles, self-satisfied in a way that takes me totally off guard. "I thought that was you," she says. "When I saw you up there. You guys got good."

"Uh," is about all I can manage.

"Talent show. Winter 1981. You did that cover of 'Prowler' that went over like a lead balloon."

Lead balloon is generous. We'd been kicked off stage halfway through our performance and had spent the next week with members of the PTA knocking down our parents' doors with concerns about Corroded Coffin trying to turn their precious babies to Satanism.

And whoever this girl is, she'd been there to witness it. I feel like I should be having a moment of recognition, but I resolutely do not, and after a few moments of dial-tone staring, Paige takes pity on me. "Paige Warner," she says. "Hawkins High, class of '82."

This, at least, rings a bell. "Warner . . ."

"My brother's still a student there," she says. "Junior. He's on the baseball team."

Which means he's probably tried to kick the shit out of one of my Hellfire kids at least once. "You want another one?" I ask, because if there's one thing I don't want to do right now, it's discuss the highs and lows of high school sports.

Her eyebrow quirks up like she knows exactly what I'm doing. "Won't it make me go blind?"

"What's life without a little risk?"

I duck around the bar with a smoothness that impresses even myself. There're about five minutes before Bev comes back from her migraine break that's really a smoke break and yells at me for screwing around, so I'm going to take advantage of every single second. "Heavy pour or light?"

"Light. I've got to get past my parents tonight."

I mix her drink, emptying nearly an entire can of off-brand pop into her glass and sliding it across to her. "So," I say, watching as she takes a sip. "You must be visiting. Otherwise I'd have seen you around."

"Mm," she hums, watching me over the rim of her glass.

"*Mm*," I imitate, wrinkling my nose at her. "Don't pretend like that's an answer. You got out of this hellhole, you're back now for . . . however long. And for some reason you decided you wanted to grab a drink *here*, even though there're tons of spots in town where you'll have less of a chance of getting puked on in the parking lot."

"What if I told you this was the only bar in twenty miles with a stage, and I wanted to hear some live music?"

I glance over at the shitty amps, the creaking stage. "I'd say, what's wrong with driving twenty-one miles?" She laughs again. "Unless you wanted to see us specifically."

"Before your ego starts inflating, *no*. This is just a happy coincidence."

"Happy, huh?"

"Sure." She shrugs, running a finger around the rim of her glass. "You're right, I'm visiting. My grandma just died, and her house is basically a war zone. Hoarder to the max. I flew out for a few weeks to help my folks sort through it all, and it is *grim*. We've found, I don't know, three dead cats?"

"That's a lot of dead cats."

"A lot of dead cats," she agrees. "And maybe it's all the animal carnage, but I'm really missing L.A. This is about as close to the Roxy as you can get in Hawkins, Indiana."

"Wow. Los Angeles?" *Wow.* "Wow." I shake my head, struggling to clear away visions of sand and surf and sunlight. "I already felt bad enough for you, getting dragged back here. But getting dragged back from California?"

She cocks her head. "It's not all bad."

Something in the way she's looking at me is throwing me off-balance, and I finally put my finger on why. It's so unfamiliar, is the thing. Typically, somebody's staring at Eddie Munson, they're seeing the town fuckup, the freak. But Paige . . . she's looking at me like I'm a person.

Like I'm a person she wants to *eat.*

I haven't exactly been a monk since my disastrous kiss with Ronnie five years ago. There'd been Nicole Summers, back in tenth grade, and—memorably—Cass Finnigan earlier this year. But both times I'd been able to tell going in that these girls had been . . . daring themselves. They hadn't wanted to get to know me. They'd just wanted to tell their friends what it was like to get with the freak.

Not exactly heartbreaking. I hadn't been looking to be anybody's boyfriend. But under Paige's gaze . . .

"So, uh." I clear my throat. "The Roxy, huh?"

"The Roxy, the Troubadour, Whisky a Go Go . . . any night of the week, I'm usually at one of them."

"That sounds . . . I'm gonna be honest with you, that sounds like paradise."

"It does," she says. "Some days, it actually is. But a lot of the time it's just my job. I'm a scout. Well, *junior* scout. Scout assistant."

"Like . . ." I raise three fingers in a salute. Her nose crinkles again in a smile, those freckles dancing.

"Like for a record label, smart-ass. WR Music. I work for Davey Fitzroy, he's—"

"I know who Davey Fitzroy is." I feel a little faint, or maybe just a little crazy. It's objectively an insane experience, to hear someone *in Hawkins* casually mention a person whose name I've only ever seen in the fine print of some of my most well-loved record sleeves. "He's a genius."

"Sure. Among other things."

Battling through my starstruck haze, I raise my eyebrows at her. "You got a story?"

"I have . . ." She breaks off with a rueful laugh. "I have two years of too many late nights dodging high guitarists and drunk drummers who think the way to get to my boss is to cop a feel on me. Not that it would even help if I was into that shit. Davey's favorite thing to do is to shoot people down, and the only way to get promoted at WR is to get somebody signed, which means I'm trapped in a fun catch-22 until Davey fires me or I quit." She gulps her drink, the words coming faster now. "Like, I go to all these shows, especially ones with the musicians people don't already know. I look for guys like you, like Corroded Coffin, who've been playing in dinky dives forever. But even if they're great, I've never found a band Davey'll take on. They don't have what he's looking for."

"And what's that?"

"Something real. You can always tell when somebody is really themselves up on that stage. When you find it, you can't look away." She taps the ice in her glass with a black-painted fingernail. "Between you and me—and this is a secret—"

I hold a hand over my heart. "Bartender-client privilege."

"—I'm not sure how much longer I can keep hitting my head against the wall. I mean, I love music. I even love the music business, or what it could be. But if there's no place for me in it—"

"Junior!"

That's Bev's voice, a whip-crack through the night. I jolt back from the bar, clutching my rag in both hands like it'll protect me from the five-foot-nothing tobacco-scented tidal wave bearing down on me. "I told you to replace the PBR ten *years* ago, and we're still dry."

"One sec, Bev—" I say, but Paige is already draining the rest of her drink and pushing back, slinging her purse over her shoulder.

"I'll see you around," she says.

"Junior."

"I'll be here," I say, and watch her sidestep Drunk Sam and sidle out the front door. And as I head to the back to pick up Bev's keg, I realize that I'm smiling.

Something real. When you find it, you can't look away.

I think I know exactly what Paige means.

—— Chapter Four ——

I'm still buzzing when I wheel the van onto Philadelphia. In another world, maybe one where it's not two in the morning, I might have been humming. Walking on air. What do they say in those romance movies?

Guys like you. That's not the line, but it's what Paige had said. Like it was a compliment. *Guys like you.*

I give myself a shake, pulling onto the gravel drive in front of the house. *Focus up, Munson. Get some sleep, you're spinning out.*

But that's easier said than done, because as I swing the car door open and jump out onto the grass, I catch a glimpse of something that sends my heart swan-diving into my stomach. The kitchen light is on, glowing dimly through the crack in the curtains when I know it shouldn't be. But this isn't what has me so on-edge; that honor goes to the two pairs of boots just beside the front door. One set is old but spotless, lined up against the wall with careful precision. The other is muddy, discarded, left boot slumped to the side.

It's that pair that's messing with my blood pressure. I know those boots. I've watched them walk out of my life more times than I can count.

My first instinct is to bust in the front door as fast as I can. But I'm not going to give those boots the satisfaction of hurrying me along. So I take my time gathering my guitar from the back of the van, slinging the strap over my shoulder, and trudging up the steps to the front door.

Dad is taking up both kitchen chairs when I stomp in, slouched low on one with his socked feet slung up on the other. There's a can of SpaghettiOs on the table in front of him, a spoon sticking out of it. He hasn't even bothered to twist off the sliced-open top of the can. It flares to the side like a razor-edged petal, guarding what was supposed to be my dinner.

My uncle Wayne hasn't bothered to fight for a seat. He's leaning against the counter, hands shoved deep into his pockets, a plastic bag of groceries slouched on the ground at his feet. It's not an uncommon sight; Wayne has a pet theory that I can't feed myself, so every two weeks or so I'll come home to find him shoving microwave dinners and canned soup onto the cluttered shelves and into the moldy refrigerator.

"There he is!" Dad exclaims at the sight of me, swinging his legs off the chair.

Wayne just nods in my direction, not taking his eyes off Dad. "Eddie," he says. He's never been quick with a smile, but now he's wearing the deeply etched frown he only ever breaks out for his brother.

"No hello for your old man?" Dad asks, and I realize I've been standing in the doorway glaring at him for the better part of twenty seconds.

"When did you get in?" I ask.

"Couple hours ago. Traffic on I-80 was a bitch."

"Joliet?"

"Who said anything about Joliet? Maybe I was in Chicago."

"State pen's in Joliet," Wayne says.

Dad sticks his tongue out at his brother. "Ye of little faith." He stands, opening his arms. "How about a hug?"

I should feel more reluctance as I pace obligingly forward. I should turn the other direction, get back in my van, and drive into the night. This story always starts the same way—with a hug that smells like leather and cigarettes and drugstore cologne. It always ends the same way too.

I hug him.

"Good to see you, kid," he says, thumping my back a few times for good measure. "I missed you."

Not enough to call, I think, then, *why the hell not.* "Not enough to call."

He backs up, holding me at arm's length. "You're too smart to need me hovering around. Right, Wayne?"

Wayne just moves his steady gaze from Dad to me. "Brought you groceries," he says.

"*Groceries.*" Dad flicks the lid of the SpaghettiOs can, sending flecks of sauce splattering across the kitchen table. "It's a miracle you don't have scurvy, if this shit's what you've been eating."

"Thanks," I tell Wayne.

"Remind me to make you a real meal," Dad barrels on. "We'll hit the Big Buy, stock up on some seasonings, sugar, flour. *Ingredients.* You remember ingredients, Wayne?"

His teasing smile invites me to join in, to laugh at my uncle just like him, and to be honest, it's difficult to resist. But I swallow back the impulse and force myself to study his face. Dad doesn't roll into Hawkins unless he's got a reason, and his "reasons" tend to detonate. The sooner I figure out what's driving him this time, the sooner I can get out of the blast radius. "How long are you staying this time?"

Dad rolls his eyes. "You've been spending too much time with your uncle. You sound just like him. 'How long this time, how long this time?'"

Wayne's shoulders are tight. "How long, Al?"

Dad shrugs. "I dunno."

At least he's being honest. If he'd said something like *I'm sticking around,* I'd have kicked him out the door. "Great," I bite out, grabbing a beer from the fridge. Normally I don't like to drink after shifts at the Hideout, since the sticky smell of spilled Bud is already ground into my pores, but it's feeling like tonight is an exception.

"Eddie—"

"Get your own beer," I say, slamming the refrigerator shut and turning back to face him. But the look on his face draws me up short.

Al Munson is a guy who takes up space. Air, attention, the second kitchen chair—if it's available, it's his. But the real Munson Magic is how hard it is to hate him for this. He could steal a kiss off a biker's girlfriend and still end the night playing pool with the guy. He's got a smile for everybody, charm out the ass. I've even seen him make hard-assed Chief Hopper laugh. You meet Al Munson, you can't help but love him.

I inherited his hair, his van, and his guitar picks. But nobody's loving Eddie Munson on sight.

Which is why it shocks me when I realize that the Al Munson standing in my kitchen right now looks honest-to-God *small.* There are cracks in his winning grin, his Munson Magic is flickering. He hasn't stopped studying the ceiling. He won't meet my eyes.

Uncle Wayne hasn't missed it either. He's shooting me a warning glance, like he knows what's coming. Because of course he does. He's done this dance more times than even I have.

"It's getting pretty late, Wayne," Dad says. "Think you should be heading on home."

There's a muscle in Wayne's jaw that's winched tight enough to snap. It takes him a few seconds, but he finally unhooks his teeth enough to say, "Room's all set up at the trailer if you need it, Eddie."

I shake my head. "I won't."

"Mhm." Wayne screws his ball cap down around his ears and stalks toward the front door. "See you around, Al."

Dad gives him a mocking little salute. "I'm sure you will."

Then the door is swinging shut. And it's just me and Dad, together in the kitchen for the first time in over a year.

He shakes his head. "Can you believe we're related to such a goddamn stick in the mud?"

But I'm not so easily distracted, especially not when there's still trouble written all over Dad's face. "What happened?"

"I—" Dad takes a deep, shuddering breath. "I fucked up."

There it is. The Reason. "Cops?"

He shakes his head. "I—I made a few miscalculations. Borrowed some money from the wrong people. Now they want it back."

I set my beer down on the counter. "What money?"

"Would you believe me if I said I gave it away to a good cause?" There's a sparkle of humor in his eyes, just for a moment. "Donated to a starving widow and her three kids?" I just look at him, and that sparkle fades. "Didn't think so. Fine. It's a gambling debt. I'd just got out of a two-month stay behind bars at the FCI in Colorado. Frankie and his boys picked me up, and we were gonna blow off some steam, hit a casino." He smiles at me, kind of pale. "I guess the casino hit me back."

"How much?"

"Ten grand."

My pulse roars in my ears. *"Jesus,* Dad."

"I know, I know, but listen—"

"Who are these people? Are they coming after you?" If they followed him all the way to Hawkins—does that mean *I'm* in the crosshairs? And if I'm in the crosshairs, is Wayne? Is Ronnie? What's the outer range on this shrapnel? "Are they coming *here?"*

"Listen." He takes a step forward, hand on my shoulder. It's steady and sure, in a way that his wan grin wasn't, and I can feel my pulse start to slow. "They won't come anywhere near us. I promise."

"Do you have ten thousand dollars lying around that I don't know about?"

"Not yet. But I will." Dad plucks my beer off the counter before I can protest, but he doesn't drink. Instead, he presses it into my hand, wrapping my fingers around the cold glass. "C'mon. Sit down a second."

I do, scraping back the chair he had been using as a footstool. He sits across from me so he can look me dead in the eye.

"There's a truck leaving Pine Meadow, Oregon, in just a few weeks," he says. "It'll be doing the full-cross-country—pulling into Baltimore about two days later."

"This is starting to feel like math class."

"Then raise your hand if you've got something to say," Dad shoots back, and I can't help but laugh. The Munson Magic never fails. "Now this truck. The thing about this truck . . . is what's on it." He leans both elbows on the table, slouching closer. "One million dollars' worth of homegrown weed, all wrapped up and ready for distribution across the eastern seaboard. All wrapped up and ready for *us."*

The roar in my ears is back. I stare at him. "You—you want to steal a *million* dollars of—"

Dad laughs, like *I'm* the one saying crazy shit in this kitchen. "Are you kidding? Even if I could turn that shit around, what would *I* do with a million dollars? No, I'm just talking about taking enough to cover this debt. With a pie as big as this one, no one's gonna notice if a little tiny slice is missing."

"A ten-thousand-dollar slice . . ." I mutter.

"Well?" Dad is watching me intently. "What do you think?"

"I think . . . nothing I say is gonna make much of a difference here." I toast him with my bottle. "So knock yourself out."

"No, kid, you're not listening," Dad says. "This job, it's not something I can pull off by myself. I need another set of hands. I need *you*."

There's a numbness spreading through me that has nothing to do with the late hour or the few sips of bargain beer running through my system. This is why the sight of his boots had sent my heart crashing through the floor. I thought I'd figured out the Reason that would send me ducking for cover this time around, but I'd been wrong.

"Wrapped up and ready for us." That's what he'd said. It's not just that Al Munson is in trouble. It's that he wants to use me to get out of it. If Dad gets his way, I'm not just going to be collateral damage. I'm going to be part of the explosion.

"This job is as low-stakes as they come," Dad is saying, oblivious to my internal crisis. "We get to the truck, take what we want—not a ton, but enough to make a difference. Some for me, some for you."

". . . for me . . ." I echo through the shock.

Dad grins. "Come on, you can't tell me a chunk of cash like that wouldn't change your life."

"It doesn't matter what it'd do," I say. "I'm not going in on this."

He shakes his head, just once. It's so close to fatherly disappointment that it sets the hairs on the back of my neck standing on end. "You can't make up your mind so quickly."

"I can. You find someone else to hold your bag for you."

"It's gotta be you, Eddie."

"Why?"

He doesn't say anything. Just sits there, looking at me with that open, self-deprecating smile that pulled a damn *chortle* out of Jim Hopper, and I very abruptly cannot be in this room anymore. I stand, draining my beer in a few gulps, and wiping my mouth on my sleeve. "Sofa's where you left it. I think there's still a blanket in there too."

"Sleep on it," Dad says. He sounds so sure of himself. I imagine throwing my empty bottle at him, just for a second, and have to settle for swiping back the open can of SpaghettiOs instead.

"Go to hell," I say, stalking toward the kitchen door.

"That's in the cards one way or another, kid," Dad says as I turn in to the hallway, so quiet that I almost miss the words. "How fast I get there is up to you."

Chapter Five

"The question is pretty simple, at the end of the day. Who do you wanna be?"

Gareth frowns at me across the expanse of the lab table. I'm starting to think that's just his default expression, and I can't really fault him for that. If I was stuck with that adorable halo of fluffy brown curls and a mouthful of chrome, I'd probably frown a lot too. "I want to be Illian."

"Illian is fish food. Work with me here."

"I don't *know*," Gareth snaps, stabbing his pencil into his pad of graph paper like it slapped his mother.

He's been in a pissy mood since he walked in the door twenty minutes ago, and he hasn't exactly sweetened since. We're squatting in the chemistry lab with the lights off because I didn't have time to sweet-talk Mr. Vick into letting us do this on the books. It's easy enough to jimmy the locks on these old doors, but I always hate doing it. For one thing, the odds of some nosy teacher walking by and spotting me are better than good. For another—

I need another set of hands.

For another, I'm not sure I like knowing how to do it in the first place.

I'd left Dad snoring loud enough to bring the house down, sprawled out on the sofa. He didn't even twitch when I opened the front door, and I'd taken a moment to watch him in the early morning light, swallowing back the complicated feelings rising in my chest.

Al Munson has come crashing back into my life in more flavors than I can count. Sometimes he's just gotten out of prison and needs a place to lie low. Sometimes he needs to borrow money from Wayne. Sometimes he's got an honest-to-God *job* (*"For keeps, this time."*) Those are always the shortest stays.

But he's never come back for *me*. And even if it's not like he's trying to pay off a quality-time deficit, he came back because he wants me to work with him. He could have gone to any of his buddies, and he came to me.

I shouldn't be happy about that, right? I definitely shouldn't. But—

"What do you mean, you don't *know*?" I ask Gareth. "You knew when you made Illian."

Gareth is perched on one of the science department's death-trap stools, and he keeps rocking back onto two of the legs. He's also favoring his left arm. I haven't called him out on either of these things yet, because I don't want Gareth to start using me as a sparring dummy instead of his graph paper.

"Jeff made Illian," he says. "He said, you can't walk into Hellfire without a character, and he didn't want to wait a billion years for me to figure out how to fill out a character sheet, so he gave me one."

"Well, that's . . . unhelpful."

"Whatever." The floating legs of Gareth's stool slam back onto the linoleum, and he shoves to his feet. "We don't have to—"

"Okay, first things first, freshman." I risk life and limb and smack my hand down on his graph paper so he can't pack it away. "I'm the DM, right?"

Gareth's eyes are wary. ". . . Right."

"So I'm the one running our sessions. I say when they're over. Understand?" Gareth nods. "Good. Now sit your butt back down and let's work this out."

He sits his butt back down. "Thank you," I say. "Now we're gonna start with the basics. Dwarf, Elf, Human, Gnome— what's calling to you?"

"Illian was a half-elf—"

"I didn't ask what Illian was, I *know* what Illian was. Illian was Jeff's. I asked what's calling to *you*."

"I . . . like dwarves," Gareth says.

"Dwarf. Awesome. May I?" I pull the pad of paper toward me and gingerly, like disarming a gunman, pluck the pencil from Gareth's hand. "Dwarf," I write, and underline it twice. "The next question is what's gonna inform your class, okay?"

"Okay," he says, easier now.

"Alignment. What are you feeling?" He stares blankly at me, and I move *yell at Jeff* a few notches up my mental to-do list. "This is, like. Who you *are*, at the core of you. Lawful, chaotic. Good, evil. So, for example, if you're playing a dwarf, then the rule book says you'd probably be more on the lawful end of the spectrum, though the good-versus-evil conundrum is something you'd make a call on for yourself. And once you figure out what combo you prefer—lawful good, lawful evil, even lawful neutral, you'll figure out the sort of . . . I don't know. Moral code? You'll be making decisions with during the game."

There's a line between Gareth's brows as he takes this in. "So if I'm a dwarf, I have to be lawful—"

"You don't *have* to be anything," I say. "That's just what's suggested. What most people think a dwarf is. Lawful good." Gareth's nose wrinkles, and I laugh. "I know. Buzzkill. Now, me? I like to mix things up. Chaotic evil dwarf? Hell yeah. Don't let yourself get boxed in by what the book says you should be, it's never worth it. Do what you think is gonna be the most fun."

"Chaotic," Gareth says the second I shut my mouth, jumping in so fast that the word clips the end of my last sentence. His eyes are glowing. The kid's got the spirit. "I wanna be chaotic. Chaotic . . . good."

"Classic choice, dude," I say, nodding approvingly. "Now let's talk classes. Have you thought about playing a thief?"

Over the next hour, Hodash the Breaker is born. I can't hold on to last night's dark cloud as I watch Gareth roll his way through his stats and scribble down ideas for backstory. His enthusiasm is infectious, and it's obvious to me now that Illian was never his to begin with—Gareth's never been so invested in a Hellfire session as he is right now, bent over his graph paper and breathing life into his chaotic little dwarf rogue.

"Question, freshman," I say, once the foundations for Hodash have been established and we're shoving papers and books back into our bags, getting ready to leave.

Gareth peers at me, wary, over the top of his humongous backpack. "Yeah?"

"It's not a pop quiz, calm down." I sling my jacket over my shoulders, shoving my arms through the sleeves. "I'm just curious. If you never played D and D before you got to high school—never filled out a character sheet or anything—why join Hellfire?"

Gareth shifts from foot to foot. "Where else was I supposed to go?"

Not sure what I'm supposed to do with that, I just ruffle his hair. "Get out of here. I'll see you next Wednesday."

He ducks his fluffy head and scoots out the door. I do a final check of the room, erasing any last trace that we were there. Then I'm following, slipping out into the hall and locking the door behind me.

Ronnie is waiting for me on a bench outside the library, like usual. She puts away her book—some bland paperback I'm definitely not bothering to read for English class—and stands when she sees me coming. "Freshman crisis?"

"Averted."

"Phew." Ronnie mimes wiping sweat from her forehead. "Can't have those little sheep wandering around in the cold." We start ambling through the halls, making our gradual way to the front doors. "I can't believe you're actually in today," Ronnie says, slinging an arm over my shoulders. "Thought you'd be shacked up somewhere with that girl from last night."

"Shacked up? Granny Ecker, is that you?"

"Granny Ecker would say, 'You better wrap it up if you don't wanna be chasing another tiny demon Munson around this town.'"

"This is why your grandma and I get along so well. There was no *shacking*. I was a perfect gentleman, and so was she."

"Bummer."

I twirl my keys around my finger. "You're not making a great case for yourself if you want a ride. *Do* you want a ride?"

She grins. "Last time?"

I roll my eyes. "Last—"

Somewhere in the abandoned hallways behind me, something thumps. Ronnie's eyes narrow. "Did you hear that?"

I just shrug. "Do you want a ride or not?"

Another thump, this time followed by a metallic crashing rattle. It's the unmistakable sound of someone getting thrown into a wall of lockers.

I look at Ronnie. She looks at me. "Do we—?" she asks.

I want to shrug again, to retreat to the van to tell Ronnie about Paige, about my dad, about every crazy thing that happened last night. But then there's another crash, and now I can hear the voices—can hear a fragment of what is unmistakably Gareth hissing "—told you, *I don't have it.*"

"Shit," I mutter. Ronnie is already stalking down the hallway, toward the disturbance, but I grab her sleeve before she can get far. "Get someone."

"But—" Her protest fades at the look on my face. Of the two of us, she's the one who'll actually get help if she asks, and we both know it. With an unhappy frown, she swivels on her heel and dashes away in the vague direction of the teacher's lounge.

Which means that I'm alone as I shove my keys into my pocket and follow the rising sounds of someone getting their ass handed to them.

Gareth's been cornered right outside the auditorium, holding the arm he'd already been favoring to his chest. He's put his back to the wall of lockers, and he's got his best glare pasted across his face.

Not that it's having much of an effect on the wall of Hawkins Tiger green surrounding him. I recognize the three guys in letterman's jackets from the few pep rallies Ronnie's dragged me to. The Hawkins basketball team. Whatever's the opposite of state champions? That's their claim to fame.

"You know what happens next, metal-mouth," the head jackass is saying. This is Tommy H, the worst point guard in central Indiana. "One punch for each dollar you owe me. What is it, twenty?"

"Twenty-five," says one of his buddies—Connor? Caleb? I'd have to start giving a shit about sports to be sure, and that's never going to happen. "Interest."

"Twenty-five," Tommy H agrees. "And that's cutting you a deal."

Gareth's shoulder blades are trying to dig a hole into the lockers. "Why don't you cut yourself a new asshole."

"Why don't I cut you in the—"

But we'll never have the pleasure of hearing whatever unimaginative rebuttal Tommy H has cooking in that noggin of his, because Gareth's spotted me, and his face has brightened like a goddamn lighthouse. It's too obvious to miss, even for these meatheads, and suddenly four pairs of eyes are slamming over to me—three belonging to Tommy H and his assorted jock friends . . .

. . . and the fourth belonging to a girl with a blond ponytail and a JV cheerleader uniform, whose face is ringing some distant bell of recognition that I cannot, for the life of me, place.

"You want something, freak?" Tommy H snarls.

Not particularly. "You okay?" I ask Gareth.

Gareth shakes his head. "Yeah," he says.

Mixed messages aside, it's pretty clear how this situation is going to go. "I think I heard your mom pull up out front. You don't want to keep her waiting—"

But Tommy H grabs Gareth's shoulder and slams him back against the lockers when the kid tries to move. "Uh-uh. Not until you pay up."

The girl tugs on the sleeve of one of Tommy H's cronies, a blond shrimp of a guy. "Come on, Jason, can we go?"

"Hang on a sec—" Jason waves his girlfriend away. "You're Eddie Munson, right?" He's got this kind of manic fire burning at the back of his gaze. It freaks me out way more than Tommy H's looming muscles.

I lean against the wall, arms crossed over my chest. If I can't actually be calm, then I can sure as hell act like I am. "What's it matter to you?"

"Munson?" Tommy H is looking at me in a new light now, a sadistic grin spreading across his face. "Oh, man. That's freaking hilarious."

The girl has two hands wrapped around Jason's wrist now, tugging hard. "Just let them go, it doesn't matter—"

"You want a *Munson* to help you out?" Tommy H sneers the question into Gareth's face, wrapping a hand in the collar of his T-shirt. "That family's all fuckups and freaks—"

I swallow back the spark of rage igniting in my gut. "I'm not looking to start any shit, dude—"

"I heard the cops keep running odds," Tommy H says, "on who's gonna bring your dad in next. Or if he'll turn up dead on the side of the highway first."

"*Stop it, Tommy.*"

The girl has abandoned her crazy boyfriend, weaseling into the circle to grab hold of the hand Tommy's got clamped down onto Gareth. "Let him go," she says again, giving his hand a pull. And maybe it's the shock of someone wearing Hawkins Tiger green standing up to him, but Tommy H lets go.

Chrissy Cunningham. The name comes to me in a rush, now that there's a spark of something beyond cowed compliance in her face. *Chrissy Cunningham.* She's just a sophomore, but everyone with a working brain cell knows she's the rising queen of Hawkins High. I'm used to seeing her as just some cutout of a cheerleader, all perfect teeth, perfect hair, perfect *everything.* It's such a fundamentally uninteresting package that my brain just kind of skips over her, yawning at her existence.

But there's another Chrissy Cunningham. I just hadn't thought she'd survived the jump to high school. I hadn't thought she'd even *existed* outside the boundaries of the Hawkins Middle auditorium.

The thing about the Hawkins Junior Talent Show was that every middle school student was required to participate at least once. Experience-wise, it was exactly as torturous as it sounded, tormenting both the angsty tweens forced to sing and dance in front of a jury of their snickering peers and the parents who'd been dragged along to make up the audience. But in the name of "building public speaking skills," the event continued year after year, and year after year another generation of Hawkins children walked away with psychological scars.

I'd put the ordeal off for as long as I could. I'd been trying to slip through eighth grade unnoticed too, but then Mr. Fleming had called me out in front of the rest of my English class and forced me to sign up then and there. But I wasn't about to go down without taking my friends down with me, so I'd roped Ronnie in, and she'd roped Dougie in . . .

And thus: Corroded Coffin was born.

By the night of the talent show we'd managed to practice a grand total of two times, had gotten the school administration to approve our song choice only by emphasizing the *Priest* in *Judas Priest,* and I had been just about ready to puke all over myself. This was the reason Dad had kept his distance when he'd dropped me off at school at five p.m.—one wrong move and he'd have driven home wearing the bag of Fritos I'd eaten for lunch.

"Here." He'd pressed a guitar pick into my fingers. *His* guitar pick. I'd held it up in front of my face, feeling a little like Gollum with the One Ring. *"You're gonna do great."*

"You're coming tonight, right?" I'd asked, and felt instantly better at the sight of his crooked smile.

"You know what they say about wild horses, kid," he'd said, and then squeezed my fingers around the pick. *"It's yours, by the way. For keeps."*

I'd still been clutching the pick tight enough that my hands were starting to cramp as, hours later, Hawkins Middle had started to make their way through its exhaustive program. Most of the reluctant performers had camped out in the hallway outside the auditorium, since the theater didn't exactly have a giant backstage. But if you knew where to go (and nobody was eager to look for you), there was a small catwalk that ringed the edges of the curtain. With good enough stealth, you'd be able to camp out there and scan the audience for familiar faces.

Which is what I'd been doing when someone settled on the catwalk next to me.

I'd almost shrieked in surprise. I'd been so focused on the brief glimpses I could catch of the audience that I hadn't even noticed someone coming up behind me. And now there was this girl perched there, her spindly arms wrapped around her spindly legs and her huge eyes shadowed by the murky catwalk lighting.

"Are you looking for someone?" she'd whispered. Below, five seventh graders clattered clumsily through a baton-twirling routine.

I hadn't been quite sure what to do. By all accounts, this was not the type of girl who should be talking to me. She wasn't Ronnie Ecker, not wearing hand-me-down overalls and a battered cap. This girl was *polished*. Her hair was blond. It *curled*. She looked like she'd skipped off the cover of some Nancy Drew novel.

But after an excruciating silence, it became clear that this girl hadn't made some hideous mistake talking to me, or at least not one she'd figured out yet. So I cleared my throat and whispered, *"My dad."*

"Where is he?" she'd asked, leaning around me like she'd somehow be able to pick Al Munson out of a sea of equally unfamiliar adults.

I'd just shrugged. Because I'd been up on this catwalk for almost an hour now, and the closest thing I'd found to Dad had been my uncle Wayne, planted way on the left side of the auditorium, watching every act with the same stoic expression on his bearded face.

"He didn't come?" I'd expected pity in the girl's eyes, and was surprised when I found hungry jealousy instead.

"He's just running late," I'd said, and it had sounded hollow even to me.

But she'd just nodded like she'd believed me. *"I came up here to look for my mom."*

"Is she running late too?"

She'd wrinkled her nose. *"I wish. She's right there."* I followed the direction of her finger, and instantly locked in on the immaculate, poised woman seated front-row-center.

"I'm sorry," I said, and that made the girl smile.

"Me too," she'd whispered, like it was a secret, like it was something she'd never told anyone ever before. One of the girls on the stage below dropped her baton for the fiftieth time, and I realized the act was drawing to a close. I'd shoved up onto my knees, flinching at the dig of the catwalk grill into my skin.

"My band's up next," I'd said. *"Uh."*

"Break a leg," she'd told me, filling in the blank. *"And—"*

"Eddie."

"Eddie. If your dad gets held up, I'll cheer for you." She'd flailed her arms, and I'd noticed her pom-poms for the first time.

"Right back atcha." I'd winced as soon as it had come out of my mouth. But the embarrassment had almost been worth it for the grin it had gotten out of her.

Later, when the last chords of "Exciter" had thumped unwillingly into the offended ears of Hawkins's parents and we'd all straggled through the final curtain call, I'd spotted the girl in the lobby, with her mom on one side and a blank-faced, suited man (her dad?) on the other. The mom had been in the middle of some lecture I couldn't hear, but from her gestures I'd been pretty sure she'd been detailing where in the girl's routine she'd screwed up.

I'd met the girl's eyes through the crowd, just long enough

to mouth *I'm sorry,* one more time. I'd caught the edge of the girl's answering smile before her mom, noticing the girl's split attention, had grabbed her by the shoulder and yanked her toward the door.

I'd thought the last four years had stamped out any trace of the unsettled, imperfect, *approachable* Chrissy Cunningham. But maybe I was wrong.

"Chris is right," Jason chips in now. "We shouldn't hang around. Harrington'll be by any second, and he won't like—"

"Harrington's not gonna do shit," Tommy H spits. "Not since Wheeler started wearing his balls as a necklace. And this kid *owes me—*"

"Wow," I drawl. "Pretty crazy to talk about some other guy missing his balls when you're the one who gets his kicks beating up freshmen."

It's a mistake. I know it's a mistake as soon as I open my mouth. The only thing I wanted to do was to get Gareth and get out of here, but now Tommy is turning his cherry-red face toward me. Any spark of the remnants of Chrissy's personality dampens and dies as Tommy's friends fall into position at his back, and now it's just me against a bunch of glowering jocks. *Wonderful.*

"I think the Freak King's been skipping school," Tommy says. "It's up to us to make sure he learns his lesson."

"Gareth—" is all I manage to get out, and then there's a shoulder driving into my stomach as Tommy dives head-on into me. My teeth clatter in my skull as I fly backward, landing smack on my back on the linoleum. All the breath explodes from my lungs, and I have enough sense to give it the shape of one word. *"Go."*

Thankfully, Gareth's got enough sense not to stick around, because I can see the flash of his Converse through the thicket of approaching legs as he darts off in the opposite direction.

"The kid owed us twenty-five," Tommy H sneers down at me. "I'm thinking we're gonna have to charge you double." He winds up to launch a kick into my ribs—

—and I grab his leg on entry and roll, taking him with me. He slams down, some combination of nine different curse words erupting from his mouth. "Is this the lesson you had in mind?" I ask.

He pushes back with a grunt, scrambling to his knees. When he regains his balance, he pulls his fist back, looming over me, and I curl up as best as I can with the basketball morons crowding in close, covering my face with my arms—

"What the hell is going on here?"

I'm not enough of an idiot to take my arms down, which means that the only thing I can see is a sea of legs parting for a pair of sensible khakis. But even though I can't see this person's face, I sure as hell can recognize his voice as his brown tassel loafers stop in front of me. "Mr. Hayes," Principal Higgins intones. "Explain."

"It was Munson," whines Tommy H. He's still crouched on his knees. What a suck-up. "He wouldn't stop hassling Chrissy—"

"Bullshit," I hear Ronnie spit from somewhere behind Higgins.

"That's not true," Chrissy protests at the same time.

"Come on, Chris," says Jason, and then he's hauling her down the hall. I finally drop my arms and shove to my feet, catching a final glimpse of her before she's dragged away.

"That's not what happened," I tell Higgins.

Ronnie is hovering at Higgins's elbow. "These guys were ganging up on a freshman. Eddie was making sure he was okay—"

Higgins raises an eyebrow. "Where's this freshman now?"

Of course there's no sign of Gareth. I told him to run.

"Thank God you came by when you did, sir," says Tommy H. "I didn't know what this freak was gonna do next."

I roll my eyes. "You boot-licking little—"

"*That's enough*," Higgins barks. "Mr. Hayes. You and your friends move along. Our Hawkins Tigers should be focused on excelling in their extracurriculars, not getting wrapped up in . . . this." The wave of his hand takes in all of me.

"Thank you, sir," says Tommy H. He shoves maybe-Connor in the shoulder and with a muttered "*Move, asshole*," the two of them are jogging down the hall.

"You as well, Veronica," Higgins tells Ronnie.

"But—"

"Ronnie." I catch her eye. "It's okay. Get out of here."

I can see the muscles in her jaw clench, like she's biting back another protest. But after a long moment, she caves. "I'll see you later," she says, like she's trying to extract a promise.

"Later," I say. *Promise.*

And then she's gone, and it's just me and Higgins under the buzzing fluorescents in this empty hallway. I shove my hands into my pockets. "How about me, sir?" I ask. "We're all Hawkins Tigers here. Don't I have extracurriculars to excel at?"

The acid in Higgins's glare could etch metal. "You're with me, Munson," he says. "You and I are going to have a little chat."

Chapter Six

The school's main office is mostly empty, save for Janice, the secretary at the front desk. As always, her fanatical devotion to the color purple is reflected in every inch of her wardrobe. Behind her Coke-bottle glasses, her magnified eyeballs scan me up and down as I follow Higgins inside. One eggplant fingernail taps a beat against her yellow legal pad. She does not seem excited by my presence.

"Is this the disturbance, Principal Higgins?" she asks.

Higgins gives a world-weary sigh. "Are you surprised?"

"Mm," she says. "Want me to pull the file?"

I might as well not be here at all. "Good afternoon to you too, Janice," I say, leaning around Higgins to pin her with my brightest grin. My shoulder protests the twist, still throbbing from Tommy H's tackle, but I ignore it. "Might I just say, that color really brings out your glasses."

"That won't be necessary," Higgins says, continuing in the

grand tradition of pretending I don't exist. "I think we've all got Munson's record committed to memory."

"Don't say it like that," I protest. "That makes it sound like we're doing this too often! And I think we both know how much we enjoy our little chats."

"Will you be needing . . . other paperwork?" Janice asks.

She doesn't come out and say it, but we all know what she means. *Is this the day that Higgins finally fulfills his lifelong dream and expels me?*

"No," Higgins grumbles, and I don't fight the savage edges of my smile. If Higgins had something to kick me out on, he'd have done it already. But bad grades aren't enough to expel a student. I'm not dealing, not cursing out teachers. And every fight I've gotten into, I've been the only one walking away with bruises.

Not that this means Higgins doesn't pull me into his office every chance he gets. "With me," he snaps. I give him an over-zealous salute, wink at Janice, and trail Higgins to his office.

Sometime in the last two years, someone has apparently suggested that the principal's office door could be less forbidding. Higgins has dealt with this note by having a large poster made with the words YOUR PRINCIPAL printed on it in blocky black letters. It's an easy sign to hate, and I can't count the number of times I've suggested Higgins swap it out.

"Close the door," he says. I close the door and flop into the rickety chair across the desk from him. For a long moment he just looks at me. I look back at him even harder.

"Should I start?" I finally ask. "I didn't prepare anything—"

"Cut the shit."

"If I had any shit, rest assured, I would cut it."

"I didn't bring you in here to listen to you flap your mouth," Higgins snaps.

"Then why did you, sir?" I ask. "Since, and I'm going out on a limb here, you don't actually care that the basketball team is beating up kids for their lunch money. Oh, but I forgot, they're *excelling*, right?" Higgins's face is turning red with anger. "Is that excelling as in academically? Or as in, Tommy H's pops owns the most successful car dealership in town, and you can't afford to piss him off?"

"Don't test me, Munson," says Higgins. "You're on thin ice, and it's already past cracking."

"Oh, gosh. Living on the edge. I've never done that before, what's that like?"

But in a real change of pace, Higgins is immune to my needling. "I brought you in here," he says, "so we can talk. Man-to-man."

It's cryptic enough to ring every alarm bell in my skull. "Uh."

"I wonder if you've given any serious thought to your future."

If I had a list of things I'd been expecting Higgins to ask me, I wouldn't have even considered putting this on it. Never once, in my four years at this godforsaken school, has this man come at me with anything but rancid irritation. And now he's put on his guidance counselor hat? There's got to be a twist.

"Something tells me you're considering it enough for the both of us," I tell him.

He snorts. "That's the one good instinct you've ever had." He laces his fingers together, leaning his forearms on the desk. It's a real *How About You and I Get Serious* move, and it sets my teeth grinding. "Let's start off in the present then, if that's the only thing you can wrap your brain around. We'll get to the future in a bit. I'm just going to ask you one question, and I want you to give it as much thought as you can muster. Are you ready?"

Ready to pop my lid. "Let it rip. Sir."

"Why are you still here?"

Maybe Higgins is right and my IQ is subterranean, because that's twice in one conversation that he's blindsided me with a question. I blink at him. He shakes his head, and the pity in that stupid gesture ratchets my jaw even tighter. "Simpler? Very well. What is keeping you at Hawkins High?"

"The . . . fact that it's still the middle of the school year?"

"Is that really something that matters to you? You obviously don't care about your classes. Your grades are in the sewer. There's no saving them, not even if you got a personalized gold star from every single one of your teachers. You're eighteen. You could go anywhere, do anything. Why do you keep showing up?"

I have an answer for him. It's: *Where else would I go?* But there's no power in the world strong enough to drag it from me. I would actually rather die before giving him the satisfaction of hearing it.

Not that he needs to. By the smug gleam in his watery blue eyes, I can tell he knows. "Are you waiting for permission to leave?" he asks. "You've got it. Go."

I force a smile. "But what would you all do without me?"

"You think you're cute," Higgins says. "But I'll tell you what you really are: a rotting apple. And it's up to me to make sure you don't spread your rot to the rest of my school. But before I take more extreme steps, I thought I'd see if there was any shred of sense beneath all that hair. Appeal to your better nature. If you've got one."

Blood is thrumming in my ears. "That's a gamble."

"I thought so too. But I want you to tell me honestly—do you think that boy out there would have run into the trouble he ran into if it weren't for you?"

You're crazy, is what I want to say, and, *so you admit that you let Tommy H skate?* But the words wither in my throat.

How long has Gareth been wearing his Hellfire shirt? At least once a week, since Jeff gave it to him back in September. How long has the basketball team been on his ass? I don't want to think it, but it's probably the same amount of time.

I remember the way the poison in their faces had curdled when I turned up to help Gareth. *Freak King*, they'd called me, like Gareth was one of my subjects. Like that alone was something worth punishing.

"Without your . . . *club*, that boy could be a valuable member of the student body," Higgins is saying. "But instead, he's wasting his time on—on—" *He can't say Satanic.* Separation of church and state and all that. But *damn*, he wants to. "—on the fantastical nonsense that you continue peddling, and he's paying the price for it. And he's not the only one."

"What is that supposed to mean?"

"How long do you think it will take before their continued affiliation with a felon affects everyone in your little circle?"

"I'm not a felon."

"You're a Munson."

Of course. This is where the tide always turns, pivoting against my last name. It happened with Tommy H and his cronies earlier. It happens with Officer Moore every time we cross paths. *Munson.* The only thing anyone needs to know about me, a name that tells the whole tragic tale.

"Your dad didn't walk out of here with a degree," Higgins continues. "Neither did your uncle. I don't think a single Munson has successfully matriculated from Hawkins High in fifty years, and I don't see that changing with you. So do us all a favor. Stop rotting out all the good apples just because you can."

My hands are clenched in my lap. More than anything, I want to take a swing at Higgins's self-satisfied face, but if I do then I'll just be living up to my last name. So instead I shove to my feet, hard enough to send my chair teetering on its back legs. "Are we done here?"

Higgins doesn't stand. "I hope so."

"Great." Without another word, I yank the door open and barrel past Janice (who I'm sure has heard everything), stomping out of the office.

I don't know what I'm feeling when I emerge back into the hallway. Anger, frustration, guilt, despair—they get snarled up in one another until they form a giant cotton ball, which plugs my ears and my eyes and my brain until all I can hear is white noise. Static.

You're a rotting apple.

It's no worse than anything else I've been told my whole life. So why is it getting to me now? How the hell has Higgins finally wormed his way under my skin?

Gareth hiding his bruises beneath his Hellfire tee. The acid in Tommy H's eyes intensifying the second he saw me. The grip on Chrissy's wrist as her boyfriend dragged her away. From me. I stand in the hallway like a dumb statue as the images loop in my mind, over and over and over—

Something smacks my shoulder, and I finally twitch back to myself, expecting to find Tommy H or his cronies closing in on me again. But it's just Ronnie, one hand clutching her cap and the other balled up to punch me again.

"Ow," I say. "Why?"

"I've been calling your name for like a full minute. Are you okay?"

You're a rotting apple, Higgins whispers in my ear, but all I say is, "I'm fine." Because Ronnie and I might have roots in the same trailer park, but she's got the Golden Ticket. She's got a future. And how could someone like that understand—

Suddenly, I know exactly what I need to do.

"You sure?" Ronnie's saying. "You look . . ." she trails off, before continuing. "What did Higgins say?"

I try for a grin. Pretty sure I miss by a mile. "Same old, same old."

She squints at me, studying my face. "Eddie—"

"I've got someplace I gotta be, so train's leaving ASAP." I jingle my keys. "You all aboard, or what?"

"Always," she says. "I just hope you know that."

Chapter Seven

It'd be nice to get a warm welcome from Bev, but all she says when she sees me is "You're not going on tonight."

I shake my head, bracing my elbows on the bar. It's what passes for packed at the Hideout tonight, buzzing with a crowd attracted by Bev's fifty-cent beer night. The uptick in business is exactly why Bev doesn't want Corroded Coffin in, scaring off paying customers.

But that's okay. That's not why I'm here.

"I'm not looking for a gig," I say. "I'm looking for a girl."

"Maybe get a haircut, see if that helps."

"She was here last night. Dark hair, boots." Bev just looks at me. "She was the only person in the entire bar who doesn't end every weeknight passed out on the floor. Come on, Bev. You remember her."

"Jeans?" she finally asks, after a long pause. "Stupid earrings?"

"I don't know about 'stupid'—"

"Way too much bullshit around her eyes?"

"Uh—" But Bev isn't looking at me. Her eyes are fixed at some point over my shoulder . . . some point in the direction of the front door.

I turn. I see her.

She's standing just inside the door, taking in the Thursday night Hideout crowd with a mix of glee and apprehension. I feel like any second she'll decide that this level of chaos isn't worth it and disappear into the night, and I'll never find her again.

I'm already moving toward her. "Still think a haircut's worth considering!" Bev shouts after me, but I ignore it, because Paige has spotted me through the crush and—*holy shit*—her entire face lights up. There's a chance I'm going to have a heart attack. But there's no time for that right now. I'm on a mission.

"I hoped I'd run into you!" Paige says. "Are you playing tonight?"

I shake my head. "I'm actually only here because I was hoping to run into *you*."

"Oh, yeah?"

Someone well past the point of buzzed lurches into my shoulder, and I have to stagger to catch my balance and to avoid the shower of beer that follows in the guy's tipsy wake. "Do you maybe want to head outside?"

"Yeah," Paige agrees fervently, and then we're slipping out the door together, stepping into the blessedly cool, quiet night.

The Hideout parking lot is more rugged gravel than immaculate asphalt, but at least it's calm. Our only company out here is a couple of low-talking, stubble-chinned guys chain-smoking near the dumpsters. I can place them both—everyone knows just about everyone in Hawkins, and these guys work with my uncle at the factory. They're so invested in their conversation that they barely look over as we crunch out into the moonlight, which means I'm free to fix my undivided attention right where it belongs: on Paige.

"How's the decluttering going?" I ask, pulling a pack of cigarettes out of my jacket and sliding one between my lips. A moment later, I'm blinking into the face of the universe's tiniest supernova, because Paige has beaten me to it with her own Zippo, lighting my cigarette with a flick of her thumbnail.

"Horrifying." I offer my pack to her, and she takes one, lighting it for herself. "Today was pizza boxes," she says on an exhale, and together we watch plumes of smoke escape up into the sky. "She ordered Ike's Slice like twice a week, and I don't think she ever threw a box out."

"No more cats?"

"Not yet. But we've barely put a dent in the house." She shoots me a sideways look. "I told my mom I'd be sticking around for a while longer. To help out."

"What about work?"

"Davey barely notices when I'm there. He definitely won't notice that I'm gone. Is this why you wanted to find me tonight? To talk about my dead grandma's hoarding and make me feel weird about my job?"

"No."

"Then why did you want to see me, Eddie?"

Why can't I just come out and say it? It should be easy. It was all I could think about on the drive over here, with Higgins's sneer still searing across my brain. But Paige is standing next to me, and my tongue's turned into a lump of lead, just dead weight sitting in my mouth.

"You asked if we were playing tonight." I force the words out.

"Uh-huh."

"You like our music. You like Corroded Coffin."

"Yeah, you guys are great."

"So sign us."

The flaring cherry at the end of Paige's cigarette abruptly dies. "Excuse me?"

I circle around so we're standing face-to-face. "We're good. Sign us."

"I—it's not that easy—"

"Why not?"

"Jesus, Eddie, are you serious?" She's angry. I've already messed this up. "I thought you wanted to—*God*, I'm an idiot— you're just looking for a way to Davey, just like everyone else—"

"No, that's not—not what I'm saying. Not the *only* thing I'm saying—"

"What *are* you saying?"

"I'm saying—you were looking for something real." I hold my hands out at my sides. "Look at me, Paige. I'm not some mass-produced piece of SoCal plastic. I'm just a kid from Indiana. I don't have shit going for me—no money, no nothing. None of this is a fashion statement. My jeans are ripped because they're ripped. I look like I have no money because I have no money." I take a deep breath. It shudders in my chest. "You said you'll know it when you find it. I'm saying you found it. And I'm saying, cherry on top of all that—you like my music."

Paige is watching me, arms wrapped around her stomach, and I might be going crazy, but I could almost believe some of that angry spark in her eyes is fading. "It's a shitty move to ask a girl outside and just try to talk shop."

"You can't tell me people don't do that in L.A."

She snorts. Then, tapping one of her incisors with a fingernail, she gives me a look that rakes from the tips of my worn-out sneakers to the top of my head. I feel her eyes as they travel, leaving a glowing warmth in their wake. "I found it, huh?"

"Yeah."

"Small-town garage band striking it big in the national music scene. Barback turned front man turned rock hero."

Hero. That sounds way better than *rotting apple.* "I'll take two."

"It's a good story."

"Think you can do anything with it? With me?"

Her gaze is back on me, lingering. "I've got one or two ideas." She drops the butt of her cigarette into the gravel and grinds it out with a crunch. "Okay."

I can hardly believe my ears. "Okay?"

Paige nods. "I'll give you a shot. One shot. But here's how it's gonna work."

I'm nodding like my head's loose. "Whatever you want. Whatever you say."

"I'm going out on a limb here. I really need you to understand that. Davey's going to think I'm cutting some of my hometown friends a break when I bring you up. Which means we've got to prove him wrong right out of the gate."

"Practice makes perfect, copy that."

"Because we're in Hawkins and WR is, you know, *not,* you'll have to put together a demo for them. And I don't just mean setting up a tape recorder in your garage. I mean you'll need a studio. A mix. Something legit."

Something legit. I'm starting to see a shape in the last trails of my cigarette smoke, and it looks a lot like a dollar sign.

"Assuming that goes well and Davey likes you—and I'm making no promises—then you'll have to come out to Los Angeles to audition for him and the other executives."

"He wouldn't sign us off the demo?"

"This isn't Battle of the Bands, Eddie. They want to know what they're investing in."

"Sure." *Sure.* That misty dollar sign is getting a lot of friends.

"But I think—I actually think you're right." Paige sounds

almost surprised to be admitting this to herself. "I think you—and Corroded Coffin—you guys have got something that people will like. We might actually pull this off." She takes a deep breath, and I realize that this is almost as much of a plunge for her as it is for me. "Let's make you famous."

She sticks out a hand to shake, and I feel like an asshole because I'm stuck standing still, with studio fees and travel expenses dancing through my head. I don't have that money. I don't have anything *close* to that kind of money, and it doesn't matter how many shifts I pick up at the Hideout, Bev is never going to be paying my way to California.

But I know someone who could.

I shake her hand. "Rock hero," I say. "It's got a ring to it."

—— **Chapter Eight** ——

The plate that lands in front of Dad is stacked so high that the tower of pancakes nearly scrapes his chin. "Line cook had a few extra going," the waitress tells him. There are still curlers stuck in the front of her hair, but she twirls the back with a long fingernail. "I threw them in before they could go to waste."

"You are a real sweetheart . . ." Dad squints at her chest, making a show of looking for her name tag. But nobody's eyesight is *that* bad, and after a long moment, the lady playfully hip-checks his shoulder.

"Stop that," she tells him. "I'm Dot."

"A pleasure, Dot," Dad tells her. "Now tell me—you got honey anywhere in this fine establishment? I've got a hankering for something sweet."

"I'll see what I can rustle up," she says, but the wink she levels at him practically screams *I'm something sweet.*

By the time she's sashaying back toward the diner counter,

my own much sparser plate of eggs and bacon has gone stone cold. I dig in anyway, hoping a puddle of ketchup will help things out.

"This diner's a shithole," Dad says through a mouthful of pancakes. "Why couldn't we go to Benny's?"

"It closed."

"You're kidding. That place is a freaking institution."

"Not after Benny put a bullet in his own eye."

"Damn." Dad whistles low, and for a second he's quiet, lost in some distant thought. "That guy owed me two hundred bucks."

"Jesus Christ—"

"Got some honey for you, hon." Dot's back, and she's got wordplay. She plunks the jar down in front of Dad and smiles. "Can I get you . . . anything else?"

"We're good," I say, mostly to remind her that I too exist. There's no red-lipped smile for me. Dot just glares and flounces off, and Dad buries his laugh in his Mount Everest of pancakes.

"You got a way with the ladies, kid."

I've got one or two ideas. Paige's voice is a whisper in my ear. "I get by."

"Yeah? Anyone you got your eye on right now?"

"Dad."

"That's a yes."

"I didn't bring you here to talk about my love life."

"Why *did* you bring me here?" It's a flippant comment, but Dad's eyes are piercing over the rim of his coffee mug. He knows something's up. He's known it all along.

And he was right to be suspicious too. We don't get *breakfast,* we're not that kind of a family. But the thought of saying what I'm about to say in our house just felt too—for lack of a better phrase, it felt too close to home. I'd needed some distance, a little bit of removal. Something to make it less personal and more procedural. Which is why I'm currently poking at scraps of stone-cold eggs while Dad faces down a Mount Everest of pancakes.

"The other night. You said. You had a line on a job." The words feel tacky in my mouth, and I fight to spit them out.

Dad's face hasn't shifted a millimeter. "I did."

"You said ten grand for you. And—if you had a partner—how much would they take home?"

"How much would this partner need?"

I've done the math—added up the eye-watering price tags for recording fees and travel, and padded in more in the pie-in-the-sky hopes that I'll be needing money to permanently settle in California too. "Five thousand," I say. It's an inflated number, one I conjured in the expectation that Dad will bargain it down.

But he just nods. It might be my imagination, but I think he's holding his breath. "Okay."

"*Thousand*, I said. Not hundred."

"I heard you the first time. *Okay*," he repeats. "You're saving my ass, I owe you big time—"

"Hang on, hang on—" I lean back, trying to get out of range of the painful relief spreading across his face. "I didn't say I was in, not yet. Before I agree to anything, I need to know what I'm signing on for."

There's an approving glint in Dad's eyes, one I'm not sure I've ever seen directed at me before. "I always knew you were a smart kid. Fine, then. Let's talk business." He wipes pancake crumbs off his mouth and shoves his plate to the side.

"And don't sugarcoat it."

"Wouldn't dream of it. You ever hear of a guy called Charlie Greene?" he asks. I shake my head. "Good," Dad says. "Because he's one of the biggest drug kingpins in Oregon. Weed, coke, heroin, speed, K—if he can't grow it or cook it himself, then he'll import it. He mostly stays in the Pacific Northwest, but he's got a few outposts—Baltimore, Des Moines, Grand Island. And he's got to keep those outposts supplied."

"You said he runs shipments," I say. "Pine Meadow to Baltimore."

Dad nods. "You wanted to know what you're getting yourself into. So here it is. His next resupply should be leaving Oregon in five weeks. Which means, if everything goes to plan, it should be passing through central Indiana in five weeks and one day."

I realize I've picked up a strip of my ice-cold bacon and I'm systematically crumbling it into bacon bits. Self-conscious, I wipe my hands off on my wispy diner napkin. "So we're supposed to masked-bandit this thing? Ride up to a speeding train on horseback, guns blazing, your money or your life?"

"It's a thought," Dad says. "Or maybe it would be if Charlie used the railway. But he likes a certain amount of flexibility. It's not a train car we're robbing. It's a truck."

I have a quick premonition of headlights barreling toward me, an ear-splitting horn blaring an unheeded warning. I blink it away. Pick up the bacon again. Keep turning it into powder. Whatever keeps my mind off images of pancaked demise. "Cool."

Dad grins. "You look about two seconds away from shitting your pants."

"Shut up. Keep talking."

The appreciative slurp Dad takes of his coffee is loud and mostly for Dot's benefit, because she's still watching us from behind the counter, chin in her hand. "Since you can't just fill the back of a truck with loose bags of drugs and expect state troopers to look the other way, Charlie's got a work-around. All the shit he ships, he packages it up to look like fruits, vegetables. Produce. Stuff you'd expect to find coming from West Coast farm country, and it's all mixed up with the real deal too. Which means, to preserve the illusion and to make sure your weed isn't dropped off in Baltimore in a giant tub of moldy carrots, Charlie's got a fleet of tricked-out refrigerated trucks that his guys use to make the drive. They keep the air circulating, keep everything chilly and fresh." The smile on his face grows. "They're called reefer trucks."

"They're not called reefer trucks."

"I wouldn't lie to you," he lies. "These trucks pick up the main line in Oregon, but once they're out of the mountains, they clear off onto the local highways. Easier to buy off a small-town traffic cop than a state trooper, and if cash doesn't work . . ." The finger gun Dad levels at me has honey on it. "Charlie's instructions are extremely clear. Once you start driving, you do not stop until you reach your destination, and if you do then you'd better have a great reason for it. It's why he puts two guys in each truck, to switch off shifts and keep their eyes on the rearview."

"And shoot cops."

Dad's shrug is way too nonchalant for me. "Only when necessary."

"So—okay, so—" I feel a little bit like my brain is going to start boiling out my ears. "I just need—to get this straight with you. Your plan is to take a run at a speeding truck that has explicit instructions to never stop for anything. A truck that's carrying a metric buttload of very illegal drugs and also two heavily armed murderers who are perfectly willing to add another body to the count, given the opportunity."

"And the timing is tight too," Dad says. "I forgot to mention that. If they're early or we're late—we miss our shot. We're done."

"Great." I run a hand through my hair, probably leaving flecks of bacon behind. I do not give a shit. "Sounds doable. Sounds fucking doable."

Dad's tricky grin has faded, and now he's just watching me again, assessing and level. "You asked me not to sugarcoat it."

I had. And from what I can tell, he's been nothing but up front with me.

"Eddie," Dad says. "I wouldn't come to you with this job if I didn't think it was something you could handle."

Well, he's wrong. This isn't something I can handle. The closest thing to pulling an actual, functioning heist I've ever done is raiding Strahd's castle with Hellfire two years ago, and even then two of my party bit the dust.

It had been so easy to talk about alignments with Gareth, under the fluorescent glow of the lights in Mr. Vick's lab. *What are you feeling?* Simple. But right here, right now, all I can think about is what I'm *not* feeling. I'm no chaotic-evil criminal, no matter what everyone else in this town thinks. I can't do this. This is too much. I can't—

"We might actually pull this off."

Paige's words whisper through my memory, brimming with suppressed excitement, with a future that leads away from Hawkins and toward golden California sunshine. But also—

"I fucked up. Borrowed some money from the wrong people." And. *"They want it back."*

The shade of that desperate Al Munson is well buried here in this sunny diner, with Dot drooling over him from five yards away. But it's easy for me to remember. I think it'll always be easy to remember.

"What do you think?" Dad asks.

I take a breath. And then I pull over his half-eaten pancakes and dig in. "I better not regret this," I mumble with my mouth full.

Dad sinks back in the booth, watching me. The gratified grin on his face ignites some warm coal in my chest that I try not to think about. "No way in hell, kid," he says. "No way in hell."

Chapter Nine

Dougie's family lives at the end of a swanky cul-de-sac on the nice side of town. I don't know how Dougie has convinced them to let us make it our rehearsal home base, but from the glares I always get through the window from Mrs. Teague whenever I pull up in front, duress was probably involved.

But there's no glare to be seen today as I jump out of the van. Instead, she's squinting in picture-perfect confusion at the faded pink fixed-gear bike leaned up against her mailbox— and at the girl standing next to it.

"Nice bike," I tell Paige.

"This lady," she mutters back, out of the corner of her mouth, "has been staring at me. For five minutes."

"That's Mrs. Teague." I hit Mrs. Teague with an over-the-top cheery wave, like I'm the friendly neighbor on some *Leave-It-to-Beaver*-type show. I can't hear her affronted huff through the picture window, but I do relish the sight of her slamming the curtains closed with an irritated flourish. "She's one of our many adoring fans. Come on—we're in the garage."

I lead Paige along the drive that curves around the house. I can already hear the rattle of drums, the crinkle of potato chip bags, the whining tune-up of Jeff's bass. Everyone's already here. Good. That means I don't have to try to sell this twice.

"Good afternoon, ladies and gentlemen!" I call, too loud and cheery, as I swing through the open garage door. Ronnie's perched behind her drum kit, twirling one drumstick in her fingers. Dougie has co-opted the other drumstick and is using it to try to hook an extension cord off a high shelf, while Jeff gives the tuning pegs of his bass a run for their money, frowning as he focuses in on the D-string.

"You're late, dude," Dougie says. "My mom's only giving us an hour before she cuts the power, she says the neighbors keep complaining—*Jesus*—" His nudging has finally coaxed the extension cord to fall, and it tangles around his head like a boa constrictor.

But Ronnie isn't distracted by Dougie's shenanigans or by Jeff's slow strangulation of his fretboard. Her gaze sharpens the instant Paige appears in the garage door before it slams right over to me. "Company, Mr. Munson?"

"Hi," says Paige. "That's a nice bass."

Jeff's hands yank away like his strings have burned him. "Um!" he says, half exclamation and half squeak.

"Are you a groupie?" Dougie asks, not even pretending not to stare, and I've really got to intervene here before my band convinces Paige that she's made a mistake in taking me halfway seriously.

"*Okay,* you freaks." I step in front of Paige. Hopefully without a direct eye line, these guys will regain some tiny sign of brain function. "Can we be normal?"

Ronnie, of course, isn't paying attention. She leans sideways on her stool until she can see Paige again. "You were at our Hideout show."

Paige smiles. "You've got a good memory."

"I always remember the girls who turn Eddie's brains into oatmeal."

"Oatmeal, huh?" Paige shoots me a warm sidelong glance.

A flush swamps me from my eyebrows down to my toes, all at once. "Shut? The hell up? Ronnie?"

But Ronnie's not about to break her let's-ignore-Eddie streak now. "It's *very* nice to meet you," she says, sidling around her drum kit to hold a hand out to Paige. "Any . . . *close friend* of Eddie's is a friend of mine. I'm Ronnie."

Paige shakes her hand. "Paige."

"Did Eddie convince you to come hear us practice?" Ronnie asks. "Because I think that counts as a war crime in some parts of the world."

"Let me just extend a blanket apology for all of them," I tell Paige, cutting Dougie off before he can chime in with something that will damage this situation beyond repair. "And *no*, jackasses. Paige is not here as—my *date*."

"So she's single?" Dougie asks.

"Well," says Paige, shifting back a half step.

"She works for WR Records." I blurt it out, because if I try to play coy any longer, my bandmates are going to run this whole thing off the freaking road. "She wants us to record a demo. To send to her boss. *At WR Records.*"

The silence that follows this is gratifying, honestly, because the fuse of this news has been fizzing in my bones for days now, ever since Paige first agreed to consider us. It's been only pure force of will that's stopped me from spilling the beans to Ronnie, but now, looking from face to shell-shocked face, I'm nothing but happy that I held my tongue.

Still, there's a point when the quiet draws on just a little bit too long. "Don't everybody get excited at once," I say, trying not to look as anxious as I feel.

"WR Records?" Jeff says. It looks like just saying it is triggering nausea. "Like . . . like *WR Records*?"

Paige puts a hand on my arm, stepping around me into the garage. "I'm a junior scout under Davey Fitzroy," she says. "Yes, for WR Records. And Eddie's right. I think you guys— Corroded Coffin—are something that he would want to know about." I open my mouth to chime in, but she shoots me a warning look, and I click my jaw closed again. "But before we take any first steps—booking studio time, hiring an engineer, even giving Davey a heads-up—I need to clear it with the rest of you. Is this something you're into?"

"Of course they're into it," I say. "It's a record deal. Right, guys?"

I look around again. The shock is starting to fade, now that Paige's words are sinking in, but the expressions settling in its wake aren't exactly the full-steam-ahead enthusiasm I would have expected. Only Dougie looks eager, his eyes burning bright. "Hell yeah," he says. I think he might be salivating. "*Hell* yeah!"

"Wait—so—" There's a deep line etched between Jeff's eyebrows, and I'm not sure if it's confusion or worry. "WR wants to sign us?"

"They want us to record a demo," I say. "Paige will send it to her boss. If he likes it—we'll fly out to Los Angeles for an audition."

"*Los Angeles?*" All of this information seems like it's logjamming in Jeff's ears, and he's struggling to filter it into his brain.

"*Hell yeah*," Dougie crows. "Let's do it. When do we start?"

But the only person I'm paying attention to right now is the person who hasn't said anything. Ronnie is standing in the middle of the garage, clutching one end of her drumstick in either hand. Her knuckles are white—if someone startled her right now, I think she'd snap the stick in half. And she's staring into the space between me and Paige with absolutely zero expression.

Of all the reactions, this is the one I'd anticipated the least. I reach out to shove playfully at her shoulder, both to wake her up and to gauge her reaction. "You alive in there, Ecker?"

She blinks, and then looks at me. "Yeah," she says, and that's all.

"So like . . ." It's starting to compute for Jeff, the line between his eyebrows smoothing. "So like, we could be rock stars."

"That's the idea," Paige says.

"Can I ask you just one question?" There's a light behind Ronnie's eyes again—not the teasing spark from when she'd thought Paige was my almost-new girlfriend, but something fiercer and more directed.

Paige smiles, approachable and laid-back. "You can ask me as many questions as you want."

"You're too kind." Ronnie starts tapping her drumstick against her thigh, a fast-paced *thwap-thwap-thwap.* "I just wanna know—why us? Why Corroded Coffin?"

I roll my eyes. "Because—"

"I'm asking *her,* Eddie."

"It's a fair question," Paige says. "I guess the simplest answer is: I liked what I saw. You—you *all*—have something that I think the music world is craving right now."

"And what is that?"

"A story," Paige says, and for a second, her gaze cuts sideways toward me. *Barback turned front man turned rock hero.* "Everywhere I look these days, I find a bunch of polished rich kids, treating their record contracts like a cute little hobby. Nobody wants to root for that, or for them. But a bunch of hometown heroes striking out for the big time? You'll be legends."

Ronnie's drumstick hasn't stopped tapping. "So what you're saying is—you're interested in us, not our music."

"I'm interested in both. That's how the industry works."

"And what happens if the story changes?" Ronnie asks. "What if it doesn't match up with WR's anymore?"

"That's not gonna happen," I cut in. "It is our story. We *are* hometown—"

"*Heroes?*" Ronnie snorts. "Who's calling us that?"

"It sounds like you all have a lot to discuss," Paige says. Her professional smile hasn't shifted, but I can see a touch of strain around the edges. "Why don't I give you some space to talk it over and then—we can take it from there."

"I'll walk you out—" I say, because it seems like I should, but Paige stops me with another hand on my arm. Even through my jacket, I can feel the heat of her palm burning all the way to my skin.

"Stay," she murmurs, and I feel that too. "Talk to them." And then, with a final squeeze, she's letting me go and walking out into the golden daylight. I watch her go until she's too far up the drive for me to see anymore.

"I'm in," Dougie says the second the crunch of Paige's footsteps fades. "I'm in. I'll sign right now. Let's go."

"I don't know . . ." Jeff says. He's been chewing on his lip so hard that it's starting to swell. "You guys are seniors—I've still got two years of school left."

"What are you talking about, dude?" Dougie demands. "School? Why are you worried about school when someone's telling you that you could be *famous?*"

"It's not that easy," Jeff shoots back. "What, are your parents gonna be over the moon when you tell them this is your plan?"

"*Screw them,*" Dougie says. "If my dad had his way, I'd slip-

'n'-slide straight from high school graduation into the passenger's seat of his HVAC truck. Teague & Son until the end of the line. No stops, no detours, no *way*. I'm in."

"School will always be there, man," I tell Jeff. "Whether we're the next Metallica and we tour for decades, or we wash out in two months—you can go back any time, get your diploma, go to college, live the nine-to-five life. But this chance has an expiration date. Just think about how you would feel in ten years, in twenty, if you woke up one morning with your class-of-'86 ring and realized you'd missed your shot at being something *incredible*."

And maybe I use my DM voice while I'm narrating this grim future, and *maybe* Jeff has been conditioned for two years to buy into whatever that voice says, but I'm not *lying*. I'm just making sure he understands all the facts.

"Okay," Jeff finally says.

"Yeah?"

He grins, a spark of excitement spreading across his face like wildfire. "*Okay*."

"Okay!" I exclaim. Then, holding my breath—

I turn to Ronnie.

"How about it, Ecker?" I ask. "Fame, fortune, glory: Corroded Coffin. What do you think?"

Ronnie's spinning her drumstick again, fast enough that it blurs. "Are you really asking? Like, do you want to know what I think? Or do you just want me to say whether I'm in?"

This is a trap. There's only one way I can answer that question without sounding like a complete scumbag. "Of course I wanna know what you think."

"I think . . ." Ronnie sighs, her shoulders loosening. When she looks back up at me, her impassive mask is gone, and I can read every vulnerable thought that bleeds from her eyes. "I think I want this to be real. I think that I want to live in a world where stuff like this happens. But I don't, Eddie. None of us do. Look around. Really look around, like, with your eyes open." She flicks her drumstick at the concrete floor, the tangle of extension cable around Dougie's feet, the rickety wire shelves. "We're not some metal savants. We're *garage*. The most we can handle is a weekly gig at the Hideout, and even that's pushing it—"

"That's bullshit!" Dougie exclaims. "That lady said we've got something special—"

I hold up a hand, cutting Dougie off before he can spiral. "Paige thinks we're real."

"But what does that *mean*?" Ronnie says. "I don't know. You don't know. I don't think she knows either. But whatever it is, it's—it's, like, a mold. It's a package she thinks she can sell. Right?"

Her reluctance is getting under my skin. "If you don't want to do the demo—"

"That's not what I'm saying. I just—I don't want to be twisting ourselves into knots, trying to be something that somebody else wants." *I don't want* you *twisting* yourself *into knots,* is what her expression telegraphs, clear as day. The concern just ratchets my irritation higher, especially when she adds, "We don't have anything to prove, Eddie. Not to the people in this town, not to anybody anywhere."

"I just want to play some music," I say. There's a bite to the words I can't take back, but Ronnie just absorbs it.

"That's it?" Ronnie's eyes are intense, searching my face for—for something I'll never understand. "You promise?"

The irritation drains away all at once, leaving me deflated and exposed. "I promise," I tell her.

And finally, Ronnie nods. "Okay," she says, almost too quiet for me to hear. "Then let's go be rock stars."

Chapter Ten

The house hasn't been so much built as it has been kind of dumped. It slumps through the trees and down the slope to the lakeshore, spilling itself along the way. I squint at it, searching for one single redeeming quality as I trudge along behind Dad up the front path. "This place looks haunted."

Dad's already rapping at the front door. "Haunted by a good time, maybe. Don't be rude."

"Rude to who? Casper?"

But the cloud that plumes out as the front door is yanked inward is no friendly ghost. Instead, it's the thickest, most impenetrable fog of weed smoke I've ever encountered, so dense I think I could slice a chunk off it with a knife.

"Is that you, Munson?" drawls a voice from somewhere within the cloud, and I'm starting to see a shadowy shape now—the outline of a tall man with a wild beard and cargo shorts, slumping just like his house. "You bring me a friend?"

"This is my son," Dad says. "Kid, I'd like you to meet Reefer Rick."

I'd thought that the first step in planning a heist would be more exciting—something involving maps or schematics or maybe a trip to a James Bond-y weapons cache. I thought it might be dangerous, or at least *tangible*.

"We'll get there," Dad had told me as I'd wheeled the van out of the drive and onto Philadelphia. *"But there's an order of operations to this shit. And there's no sense in jumping straight in if we don't have a buyer lined up on the other side."*

I don't know what I'd expected from the word "buyer," but it wasn't anything like the beaming, friendly face I'm looking up into now. Reefer Rick is a giant of a guy, with big smiling eyes and a T-shirt printed with a faded Smokey the Bear and the words SAVE OUR FORESTS.

"Munson Junior!" Rick exclaims, grabbing my hand and pumping it in a handshake so exuberant that it joggles my shoulder in its socket. "I feel like I'm meeting royalty right now!"

"It's just Eddie," I say through my clattering teeth.

There's no sign that Rick's actually heard me. "Come the heck on in!" he says, shuffling back to let us pass through the door. "Welcome to the Reefer Residence!" I'm not entirely sure why—maybe it's Rick's overwhelming friendliness—but I scrape my shoes against the sill as I step inside, hyper-conscious of tracking mud into the house.

Maybe I've been watching too many movies, but when Dad told me we'd be heading to a drug dealer's house, I'd expected to find something dark and dreary. Instead, the space we step into is open and bright, though the low-hanging haze of smoke turns the sunlight into kind of an orange blur. It's not orderly by any means, but it's certainly not messy—there's no film of dust, no sticky spills, and the scattering of beer cans and dirty plates I can see all look to be no more than two days old. In my book—the book of a teenager who's been living on his own for months—this is practically a drill sergeant level of hygiene.

A regimented line of bright blue pill bottles stands at attention on a side table, and Dad taps the lid of one of them as we pass. "Branching out? What are these? Bennies?"

"Times are hard, my friend," Rick tells him, not breaking his shuffling stride. "I'm here to lighten loads and brighten days, not pass judgment."

Rick's bed sits, unmade, between a couple of wide windows along the far wall, but the majority of the space is gobbled up by a hulking pool table. This is where Rick heads now, shuffling in his slippers toward the pool cue that's been discarded against a rickety china hutch.

"You play?" he asks me, picking up the cue.

I shrug. "A little."

"Right on." He hands the cue to me and produces another one from somewhere beneath an overstuffed floral sofa, straightening with a loud grunt. "Don't get old," he tells me.

He can't be more than thirty-five, but I nod. "I'll keep that in mind."

"How you been, Rick?" Dad asks. He moves a stack of old magazines off an armchair and settles in, leaning as far back into the plushy cushions as he can.

"Shh," Rick says, eyes sharp as he fills a beat-up rack with pool balls. They clack against one another, nestling tighter and tighter as he goes. "You wanna break?"

Is it possible for this conversation to head off the rails if it was never on them in the first place? "I don't care," I say. "Sure."

"Be my guest." He removes the rack with a flourish, stepping back from the table and hanging off his pool cue like a walking stick. I shoot Dad an uncertain look.

"Break if you're gonna break," Dad says.

I guess I'm going to break. It takes two seconds to line up my shot. Then there's a loud *thunk*, and the balls are splitting every which way, so chaotically that I can credit the green six that plummets into a pocket only to dumb luck.

"Solids." Rick nods his approval like this is something I've done on purpose. "Excellent choice. Nah, I've been awesome, man." It takes me a second to realize that he's talking to Dad, answering his earlier question. "Just chilling, you know. Business is good, life is better."

"I'm glad to hear it," Dad says as I line up my next shot.

"I gotta admit, I was worried when I didn't hear from you," Rick says. "Two years, radio silence? Those were some dark thoughts that started creeping in. I'm very glad to see you're still walking around."

"You know it takes more than one dumbass enforcer to keep me down."

Thunk. I sink another ball. Rick is watching Dad when I look up, hazy insight burning in his bloodshot eyes. For his part, Dad doesn't seem bothered. He just lounges back in the armchair, hands clasped behind his head, like this is his house and not Rick's. "Sure," Rick finally says. "I know that."

My next stroke scratches. "Damn," I say, straightening up. "Your turn."

"Speaking of business," Dad says, as Rick chalks up the tip of his cue, "Eddie and I, we've stumbled upon something of an opportunity we think might interest you."

"Mhm." Rick is squinting down the length of his cue, angling a shot for the twelve ball near the far corner.

"In a few weeks, we're going to come into possession of . . . call it twenty pounds of weed. I'm not talking backyard shit. No seeds and stems. More like twenty beautiful pounds of Golden Ambrosia. All the way from Oregon."

"Why are you telling me this, man?" Rick asks. *Thunk*. The twelve disappears into the pocket, and Rick rotates around the table, his eye on the fifteen that's been tucked up behind a wall of solids.

"Why do you think?" Dad asks. Rick just bites the inside of his cheek and crouches to the same level as the table.

"I think you want me to buy it off you," Rick says, and then his shoulder is jerking and the cue is twitching and the cue ball is doing an improbable hop over the line of defenders, smacking into the fifteen and sinking it out of sight. "For . . ."

Dad's easygoing mask has thinned, the tension underneath starting to poke through. "Fifteen thousand."

"Fifteen thousand for twenty pounds of Golden Ambrosia." Rick whistles low, but he's still not looking up from the table. "Quite a deal you're cutting me. I'd have to be a moron to pass that up."

"So don't be a moron." Dad stands, the armchair creaking beneath him. "Come on, Rick. Have I ever led you wrong before?"

Now Rick glances toward him, and the look on his face says that Dad really doesn't want him to answer that question honestly.

"Dad was in lockup." I blurt the words out without really meaning to. The only thought in my mind is that, for some reason, this little meeting seems to be going not so great, and if Dad isn't going to explain his way out of it then I should give it my best shot. "In case you're wondering why you didn't hear from him. It's because he got arrested. In Colorado."

Rick turns his easygoing smile toward me. "I'm never one to wonder why Al Munson's disappeared off the face of the planet, Junior," he says. "Are you?"

Yes. No. I don't know. "Then what's the holdup?" I ask. Rick snorts. With barely a glance at the table, he lines up and sinks another shot, and I step back so he can do it again, rambling all the while. "You said it yourself, this is a sweet deal. We do all the work, you get the product. You could get rich off twenty pounds. All you have to do is say yes."

Rick lolls his chin on the tip of his cue. "And then what? We do our business, we hit the happily-ever-after, then what?"

"I don't—"

"It's a rhetorical question, guy," Rick says. "I know the answer. *Then* the problem of where-did-Munson-and-company-steal-the-shit-from-in-the-first-place becomes *my* problem when the wolves chase me down. I'll be sitting here, living my life, getting by, and all of a sudden a couple guys come knocking on my door, asking me where their weed is. And when it's already gone, what happens to me?" I don't have any answer for him, so he just shakes his head. "Nothing good, I'll tell you that much."

"That's not gonna happen," Dad says.

"Whatever you say, dude." Rick's tone is agreeable, but his eye roll is not. He takes another shot at the pool table. This one misses.

"Think about it, Rick," Dad says, sauntering up beside me and taking my cue. "There's no way in hell this could ever trace back to you. When Eddie and I grab the shit—"

"*Don't* tell me who you're getting it from—" Rick cautions.

"—*our mysterious benefactors* won't even know it's gone until it's too late. They won't know who we are, or where the weed went missing. Maybe they didn't even have a full payload to begin with? Who's to say? But at no point is anyone gonna hear your name or see your face."

Dad's not taking a shot, which means we're effectively at a standstill. Rick twirls his cue between his fingers, studying the spread of balls across the green felt. He still doesn't look convinced. He's never going to *be* convinced, not by Dad—not by the guy with a track record of evaporating into the night and (if my read is right) leaving Rick hanging high and dry. This plan is DOA, dried up before it had a chance to bloom. *Good-bye, WR Records. Goodbye, L.A. Goodbye, Paige Warner.*

I'm midspiral when the weirdest memory hits me, so vividly that it practically walks up and taps me on the shoulder.

One punch for every dollar you owe me.

That's what Tommy H had said. And then Gareth had spat a curse at him, and Tommy's face had plunged deep purple. After that, he hadn't cared about whatever stupid milk money Gareth might have had on him.

He'd just wanted the kid to hurt.

"It's not gonna trace back to you," I say, echoing Dad, "because they're not gonna care about you."

Rick's got his chin perched on the end of his pool cue, and he squints at me through the hazy sunlight. "How do you figure that?"

I reach out to poke at the cue ball, bouncing it off the rail with my finger. "If they figure out who stole from them, they'll be pissed, right? But pissed at Dad—pissed at me. They might come after us for the money, but what they'll really be looking for revenge on is their pride. You're not a part of that, you're just, like, a random lucky bystander. If there's any shrapnel, you won't be the one catching it." I take the cue back from Dad. Line up a shot. And hope to hell that I make it, because this speech is going to seem a *lot* less cool if I don't. "Of course, if that all still feels too risky for you, we'll just go somewhere else. You're not the only supplier in Indiana. You're just the closest."

Click. I hit the ball and straighten to face Rick before I can see whether my shot has landed. My heart is hammering in my chest, but I screw my best Al Munson smile onto my face and keep it there.

Rick watches me for a long beat. Then, all at once, he starts to laugh. It's loud and goofy, bubbling from somewhere deep in his chest. "Damn, Junior!" he says. "You're a hell of a salesman! I almost believed that!"

Dad claps me on the back. I can feel how clammy his palm is through my shirt. "He's really something, huh?"

"I'll tell you what. Whatever you got cooking with your old man goes south, you come to me for a job. I'll set you up good."

"And before then?"

Rick's still chuckling as he digs the end of a joint out of his cargo shorts pocket and sparks it. "It's twenty pounds of Golden Ambrosia," he says through a mouthful of smoke. "What am I gonna do, pass it up? You bring it here, I'll take it off your hands."

Relief swamps me in a wave. Maybe I don't have to dismiss my California dream just yet. "Pleasure doing business with you, Rick."

"Pleasure is the business," Rick says, leaning down to take the next shot. "And don't you forget it."

Chapter Eleven

Business is still on my mind two days later, as Paige and I pull into a gravel lot somewhere on the outskirts of Lafayette. I pull the parking brake and kill the engine, and then we're just sitting in my van, staring at a two-story brick box of a building that's about as boring as they come.

But if appearances were all that mattered, then Paige and I wouldn't have left town at seven in the morning and driven more than an hour to be here right now. And if appearances were all that mattered, then I wouldn't be nervously sweating just sitting in the parking lot.

LIVE MIKE STUDIOS says the yellowed sign above the door. I think it's watching me.

"You *sure* we can't just record in Dougie's garage?" I ask.

Paige, who has spent the better part of our trip snoozing in the passenger's seat, shoots me this Look-with-a-capital-L. It says without words, *Stop being a coward,* and also, *If you were going to wimp out, you should have done it before I had to wake up at the ass-crack of dawn.* "I'm serious," I say. "I can borrow some sound equipment from the AV nerds. We churn this out in an afternoon and—"

"Where's this coming from?" Paige asks. She produces a compact mirror from somewhere and uses it to unrumple her postnap hair.

I chew at the inside of my cheek. It's coming from my bank account. Over the last two days, I'd scrounged together every penny I could find, and once all the sofa cushions had been overturned and every pay phone coin return in town had been raided, I'd put together a grand total of one hundred and eighty-four dollars. And thirty-nine cents. When Paige and I had left Hawkins earlier this morning, I'd had all this tentative conviction bubbling inside of me, a hope that maybe that would be enough to cover whatever price quote was about to get dropped on my head.

But now that we're sitting outside the studio, reality is kind of . . . starting to crush me. There's no way I have enough cash, right? There's no way.

"If you're nervous," Paige says, picking up the slack while I just sit like a catatonic lump and stare out the windshield, "don't be. The manager of this place can't be worse than the guys I have to deal with in L.A. Just let me do the talking. I'll get us a good slot. And a good rate too." I glance over at her at that last comment. She's still studying her reflection in the compact mirror, avoiding eye contact so steadily in a way that has to be on purpose. "We're already here. Do you honestly want to turn around and leave now?"

It's a dare. She's daring me to stick around, to take the next step. And so I do what I do best. I roll the dice.

The van's hinges groan as I swing the door open and climb down. "Coming?" I shoot back over my shoulder. Behind me,

Paige laughs through a swear, clicking her compact shut and following me into the building.

Live Mike Studios should be owned by someone named Mike, but it's a guy called Nate Caputo running the show. He's in his midsixties, a washed-up hippie type with a full head of gray curls, a fringed jacket, and a permanent scowl. The scowl only deepens as Paige makes introductions; we'd had to schedule this meeting for before his nine a.m. recording session, and Nate is *not* a morning person.

"Quieter," he grunts, when Paige and I launch into a description of Corroded Coffin and our demo. But when I lower the volume and try again, he just grumbles, "Ugh," and stalks down the hall, toward the smell of brewing coffee.

"I'll handle this," Paige says. Then she's trotting after Nate. And I'm alone.

I don't plan on wandering. I'm just going to hang out, wait for Paige, maybe do a little thumb-twiddling. But then—

I see the door.

It's open, just a crack, just far enough for me to peer through. And inside—

The drum kit is the first thing I spot. Then the rugs laid out on top of one another, stacked high on the floor. Then the spindly leg of a microphone stand. And then I'm pushing the door open and stepping into an honest-to-God *recording studio* for the first time in my life.

It's not a big space, but even with all the equipment and the instruments and the scarf-draped lamps, it doesn't feel cramped. My sneakers scuff across the layered carpets with a *shushing* sound that feels too loud, and I realize that the room is completely soundproofed. Wanting to test this, I tap my fingernail against the hi-hat, and grin at the raspy *chk-chk-chk* that follows.

It strikes me hard, like, right between the eyes, standing here in the middle of this stack of carpets, cushioned air pushing in on all sides. I'm in a recording studio. A real one. I've only ever seen them in pictures or in movies—glossy photographs plastered across old issues of *Rolling Stone,* or grainy making-the-band snippets on MTV. But this isn't two-dimensional. It's not low-fi. It's—

"It's kind of a shithole."

The words come, staticky and broken and *way* too loud, through the intercom set into the ceiling overhead. I look up, startled, to find Paige watching me through the observation window. She's standing in the control room, leaning over the audio console. It's dark on her side of the glass, but the warm light from the studio illuminates her face, making her skin glow like she's got the sun burning somewhere inside.

"Hah," I say, and then realize that, with all the soundproofing, she can't hear me unless I'm talking into the mic. I lean closer and try again. "Yeah." It's the best I can manage without admitting the fact that, inside, I'm completely freaking out. This place might be a shithole, sure. It could be Abbey Road, and I'd be having the same reaction. I'm standing in a recording studio, like a real honest-to-God rock star. Did Munson Junior ever think he'd end up here?

She cups her hands over her ears, making big eye contact with me through the window. "Huh?" I say, remembering to speak into the mic this time.

Paige gestures and covers her ears again, and *finally* I think to look where she's pointing. *Oh.* There's a set of oversize headphones hanging off the corner of one of the amps. I hook them up with my fingers and slide them over my head.

"How's my hair?" I ask, grinning over the mic. Paige rolls her eyes, but her heart's not in it; I can see the smile she's fighting.

"Luscious."

"What did Nate say?"

"He's, like, catatonic. I'm not even gonna try until he's chugged at least one cup of coffee." She cocks her head, nodding toward something behind me. "You see that guitar over there?"

I'd spotted it as soon as I'd walked inside, a Strat dangling from a mount on the wall. It's a little worn—a few scratches etch the body, and the threads on the strap are starting to fray. *This baby's seen some wars.* But when I sling the guitar around my neck, plug it in, and play a chord, the sound that emerges is pure and clear and perfectly in tune.

"What do you think?" I ask, striking a pose.

"Looks good," Paige says.

"Even for a shithole?"

"I wasn't talking about the studio." She cocks her head, studying me through the glass. "You look good. In there, behind the mic, with a guitar. You fit."

I'm not sure I can answer that right away, not without my voice cracking. So I turn my attention back to the guitar, walking my fingers up the fretboard as I pick out a bare-bones take on the intro to "Number of the Beast."

"Can I ask you something?"

Her voice is low, but unmissable, hazing out of the headphones and into my ears until it's everywhere. I miss a note. "Shoot," I say, and whether I'm swearing in reaction to my screwup or inviting her to go ahead, I'll leave up to Paige.

"Why music?"

It's such an oblique question that I have to give up on Iron Maiden for a full thirty seconds as I try to figure out what she means. "Everyone likes music."

"Not everyone likes it the way you do." She cocks her head, and her short hair sways sideways in a dark ripple. "Fine okay. Rephrase. Why *this* music?"

I hit a power chord and let it reverberate, filling every corner of the recording studio. "Because it's badass," I shout over the noise.

"For sure," she says, once the last echoes have died away. "But that's not the only reason, right?" When I just stare blankly at her, she huffs a sigh. "Help me out here, Eddie. If I'm gonna sell this package, I need some copy to write on the side."

Why music? Why this *music?* I flip my pick around in my fingers as I try to put my thoughts in some kind of order.

Because, weirdly enough, I've never actually asked myself this question before. For eighteen years, music has just kind of . . . *been*. Like, eating, breathing, taking a piss . . . music. Listening to it, playing it, talking about it. It's a fact of life. But why?

"My mom."

I'm not actually sure I mean to say it. It just kind of comes out, murmured into the microphone like I'm in a weird rock-and-roll-flavored confessional. I can imagine the words filling the air in the control room, the same way that Paige's voice is filling my head, delivered direct to my eardrums by the headphones.

"My dad was the one who taught me how to play guitar, but my mom, uh." I clear my throat. "She was living in Memphis when she met my dad. She'd grown up there, nineteen years surrounded by music, everywhere she went. Country, bluegrass, rock . . . but her favorite was blues. Like, Chicago blues, the hard kind that gets into your bones, you know?"

Paige has straightened up on the other side of the observation window, pulling out of the light filtering in from the studio. I can't see her face anymore. It's just a silhouette that answers me. "Yeah."

"So—when she left, when she moved up to Indiana, she

took the music with her. It's like a nine-hour drive from Memphis to Hawkins, and she and my dad spent all of that time squeezed into a tiny car with twenty boxes of records. And then when I was born, she started sharing those records with me." I'm still plucking out a tune on this beat-up old Strat, but it's not Iron Maiden anymore. It's a Muddy Waters riff, and as it reverberates from the studio speakers, I can hear the static from Mom's record player fuzzing underneath, familiar and comfortable as an old sweater. "I still have them. I still listen to them. They're stashed next to the TV. She called them her plane tickets. Even when she was stuck in Hawkins," *waiting on her husband to come home from some dumbass scheme,* "that music told stories. It helped her see the world.

"I didn't get it, when I was a kid," I go on. "All I heard on those records were people singing about sadness, about how shitty life was. And then, uh. She got sick and. Died. When I was like six. I got it then." I pause. Typically there's a chorus of sympathetic crooning following that reveal, one that sets my teeth on edge. But Paige is still and silent inside the control room, watching me. Listening.

So I give her something to listen to. The guitar line for Black Sabbath's "Paranoid" trips off my fingers, half blues and half metal, and it might be my imagination, but I think I can see the shadow of Paige nodding along to the beat.

"I like *this music* because it's about sadness and how shitty life is. And things are sad, life is shitty. It's *real.* But also, it tells stories. This music takes you on an adventure, to another world where you're, like, facing down demons. Traveling into the depths of hell. My mom's music was plane tickets. I guess that makes my music a portal to another dimension."

"You like it because it's badass," Paige says.

"I like it because it's *really fucking badass.*" I finish the riff and let my hand fall away. "Is that enough copy for you?"

She leans forward again, into the light, and now I can see the expression on her face. She's not smiling, not really. But there's this glow in her eyes, this soft radiance that has nothing to do with the scarf-draped halogen lamps here in the studio. "I think—"

The door behind her swings open, and a moment later, someone hammers the light switch on the wall. All of a sudden, I can see every detail of the control room, every rogue wire that sprouts from the back of the audio panel, every rip in the secondhand sofa oozing stuffing in the corner . . .

And Nate, who is done with his coffee and ready to talk. I watch through the window as he says something to Paige, who nods a response. "Should I come in?" I ask through the microphone, feeling awkward. Just a second ago, my voice had been filtering through the speakers in that control room for Paige's ears alone, and it had felt like we were the only two people in the world. And Nate . . . I don't want to be rude to the guy, but he's not exactly gelling with that particular vibe.

Paige leans over the microphone just long enough to say, "Hang tight for a second." Then she's turning her attention to Nate and her back to the recording studio. I'm suddenly very aware of the fact that I'm standing smack in the middle of an empty room, holding a guitar that isn't mine, wearing headphones so oversize that they're slipping down over my ears. *Oh, God. I poured my heart out to Paige looking like a kid playing dress-up.* Feeling extremely childish and even more foolish, I begin the process of putting everything back where I found it. Tidying up the toy box.

By the time the amps are disconnected, the headphones are replaced, and the Strat is back on the wall, Paige and Nate's conversation is at, like, a twelve on the intensity scale. He's shaking his head pretty much nonstop, shifting from foot to foot, fidgeting with the scrap of fake leather that's peeling off the sofa. Paige, on the other hand, is planted like a tree. Nate's got at least a foot on her and still, she's staring him down like he's an ant and she's a magnifying glass, saying one word to Nate's ten.

So I guess it's no surprise that Nate's the one to break first, throwing his hands over his head. He says something I can't hear, but my amateur lipreading tells me it's either "Fine!" or "Fuck!" Then he's spinning on his heel and stalking back out into the hallway.

Paige sags, just enough to notice, as soon as the door slams shut behind him. A little at loose ends, I tap on the glass to get her attention, and her face is inscrutable when she looks up at me.

Well? I mouth.

She doesn't mouth anything back—just waves a hand, beckoning me into the control room.

Ominous. I hustle out into the hallway. Nate is there, lighting up a cigarette as I beeline for the control room doors. "How'd you end up with that one?" he grunts, nodding in Paige's direction.

"Won the freaking lottery, man, I don't know."

He exhales a stream of smoke just as I pass. "Then how'd she end up with *you*?"

I just power forward, blinking stinging fumes out of my eyes and shoving into the control room.

"We can rent the studio," Paige says, as soon as I'm inside, and I can't help the *whoop* that bubbles out of me, loud in this small space. "They've got a slot in about a week, so if the rest of the band is free—"

"They're free."

"You haven't asked them, Eddie."

"They're free. Trust me."

She smiles, the first trace of softness dawning through her rictus of impassivity. "I do."

I take a deep breath, bracing myself for the hard question. "How much?"

Paige fiddles with one of the dials on the control board. "Sixty."

"Sixty? That's not bad at all—"

"An hour."

"Oh."

"With a five-hour minimum."

Which comes to three hundred dollars. That's *way* out of my price range, even if I pick up every shift Bev's got going between now and next Sunday. "Can you—" My voice cracks. I clear my throat and try again. "Can we bargain him down?"

Paige shakes her head. "That is bargained down."

My stomach turns over. "I can't afford that, Paige."

"I know." The news is bad, but Paige is still smiling, soft and a rueful. "Which is why I'm covering it."

Because my brain is busy running in circles, hamster-in-a-wheel-style, it takes me a second to process what she just said. "You're—" is about as far as I get before the words run out. She's joking. She's playing a prank on me. There's no way in hell that anyone would ever offer to front *three hundred dollars* for *Eddie Munson*. "No you're not."

"I already paid the deposit."

But—but—"*Why?*"

"Don't ask me that," she says. "Ask me, 'Why music, Paige?'"

"Why music, Paige?"

"Because things are sad. Life is shitty. And music—"

"Is real?"

She shoulders her bag, looking up at me with the same steadfast tilt to her chin I've just seen her use to reduce Nate to dust. "And when you find real," she says, "you can't look away."

Chapter Twelve

The news that we've set a date to record hits Corroded Coffin like a freight train, and every afternoon the following week finds the four of us tucked up in Dougie's garage with the wide doors flung open, practicing until our fingers give out or Mrs. Teague cuts the power, whichever comes first. Corroded Coffin has always been good—good enough for Paige to sign off on—but now we're good and *focused,* and the combination feels intoxicating.

I can still feel the buzz of music in my veins on Thursday as I rumble the van through the entrance to the trailer park. It's only the threat of a potential crash that's stopping me from joggling my knee to the music in my head, but Ronnie, in the passenger's seat, has no such restrictions. She's got her drumsticks out, and she's beating out the rhythm to "Fire Shroud" on the dashboard on repeat, just like she's done the whole way home.

"It's feeling good, right?" I ask, once Ronnie gives her sticks a final spin and shoves them into her bag.

"It's feeling really good," Ronnie says.

"I thought Jeff was gonna shit the bed on the bridge, but I think he's been practicing."

"Yeah."

"Oh, hey, what do you think about switching up the lyrics in the last verse? Like, instead of *'Raging through my skin, Burning through my veins,'* it's *'Raging through my skin,* Blazing *through my veins'*?"

"They both sound good to me."

"But there's that rage-blaze, like. Half rhyme. I think I'm gonna change it." I pick up the rhythm Ronnie's dropped, tapping it out on the steering wheel. "Maybe I'll ask Paige. She knows this shit, she could probably give us some pointers." When I glance over at Ronnie, she's kind of just watching me out of the corner of her eye. "What?"

"Nothing. You're just—really excited about this. It's nice to see."

"What happened to 'we're too garage for this'?"

"Don't use my own words against me, I thought we were friends." I laugh, pulling to a stop in front of her trailer. She starts to gather her things. "Shit, did you grab the bio homework?"

I hadn't even known there was bio homework. Every moment I'm at school, I'm thinking about either the demo, Dad's job, or Hellfire, which means that my class lectures are basically just white noise. Like the grown-ups in a *Peanuts* cartoon. *Wah-wah-wah.*

The blank look on my face must answer Ronnie's question, because she rolls her eyes, opening the van door. "Why do I ask."

"Why *do* you ask?"

"I'll get it from Jeannie." She opens the van door. "Then I'm gonna call you and pass it on and *then* you're going to give me a two-minute monologue on the difference between DNA and RNA when I see you tomorrow. No excuses, Munson. I've heard you talk for half an hour about the intricacies of elven politics in Tolkien."

"What you don't understand is that, as High King in Lindon, Gil-galad may have had a claim of rulership over the Sindarin dynasties in Mirkwood and Lothlórien—"

"Uh-uh, I'm done." Ronnie jumps out of the van, slinging her bag over her shoulder.

"—but those two Sindarin dynasties had originally been established to escape Noldorin influence, and since Lindon contained a fair number of Noldorin elves—"

"Is that Eddie Munson?"

The front door to Ronnie's trailer is open, and Granny Ecker is standing on the top step, hands on her hips. Despite being on the far side of her seventies, she still stands almost as tall as Ronnie does, and there's a lot of wiry strength packed into her ropy frame. I know this from experience, since Granny Ecker was usually the only one to check me when I was running wild as a kid. I still shudder every time I see a wooden spoon.

"Guilty as charged, Granny!" I say, leaning out the window.

"Get out of that car and come in for some dinner," she instructs me in a voice that leaves no room for argument.

I find some room anyway. "I can't, I'm sorry—Bev's got me working tonight." Actually, Dad and I are making a run to the War Zone to pick up some supplies, but there's no way I can explain that to the Ecker ladies in a way that doesn't unravel my whole entire life.

"Hmph." Granny Ecker's grunt tells me everything she thinks about Bev, the Hideout, and my priorities as a whole.

But before I can shatter into pieces under her icy glare, she twists to grab something off the counter just inside the door—an aluminum tray covered in tinfoil. "Ronnie," she says, and Ronnie obediently rushes over to take it from her, ferrying it back to me with careful hands.

"I don't know if I can show up to work with a hot dish," I say.

"Don't be foolish," she says. "That's for your uncle. My best turkey casserole. You bring it on over to him."

My uncle Wayne's trailer is just a few lots down, but the sun is already starting to set, and I promised Dad I'd be back before it did. "Can't you give it to him yourself?"

"That man won't accept a thing from me," Granny Ecker says. "But you and I both know he needs feeding if he's not gonna turn to skin and bones. You want me to ask again?"

I have a vision of that wooden spoon. "No, Granny," I say, turning the van off and sliding dutifully out of the driver's seat. Ronnie presses the tray into my hands.

"And he'll have that tray back to me within the week," she says, already stomping back into the trailer. "Or I'll have something to say about it."

The screen door swings shut behind her before I can respond. Ronnie gives me an apologetic smile, following her grandmother up the front steps.

"RNA. DNA," she calls back to me.

"Sauron used the Noldorin elves' resentment of Gil-galad to earn their trust!" I call back, but she slams the trailer door closed before I can inflict any more psychic damage on her. Then, with an aluminum tray of turkey, cheese, and macaroni warming my hands, I trudge in the direction of Wayne's trailer.

I don't bother knocking before I try the door. Uncle Wayne always leaves it unlocked, even when he's at work or out drinking with his friends. *"I got nothing anybody'd wanna steal,"* he always says when I question it, and since it's his life, I always let it drop.

He nearly upsets his bowl of Cheerios when I shove the front door open. "For the love of God, Eddie. Someday you're gonna give me a heart attack." He's sitting at the tiny card table he's got shoved into the corner of the kitchenette, and from the bags under his eyes, I'd bet he's just gotten off work.

"Mrs. Ecker sent me over with this." I hold up the aluminum dish. "Turkey casserole, I think?"

"Someone's gotta tell that woman I'm not about to waste away over here," Wayne grumbles, but from the empty box of cereal tipped over at his elbow, I'm not convinced. For someone who's so hung up on making sure my kitchen is at least halfway stocked at all times, Wayne has a real blind spot when it comes to his own shelves.

"It's not gonna be me. I can't spend my life playing go-between for you two." I nod toward the yellowing door of his fridge. "You want it in there?"

"Yup." He scoots back to let me into the kitchen. Sure enough, the refrigerator is bare, save for a couple cans of PBR and an ancient box of baking soda. There's no issue in finding space for the tray. I slide it onto the bottom shelf and swing the door closed again.

Wayne is watching me as I straighten up. "I'm glad you came by," he says.

"Thought I gave you a heart attack."

"Don't be a smart-ass. I wanted to talk to you."

". . . Okay . . ."

He fiddles with his cereal bowl. "You been all right?" he finally asks. "Over at the house?"

"With Dad, you mean?"

"Sure."

"Yeah, we've been good."

Wayne hasn't stopped messing with his bowl. The *clink-clink* of his spoon is going to give me a headache. "And you've been—spending a lot of time together."

I cross my arms, leaning sideways against the fridge. "Well, he's my dad, so . . ."

Clink-clink. "Has he talked to you about why he's back this time?"

"I guess he missed me."

To his credit, Wayne doesn't laugh at this ridiculous lie. *Clink-clink* goes his spoon. "I guess he must have."

That headache is starting to take root somewhere in my left temple. I reach down and pluck the spoon out of Wayne's bowl before things can get any worse. "I thought you wanted to talk," I say, tossing the spoon into the sink. It clatters against the bottom, loud in the close air of the trailer. "Is this what you wanted to say?"

"No."

"Then could you spit it out? If I'm not at the Hideout in thirty, Bev's gonna eviscerate me."

"I ran into Rick Lipton at Melvald's yesterday."

It takes me a second to place that name. Rick Lipton. *Reefer Rick.* "Yeah?" is all I say. I screw the lid down tight over the wellspring of panic that bubbles up inside me and hope that none of it shows on my face.

"He said to tell you, swing by if you want to lose at pool again."

I shove my hands into my pockets. "That it?"

"Eddie." Wayne pushes his cereal bowl back and stands. He's trying to do meaningful eye contact with me, and I oblige, widening my eyes so he can see how ridiculous this whole situation is. "You hanging out with Rick Lipton now?"

"Jesus Christ, is that a crime?"

"You know what that man does, don't you?"

I roll my eyes. "Going off the sandwich baggie on your bedside table, *you* definitely do."

But needling isn't working on Wayne, not right now. His gaze doesn't waver. "I'm not passing judgment like that," he says. "But you can't blame me for putting some pieces together here."

"What pieces are those?"

"Al comes back to town. You won't tell me why, and he sure won't tell me. But I'm no idiot. I can tell when my brother's in trouble. And then a few days later, you're playing pool with Reefer Rick?"

There's no anger or frustration in Wayne's face, just blazing concern, and somehow, that's even worse. A ball of something that tastes a whole lot like shame is lodged in my throat, and I try to swallow it back. *It doesn't matter,* I tell myself. *He can disapprove and worry all he wants, but he can't control me or what I do.*

So I just shrug. "What's the big deal?"

"I'm looking out for you," Wayne says. He's crossing his arms tight to his chest now, a protective shell. "I know how Al can be, when he gets a scheme in his head. He'll sweep you up and whirl you around, but he won't be there when things spit you back out again. It's happened to me more times than I can count. I don't want you to wind up the same way."

"Got it. No schemes," I say, with a mocking three-finger salute. "Scout's honor."

But Wayne just shakes his head. "I'm serious, Eddie. You're old enough—you've already learned this for yourself. Your dad's not the guy you can hang your hat on. Not if it's a hat you don't want to lose."

The flash of temper that burns through me is bright and scorching. "I said *I got it,*" I snap. I'm not a kid, and I'm definitely not *Wayne's* kid. I don't need lecturing. "Are you done?"

"You can tell me stuff, Eddie. You know that, right? Even if you don't want me to—to say anything back." I just look at him, watching as his shoulders slump in the silence. And maybe it's the light in here, but I realize that there's more gray in his beard than there was even a few months ago. More lines on his face. Weird how that happens so fast. "Yeah," he finally says. "I'm done."

He's done. We're done. I'm definitely done. There's a short-tempered goodbye, and then I'm back outside, stomping toward my van like the ground under my feet did something to piss me off.

Break if you're gonna break, Dad had told me over the pool table. Well, I've broken. The game has started. And nothing's going to stop me from playing through to the end.

Chapter Thirteen

"Stop, stop, stop—"

I rip my hand away from the strings with a frustrated growl. "Jesus Christ."

"What now?" Dougie demands.

"I thought we were supposed to be recording," Jeff asks, genuinely confused. "Why isn't she letting us record?"

On the other side of the control room window, Paige absorbs this whining. "Because you're not where you need to be yet," she says, leaning over Nate's shoulder to speak into the mic on the audio panel. "You're flat. You sound rehearsed."

"We are rehearsed," Ronnie mutters. I can see her knee starting to jig up and down behind the floor tom. She's only barely biting back her temper.

"The song is called 'Fire Shroud,'" Paige says. "So let's see some fire. From the top—"

From the top. I hit the opening chord and we're off. Again. For the one millionth time this morning.

The atmosphere had been off ever since we'd all pulled up in front of Live Mike Studios, blinking in the sunlight. Jeff and Dougie had rolled out of Dougie's pickup, staring up at the sign above the door with the same apprehension I'd felt when Paige and I had first toured it a week ago.

"You sure we can't just record this in my garage?" Dougie had asked.

I'd nudged his shoulder with my own. *"We're already here. Do you want to turn around and leave now?"*

His face had twisted in a *maybe* kind of way, so I just clapped him on the back and turned around to help Ronnie load her drums out of the back of my van. I'd caught Paige's eye and her smirk of recognition as she clambered out the passenger's side door. *"Very wise words."*

I'd stuck my tongue out at her. And that had been the last fun moment of the day.

Maybe it's the utter disinterest blazing out of Nate from his slouch behind the audio panel. Maybe it's the pressure of the blinking red light on the video camera that Paige has trained on us through the window. Maybe it's the oppressive awareness of the timer on our recording session counting down.

Maybe it's all three of these things, plus a million others. But no matter the reason, as soon as Corroded Coffin takes up their places in the recording studio—

We *suck*.

We're out of sync. And when we're in sync, we sound like robots. And when we don't sound like robots, we're out of sync.

It's a nightmare of a cycle, and it doesn't make sense. We've spent years effortlessly whipping up those hurricane-force winds and riding them through our songs—we'd done it the first night Paige had seen us at the Hideout, for God's sake. But here in this studio, it's like we've got lead weights in our pockets. Like we're nailed to the ground. And I can't, for the life of me, figure out *why*.

This stab at "Fire Shroud" isn't going better than any of the others. We're only a third of the way through, but I'm the one who pulls back this time. "Okay, okay—" I step away from the mic, turning to pinch Ronnie's hi-hats shut. The glare she shoots me is mutinous and reflexive, but it softens at my next words. "Let's take a break."

"What's up?" I hear Paige's voice through my headphones, filtering in from the control room.

"We're taking five," I say into the mic. "Could you guys—" I don't say *give us privacy*, not out loud, because I'm not sure how Nate would feel about being told to take a hike in his own studio. But even if Corroded Coffin isn't on the same wavelength right now, Paige, at least, is reading my mind. Through the window, I see her ask Nate a question. Nate doesn't hesitate a single second before digging out a pack of cigarettes in response and heading for the door.

Paige leans over the mic. "Smoke break," she says. "We'll be back soon."

"Thanks," I say, meaning it. She nods, and then the control room is empty.

I take a deep breath. I face the rest of the band. And I try not to grimace at the tangible dejection scribbled across every single person's face.

"It doesn't make sense," Jeff says. He's staring somewhere into the middle distance, like the last few hours have actually sent him into shock. "We practiced. We were *good* at practice."

"That's the *only* place we're good," Dougie says. He's digging at a hole in the rug with the tip of his sneaker, his Les Paul dangling loose from the neck strap. "Look at this place. We don't belong here. We're garage."

I want to rush out a blanket denial—*of course we're good enough for this place, of course we're not just "garage."* But with the memory of Nate's bored disinterest and Paige's shifty anxiety fresh in my mind, it's hard to get my thoughts together. It's hard to believe.

"Bullshit."

But it's Ronnie who finds the right words first. She's still seated, staring out at us, eyes intense and forehead sweaty with effort.

Dougie scoffs. *"You* were the one who said—"

"And?" Ronnie says. "We don't have to be perfect. We came here to play some music. We just have to get out of our own way and *do it."*

A scrap of guilt twists in my stomach. *I just want to play some music.* That's what I'd promised these guys back in Dougie's garage. And if that's *all* I wanted, then this—being here in this recording studio, having even the slightest *taste* of a chance to make something out of our homegrown band—would be enough. But—

Barback turned front man turned rock hero.

If that's my story, then "just playing music" is never going to be enough. Rock heroes make it to the end. They make it big. They don't flame out in a shitty recording studio in central Indiana.

"Ronnie's right," I say. "We're getting in our own way. And it's killing us. All that practice, all that pressure, all—*this"*—I wave my hand at our surroundings—"we're letting it get in our heads. It's like we're weapons, right? Badass weapons. Swords. A little bit of stress and practice, it keeps us sharp. But if you sharpen a sword too much or too often, it'll just get dull again. And that's what's happened to us. But, my friends—we don't have to let it."

"We don't?" Jeff asks. He doesn't look so sure.

"I know we don't," I say. "We've done it before. We do it every week at the Hideout. But we don't have to be Hawkins,

Indiana's best-kept secret forever. We can let the world know what they're missing out on, and we can do it *right now.*"

It's not exactly an "I just want to play some music" kind of speech, and that's not lost on Ronnie. I can feel her studying me closely. "We are Corroded Coffin," I tell the band. "We are gonna do what Corroded Coffin does and *kick ass.* Jeff—I want to see the kid who showed up at practice two years ago and refused to leave until we admitted we needed a bass." Jeff smiles, bashful and pleased. "Dougie—I want to see the guy who called Mr. Lowe a fascist *to his face* when he stopped letting us use hall passes during geometry."

Dougie snorts. "I called him a fascist because he was *being* a fascist."

And then there's just—"Ronnie—"

She rolls her eyes, but the effect is totally trashed by the fact that she's laughing. "Spare me, I'm begging you."

"—I want to see the girl who got the cops called on her for playing her drums at eleven p.m. behind her granny's place. The girl who bit Daniel Cirelli on the arm when he catcalled her. The girl who started this stupid band with me.

"Forget practice. Forget where we are, forget the camera, forget the stakes. It doesn't matter who the audience is or where we are, because if there's anyone who can play kick-ass music *anywhere* to *anyone*, it's—"

"Guys?"

Paige's voice crackles over the speakers. She and Nate are back in the control room. Nate's flopping into his chair, still looking like he'd rather be anyplace else.

"You ready to go again?" Paige asks.

I look back at the band. The suffocating dejection is gone, replaced by an electric spark that burns bright in every face around me. I can even feel it in myself as I grin. "Corroded Coffin," I say. "Let's kick some ass."

Then I turn back to the control room and—

It's not a chord that rips out of my baby; it's a falling scream. Out of the corner of my eye, I see Nate's head in the control booth whip around to stare, eyes as wide as plates, goggling through the window. Even Paige looks surprised, straightening up, watching me with a heat that feels familiar radiating from the other side of the glass.

My fingers dance down the fretboard, moving on pure instinct. Within a split second, Jeff is there too, his bass thrumming out a monotone, menacing heartbeat that twines with Dougie's backing guitar, twisting and melding for a second before—

Silence. For two . . . three . . . four . . .

The first stirrings of a hurricane whisper against the back of my neck. And then—

Ronnie's drums come in like rolling thunder. I can feel them shaking the air, reverberating against my skin. And it's not my imagination—Nate sits up in his chair, leaning forward across the audio board. *Listening.*

Well, that got his attention. Let's see if we can keep it.

The rumble of Ronnie's drums plows into a syncopated jackhammer, worming its way through my ears and into my bones until, under its own power, my foot is tapping along. Dougie's guitar wails the harmony and Jeff's bass carves out the spine, standing the song up on two legs in a way we haven't been able to manage all day—

But the real test is coming. We've burned through the opening, and now—

I step up to the microphone, whipping my hair out of my face. Then—

It's not so much that I sing. I've been singing all morning. But that's felt like *work*, like I've had to force the words out every time I opened my mouth.

This time, though. It's not hoarse. It doesn't falter. My pitch isn't wandering all over the landscape. The song pours of out me, savage and pure and white-hot. And I can *feel* the response from the control booth, like the night at the Hideout when Paige and I first met . . . but amplified, magnified by Nate's presence, by the fact that he'd been ready to dismiss us two minutes ago and now he can't tear his eyes away. The golden spotlight of focus is glowing on me, and I think I could live in this moment forever.

I tear away from the mic to take what feels like my first breath of air in fifteen years. But there's no time to linger— we're barging up on the solo, Ronnie's drums marching us closer and closer to the edge. And it's *effortless*, the way I launch, ripping into the solo, spreading my wings, letting the energy buoy me toward the sky. The rest of the band feels it too—I can tell by the fierce grin Ronnie gives me, by the way that Dougie's gone somewhere inside himself, lips moving with every note he tears from his guitar, by the way Jeff's head is bobbing on his neck like a damn marionette.

Facing down demons. Traveling into the depths of hell. That's what I'd told Paige this music felt like to me, and that's never been more true than in this moment. And as the solo burns to a close, I look to Paige in the control booth.

It's not hard. Her eyes are like flaming beacons, boring into me, fixed. I stare right back as Jeff's bass walks us toward the conclusion, and suddenly it's like we're back in this studio a week ago—just me and Paige, telling secrets through the head-phones.

There's only the final chorus left now, Jeff's bass walking us inexorably toward the finish line. So I lean into the mic and I sing it for her. I sing it *to* her. I sing until I think my voice is going to give out, and then I keep singing, and then—

The song is over.

My arms drop like a couple of overcooked noodles, my pick dangling precariously from my fingers. But even though I can feel, objectively, the cloud of exhaustion looming on the horizon, none of that is breaking through the adrenaline swamping my veins.

"Hell yeah!" Dougie exclaims, throwing his arms into the air. *"Hell yeah!"*

"That was great," Jeff says, smiling shyly.

"That was *awesome*," Ronnie echoes, using one of her drumsticks to rap me on the shoulder.

But I barely register the impact. My eyes are still fixed on the window, where Nate is doing all sorts of little adjustments on the audio board, more energetic than I've ever seen him.

Where Paige is grinning, leaning forward, both arms braced on the back of Nate's chair.

I lean in and, just for the pleasure of watching that smile winch a little wider, ask, "What do you think?"

Paige reaches toward the mic, but Nate beats her to it, jamming the talk button down with a stab of his thumb.

"Badass, brother," he says, his voice crackling through our headphones and through the ceiling speakers. "That was. Fucking. Badass."

Chapter Fourteen

"Do I schedule my tetanus shot now? Or should I wait 'til my blood turns black?"

Dad huffs a laugh, his old binoculars pressed against his eye sockets. I have no idea how he can see anything through those things—one lens is cracked to hell. But maybe he's been eating his carrots in lockup, because he drops the binoculars into his lap with a satisfied nod. "Lights out."

It's a weird thing to say because the sun is blazing overhead, so hot I feel sweat dripping down the back of my neck. We've been sitting in my van since four a.m., parked in a stand of trees off a two-lane highway somewhere in eastern Illinois— safely out of sight of the decaying barn a ways down the road, but close enough to keep an eye on the mountains of rusting car bodies that litter the grass.

On first glance, the place looks like any other run-down property out in the boonies. This part of the state is riddled with them, sprawling acres of land that nobody gives enough

of a shit about to maintain. But this particular shithole fea-
tures a warehouse with boarded-up windows and wide double
doors, a generator large enough to run all of Hawkins, and a
stockpile of power tools that would make Uncle Wayne sali-
vate.

All the telltale signs of a chop shop. And chop shops run at
night. Which means that right about now, as the clock ticks
toward eleven, the upstanding members of society who run
the place should be all tuckered out and ready for bed.

"You ready?" Dad asks.

The honest answer is *no, I am not* ready *to rob a chop shop*,
but then I think about the demo tape that's currently on its
way in a padded envelope to some windowed, spotless office
building on Sunset Boulevard. The sun probably doesn't feel
so harsh in California. "Yup," I say. And I follow Dad out of the
van and through the trees along the side of the road.

I'd thought he was joking the first time he'd mentioned this
plan. I'm starting to realize that I have that reaction a lot when
Dad tells me something, and that unless there's a priest, a
rabbi, and a sailor involved, he very rarely is. *"We need a tow
truck,"* he'd said as we rummaged through the shelves at the
War Zone, piling spike strips and coveralls into an oversize
shopping cart. *"A big one."* I figured that meant we'd be paying
another visit to Reefer Rick or another one of Dad's . . . associ-
ates. Since his buddies came in every flavor of crooked on the
face of the earth, "oversize tow truck guy" didn't seem like too
big of a buy.

Put another point in the idiot column, I think, trudging along
behind Dad. My dreams of "tow truck guy" had imploded
pretty spectacularly the second Dad said that, for this errand,
we'd be crossing state lines. *"That's a pretty shady way to start
things off,"* I'd said, loading a pair of pliers into the shopping
cart.

But he'd just grinned at me. *"It's cooler in the shade, kid."*

The issue was, he'd explained, that tow trucks are hard to come by unless you have a wad of cash burning a hole in your pocket, and even then the authorities'll take notice. Jacking one from a reputable mechanic isn't a much better solution, especially if you're trying to fly under the radar the way we are. No, there's only one type of person guaranteed not to call the cops on a thief.

Other thieves.

"And it just so happens," Dad had said as we'd pushed our purchases across the parking lot toward my waiting van, *"I've got a line on a chop shop in Illinois that has exactly what we're looking for."*

We emerge from the trees right on the property line. Dad has his eyes fixed on the warehouse's padlocked barn doors, but I'm more preoccupied with the dingy trailer rusting into the grass a dozen yards away. This is where the two figures— one man, one woman, both in grease-stained coveralls—had disappeared once the sparks and grinding in the warehouse had paused for the night. It's only been about forty minutes since they slammed the door shut behind them, but I can already hear their snores filtering through the cracked windows. They're sacked out.

Let's just hope they stay that way.

Dad smacks my shoulder to get my attention. Then he's trotting across the grass toward the warehouse. A beer can crunches under his boot, and the tall weeds are *shushing* loudly at the legs of his jeans. But there's no falter from the snores in the trailer, and so I follow, keeping a step or two behind him until he stops in front of the padlock on the warehouse doors.

From one of the bottomless pockets of his leather jacket, Dad produces a couple long strips of metal. I keep one nervous eye on the distant trailer as he slips the picks into the padlock and gives them one twist, then another—and then the lock is clicking open, unlatching in the space of a breath.

"How are you so good at that?" I mutter.

"Guitar picks, lock picks." He waves his hands, and the picks disappear. *Munson Magic.* "You figure out one, you figure out the other."

"That's bullshit."

"Things can be bullshit and true at the same time."

It takes both of us to open the warehouse doors. This time Dad is careful to be quiet, moving slowly and oiling hinges so that no wayward creak of metal gives us away. By the time we step into the dusty barn and prop the doors closed with a brick, the drops of sweat running down my neck have transformed into a river, and my T-shirt is soaked beneath my arms. I'm a mess.

And Dad looks fresh as a daisy. He's got a crooked grin on his face, and there's an unsettling moment where I realize I've seen it before—on myself, in the mirror, when I've just come offstage at the Hideout or finished running a crazy session at Hellfire. It's a smile with an edge, with a bit of twisted heat.

"You bring that light for a reason?" Dad asks me. "Or is it just a pretty accessory?"

I roll my eyes and click the flashlight on. The beam cuts a dusty swath through the warehouse gloom, illuminating stacks of skeletal car carcasses piled three or four high. Workbenches jut at odd angles. The only clear route through this chaos is a path about six feet wide, which runs from the doors toward the back of the shop. Just large enough for a truck.

"Here," Dad says. Sure enough, the waving beam of my flashlight has landed on a fragment of what can only be the tow truck's hulking frame, and Dad trots around the driver's side to peer in the window. "Check the wheels," he orders over his shoulder.

I give him a mock salute. "Yes, sir."

"Don't be a punk. This is educational."

I could argue, but this doesn't feel like the place for it. Instead, I drop into a crouch, shining my flashlight into the wheel wells to search for the metallic glint of keys.

"No luck." The wheels are bare. But Dad just snorts and snatches up a discarded car antenna.

"Munsons don't wait on *luck*," he says. "We make our own." He shoves the antenna down into the window, and after a few seconds of jimmying, the door's lock is popping open, just as smoothly as the padlock on the warehouse door.

"That a guitar pick thing too?" I ask.

"That's intermediary." Dad wrenches the truck door open. "Come here. I wanna see if you can jump all the way to advanced." He slides up onto the bench seat. "We're not swimming in time, kid," he says when I hesitate. I resist the urge to stick my tongue out, and climb up next to him.

"All right," he says. Using a screwdriver, he pries open the plastic panel beneath the steering column. It lands across my knees, and I shove it aside. "Start her up."

The bottom drops out of my stomach. "Dad, I can't—"

"Sure you can. We've been over this. Or are you telling me you don't remember?"

Of course I remember. It had been my tenth birthday present from Dad: car-boosting lessons. I hadn't needed to ask around at school to know that this wasn't a widespread coming-of-age tradition.

"One day, you're gonna need a set of wheels," Dad had told me, his eyes solemn. I'd taken this as gospel at the time—of course I'd need a car, everyone needed a car. It hadn't occurred to me until later that *not* everyone *got* a car by stealing someone else's.

"Silly me, I guess I forgot to practice." I try to laugh through the heavy boulder sinking in my gut. "How ever will I get to Carnegie Hall?"

"I ain't joking, Eddie," Dad says. "I don't work with guys who don't pull their weight. You want a cut of this job, you're gonna help out. So I'll say it again: Start her up." He shoves a pocketknife into my hand. "Notice how that wasn't a question."

I gritted my teeth against a bitter retort. And then I reach down and extract two red wires from the bundle dangling below the steering column.

These'll jump-start the battery. I hear it in Dad's voice, echoing back from that sunny morning eight years ago. I'd watched him strip the ends with a flourish and twist them together. That's what I do now, flicking open the knife with my thumbnail and connecting the red wires.

"Good." Dad's approval washes through me. I wish it didn't feel as good as it does.

Ignition first. It's a yellow wire, easy enough to pinpoint. I tease it out of the snarl and twist it in with the battery wires. My stomach twists right along with the tangle in my hands, and I realize that the thing it's rebelling against is disgust. I'm *disgusted* with myself, with how easily this comes to me, with how much of this shit I remember, crystal clear and vibrant. There'd been a reason I hadn't practiced. I'd been telling myself that I wasn't anything like my dad, that if I needed a car, I'd just buy one.

Now look at me. I'm not Eddie, not here in the cab of this about-to-be-stolen truck. I'm Junior, the kid wearing Al Munson's crooked smile.

And Junior's got a job to do.

I strip the starter wires. *Now all you have to do is connect them and rev the engine a few times,* whispers that helpful memory, but this time I can hear shades of my own voice laid over Dad's. My stomach twists again, but I'm about to follow through—

When something *creaks*.

The hairs on my arms stand on end. I glance into the rearview mirror and see—

"The door's open." Not a ton, just enough to let a crack of sunlight inside. The weight of the warehouse door must have shifted the brick.

"Forget the door."

"You want your friends to find out what we're up to?" I'm already swinging my legs out of the truck. "I'll be right back."

He doesn't say anything. He just looks at me, all serious and disappointed as I jump to the concrete floor. I try not to feel like a coward, keeping my spine straight, trudging toward the warehouse door. But we both know this is a retreat.

You signed up for this, I think, in a voice that sounds a lot like Dad's. *You made the plan, you convinced the dealer. Why are you running now?*

I don't have an answer, not a solid one. It's something about *"You're gonna need a set of wheels."* Something about *"I don't work with guys who don't pull their weight,"* and the sense that the road that runs through this job actually keeps on going once we're on the other side, if I want to keep driving. Something about the feeling, after I'd stripped the ignition, that it wouldn't just be Dad's smile I saw the next time I looked in the mirror. It would be his whole damn face.

All that bullshit, apparently, is enough to tick my fight-or-flight switch firmly over to *flight*. So yeah, I retreat. I retreat toward the only slice of sunshine in this hellhole of an automotive graveyard.

It takes my eyes a second to adjust to the light, as I peer through the crack in the door. In my narrow scope of vision, I can see that the brick has shifted more than I thought, because I can't see it anymore. It's moved so much that it's flat-out gone. Frowning, I edge the door open a bit more, just enough so that I'll be able to grab the brick, wherever it's scraped off to, and drag it back—

—and stop short. Because what I find is not a wayward doorstop.

It's a gun. And it's pointed right between my eyes.

"You were right, Sammy," says a voice from the other end of the gun. "Looks like we got a rat."

Chapter Fifteen

I laugh. I can't help it, it just bubbles out of me. This whole day, I've been waiting for the other shoe to drop, and when it does, it's named *Sammy*?

"I'll still shoot you if you're crazy, kid," the gun says, and that shuts me up real quick. "Outside. Now."

I'm outside now.

The formerly snoring proprietors of this chop shop are both about Dad's age. The one with the gun is a woman rocking a greasy mullet that would make Bob Seger jealous. The whites of her eyes are bloodshot, but her finger is steady on the trigger—steady enough to dismiss all thoughts of making a break for it. Her buddy Sammy looms at her shoulder, so tall and wide that he casts a shadow over both of us.

Neither of them look happy to see me.

"Hey there," I say. My brief manic insanity has faded. Now I'm just a kid in a junkyard staring down the barrel of a semi-automatic.

"He doesn't look like a cop," Sammy mutters.

"Who the fuck would think he's a cop?" Miss Mullet shoves the gun against my chest. "You here alone?"

Somewhere in the darkness behind me, Dad is still sitting behind the wheel of a lifeless tow truck, and if these guys find him, we're toast. Any hope of getting out of this situation is with him.

So I do what I always do when there's a jock gunning for one of my Hellfire kids. I'm too big of a bastard to ignore.

"All alone except for you, sweetheart."

Sammy snorts a laugh. He's my favorite. Miss Mullet, on the other hand, turns scarlet. "Funny guy, huh?"

"You really think so?"

"Did you miss the part where I'm gonna kill you?"

I really, really didn't. But I'm hoping that the faint grinding sound I hear in the warehouse behind me is not my imagination, and so I just say, "I've heard a lot of promises. Not a lot of follow-through."

It's not my imagination. The grinding is louder. Sammy's substantial and singular eyebrow buckles in the middle in concern. "Hey—" he starts.

"But if you're having second thoughts, I wouldn't blame you," I say, loud enough to cut Sammy off. "Killing me sounds like it'd be messy as hell, and I've seen the inside of your operation. I'm sure you folks are very talented mechanics, but cleanup is not your strength."

Miss Mullet cocks the gun.

Which is when the warehouse doors *blast* outward and Dad rockets through, as fast as a freshly carjacked tow truck can carry him. One of the doors slams into Sammy, sending him hurtling into the grass with enough force to shake the earth. Or maybe that's just my own skull rattling, because I'm hitting the deck, covering my ears as Miss Mullet's surprise squeezes the gun's trigger for her, and a shot ricochets off the corrugated steel wall a foot above my head.

My ears are still ringing as I shove to my knees, ready to wave down my ride. But all I see, once I clear the grass, is the taillights of the truck zooming away, back toward the two-lane highway.

He's not stopping for me. He's not even slowing. He's ditching me here, in this godforsaken junkyard, with two people who want to turn my head into red confetti.

"Your Dad's not the guy you can hang your hat on." That's what Wayne had said. *"Not if it's a hat you don't want to lose."* I'm starting to understand what he meant.

I'm still staring toward Dad's disappearing taillights when something flashes hot and bright across the side of my face. The dull pain follows, and then the realization that a) Miss Mullet has just smacked me in the head with the butt of her gun, and b) I'm lying in the dirt.

"You little shit," she hisses. She's standing over me now, one boot planted on either side of my head. I've got a great view up her nose and also up the gun barrel. I could do without either.

"Listen," I say, but I don't have anything to follow it up with. If this was school, we'd never get to this part. This fight would already have been broken up. I'd already have been hauled off to Higgins's office to stand trial for my nonexistent crimes.

But right now I'm alone. There's no one coming to help me out. I'll die here, and worse than that, I'll disappear. And I doubt anyone will even look for me.

"I'm gonna put a hole in that stupid haircut," Miss Mullet grits out. Pretty hypocritical as far as insults go, but I'm too busy trying not to piss my pants to point this out to her.

"Listen," I say again. It's the only word I can seem to remember.

"Then I'm gonna find your partner and do the same thing to him. And your family. And everyone you've ever met in your entire miserable life."

"Listen."

And I mean it this time. Because that sound is back—that grinding, choked-engine sound, growing louder with every passing millisecond. Miss Mullet has just time to look back over her shoulder—

—and then the tow truck is *barreling* into her, sending her rag-dolling through the air. I take a dazed and shocky moment to appreciate the sight of the wind fluttering her hair like a greasy banner. Then she slaps into the side of the warehouse hard enough to dent the steel wall, smacks into the ground, and lies still.

"Nice work!"

I'm blinking up at Dad's upside-down face in the upside-down window of the upside-down truck cab. "I thought you left," I say, without entirely meaning to.

He rolls his eyes. "You sound like Wayne."

A few yards away, the mountainous silhouette of Sammy is starting to stir. Dad revs the truck. "You comfy down there?"

"No."

"Then get off your ass, kid, let's *go*."

Sammy mumbles, and that's the spark I need. I scramble to my feet, and the growing knot on the side of my head makes the world swim. But I power through, throwing myself into the truck cab. I don't even get the door closed before Dad is hammering the gas, and we're lurching forward, fishtailing around discarded car parts and rotting logs toward the road as Sammy and Miss Mullet moan and groan behind us.

"You good to drive?" Dad shouts over the roar of the engine.

"Huh?"

"Your head. You good to drive the van?"

Common sense says no, absolutely not. But there's adrenaline singing in every single one of my veins, and I'm still alive even though twenty seconds ago it seemed like that was not a good bet, and *Dad came back for me* so—

"Fuck, yeah."

"Fuck, yeah," Dad echoes, and this time I don't feel bad when I match his crooked grin with my own because, against all odds, I'm starting to believe that we can actually do this.

All it needs is a little Munson Magic.

Chapter Sixteen

"Would you quit it?" I swat at Ronnie's finger, which hasn't stopped prodding at the knot on my skull since I picked her up that morning.

"I can't look away," she says, and her next jab lands a bull's-eye in the middle of the bump. I hiss and jerk back, but this doesn't seem to faze her. "It's hypnotizing me."

"You're hypnotizing *me* every time you poke it," I say. "You're *concussing* me."

"I'm reminding you to fix the door of your van." She finally drops her finger, and I relax. "The next time it clocks you, it could take the top of your skull off."

"You wanna tie a string around my finger? I'll remember. Hurry up, we're late."

We're trotting through the emptying school hallways, booking it double-time toward the lucky location of today's Hellfire Club: Mr. Vick's chemistry lab. (Price: A full hour of scrubbing out beakers as well as some light sweeping. If I didn't know how overworked the Hawkins High janitorial staff already is, I'd file a complaint.) I'm trying to ignore the fact that the world still spins a little bit if my foot lands just a touch too hard, but it's getting better every hour, so I'm just going to assume that I don't need to go to the hospital. Anyway, I don't want to give Miss Mullet the satisfaction.

But Hellfire Club isn't settled inside the classroom when Ronnie and I arrive, like they should be. They're loitering in the hall, backpacks discarded against the wall. Jeff and Dougie are playing some weird game of catch with a rubber band ball, bouncing it off the ceiling and into the other person's hands. Gareth's huddled on the floor, a spiral-bound notebook spread open across his knees. As I get closer, I can see the rows and rows of cramped scribbles that cover the pages, complete with an amateur pencil sketch of a scowling dwarf. *Character notes.*

He's the first one to notice our approach. "Eddie!" he calls, scrambling to his feet. Jeff and Dougie quit their dumb game and wheel around as well.

"What's the holdup?" I ask. "You don't have to wait for me to get set up, you know that."

"Door's locked," Jeff tells me. "We thought maybe Mr. Vick gave you the key."

He hadn't. He'd just said, *"See you Wednesday,"* and we'd left it at that. It had always worked for us before.

"He must have forgot," I say, and try to make myself believe it.

Ronnie slings her bag to the ground. "Where's Stan?" she asks, digging out Stan's Trapper Keeper.

I do a quick scan of the hallway. Sure enough, no Stan. "Is he coming late?"

But Jeff shakes his head. "I didn't see him today."

"He must be sick. Or maybe he couldn't sneak past his parents."

Ronnie frowns. "He always calls when he's gonna have to skip."

But if he's called, I haven't been around to answer it—either out trailing after Dad, rehearsing with Corroded Coffin, or haunting the Hideout in case Paige decides to swing by. A shadow of guilt wells up inside me, but I push it down. "Whatever it is—we honor our fallen warrior by kicking ass in his name. Would Arick Windward, the First Mage, want to know his compatriots were sitting around on their asses when they could be ripping tentacles off a Beholder?"

Gareth straightens up so abruptly that I think he might topple over. "No!"

"That's what I thought." I study the door. There's a chance Mr. Vick is still hanging around the teacher's lounge, but it's a slim one. If he ran out of here without leaving the door open for Hellfire, odds are good that he's gone for the day, and if I leave to track him down, I'd just be wasting precious time.

But. The lock on the handle isn't complicated—definitely nowhere near the lock on the chop shop garage. I can open it. I've done it before.

"Hold please, ladies and gentlemen." I dig an old Family Video card out of my wallet and kneel down, sliding the card into the crack between the lab door and the doorjamb.

There's a part of me that protests the thought, the way it always does. This time, it's drowned out by the memory of Dad's voice. *Guitar picks, lock picks* . . .

"Would you look at that. A Munson breaking and entering." *God damn it.*

Somewhere inside the space of my tiny inspirational speech, Tommy H and three of his basketball goons have appeared in the hallway. Now they range out around us, their letterman shoulders forming a semicircle that blocks us in.

"Must be a Wednesday," sneers the one who might be Connor.

"What the hell do you want?" Gareth demands. He's got his chest puffed out so much that he could probably float away on a strong enough breeze.

But Tommy H just grins down Gareth's glare. "You wanna watch yourself."

"Okay, slugger." I tap Gareth's shoulder until he blinks out of his blind fury. "Let's take it down about twenty notches." Once the kid has deflated enough to put me at ease, I stand, facing the squad of jocks with my best Al Munson smile. "If you wanted to jump in on today's game, I'm *terribly* afraid we're all full up."

"You think we want in on that Satanic shit?" demands the shrimpy little jock—Jason, I remember, the one who hauled Chrissy away like a sack of dirty laundry.

"If you don't, then I'm gonna have to repeat my young friend here. What the hell do you want?"

"Not much." Tommy H shoves his hands into the pockets of his jacket, like he doesn't have a care in the world. "We were just passing by and I remembered—you and me, we're not square."

"I know *I'm* not square," I say. My heart rate is rising. "Not sure about you."

"We're just here to play some D and D, guys," Ronnie says, stepping up next to me. "That's all. We're not trying to start anything."

"It's already started, sweetheart," Tommy H sneers. "It's *been* started. You can thank your dick-hole boyfriend for that."

"If that's the case, then why the entourage?" I ask. "Sounds like, whatever your damage is, it's only with me."

"You think things are that simple, freak?" maybe-Connor says.

"Your club is a stain on the good name of this school," says Jason. "On the good name of this entire town."

"Talk to us about the good name of the school after you've won one single basketball game," Dougie mutters somewhere behind me. If I could kick him, I would, but since I can't, Ronnie does it for me. *"Ow."*

"There's no place here for freaks," Tommy H says. His buddies shuffle in, shrinking the gaps between them, closing in on us. "But it seems like you're having a hard time learning that lesson, so—"

I run.

It's not glamorous and it's not brave. But it *is* a calculated gamble. *Judicious retreat.* I'm counting on the fact that Tommy H is focused on me, that if I make a break for it, he and all his cronies will bolt after me without a second thought. Maybe it'll give Ronnie and Dougie and the rest of them enough time to get away. Maybe it'll give *me* enough time to get away.

Maybe not, though, because a split second later, I hear the shouts and pounding footsteps as all four jocks take off after me. And they are gaining *fast.*

Linoleum squeaks under my sneakers, the multicolored tiles blurring as I rush by. My breath is already burning in my chest—*it's what you get for skipping P.E. every day for the last four years*—but I can't slow down and I definitely can't take a break, because there are four muscle-bound commuter trains barreling down after me, and if they catch up then I'm going to get pancaked.

I take a corner, arms windmilling, and the distant glow of sunlight catches my eye. *Escape.* That's east exit, a fire door propped open by Mr. Terry's yellow mop bucket. If I can make it, then at least I won't be in this locker-lined death funnel.

But the pounding and the turning and the racing are really doing a number on my throbbing head. My knees give out—just for a split second, just long enough to break my stride. I catch myself and take off again—

"Grab him—"

But it's too late. Hands clamp down on my arms, tight enough to bruise, and then I'm slammed forward, hitting the wall of lockers face-first, hard enough to rattle locker doors all the way up and down the hall. *"Fuck,"* I hiss, the word involuntarily bursting out of me with every scrap of oxygen in my lungs.

They don't even bother turning me around to face them before the first punch lands. I feel the dull pain on a split-second delay, registering that somebody—probably Tommy H—has just driven his fist into my side. Someone else kicks at the backs of my knees, and I have to catch myself against the wall again. If I go down, I'm not sure that I'll ever get back up again.

"You think you can outrun us?" Tommy H is breathing hard. I can smell sour sweat radiating off him. "Big mistake, freak." I hear rather than see him gesture to his cronies. "Hold him still." And as those hands on my arms tighten, I brace myself for impact—

Which is when I hear the scream.

The sound is so piercing that if maybe-Connor didn't have a bruising-solid grip on me, I'd have clutched at my ears. It's an ungodly decibel, something typically reached only by dying rabbits.

And by freshmen with a death wish, apparently.

Gareth hurls himself into the fray like the Tasmanian Devil, a whirl of scrawny limbs punching and kicking. *"Leave. Him. Alone!"* Between the wall of shoulders, I catch only glimpses of his aluminum-buttressed grimace, which twists and twists with every blow he lands. The kid already knows that getting punched hurts. I'd bet he's figuring out right about now that doing the punching hurts too.

"Gareth!" And now Ronnie's here too, pounding up behind Gareth and making a grab for the edge of his shirt. She tries to haul him back, but the kid's too determined. He wiggles out of her grip and manages to slam his elbow into the base of Tommy H's stomach.

The sound of air exploding out of Tommy H is concussive. "Son of a *bitch*—" he gasps, and maybe basketball is good for something after all, because *he* has no problem getting a handle on Gareth. One hand wraps around the freshman's collar, lifting him up so that Gareth wobbles, scrabbling to keep the tips of his sneakers scraping the ground.

I manage to shove maybe-Connor back enough to turn around. "Get off of him."

Tommy H leers down at Gareth. "Your freak king thinks I should do what he says."

Gareth spits in his eye.

The yelp that comes out of Tommy would be hilarious in any other situation. He stumbles back half a step, wiping desperately at his face with his free hand. His other hand, unfortunately, does not loosen its grip on Gareth, and he drags the kid along with him. "You little shit!"

"Let me *go*." Gareth claws at Tommy's fingers.

"I'm gonna *kill you*."

And in that moment, I'm not sure he's being dramatic. There's something in Tommy H's face—the same something I saw in Miss Mullet's, right before she shoved her gun right between my eyes. Something that says, *you're not gonna be walking out of here alive*, and means it.

Shit.

I push at maybe-Connor, struggling toward Gareth, but Tommy's knee is already driving into the kid's chest in a blow that sends him to his knees. For a moment, I fool myself into thinking that'll be it, that this whole chaotic scene is wrapping up, that Tommy and his goon squad will walk away. But then Tommy is pulling back, winding up, and I only have enough time to say, "Don't—" before—

Tommy kicks Gareth in the head. Or at least he tries to. The kid has enough room to twitch backward, which means that the blow catches him in the shoulder instead of the nose. He hits the lockers behind him with a dull *thunk*, but it's the sound that follows as he ping-pongs to the ground that turns my stomach.

It's the unmistakable noise of a bone cracking. Gareth gasps, curling up on his side like a roly-poly bug, clutching his wrist to his chest.

"Shit," I hiss, trying to shove forward toward him. But maybe-Connor is still holding me back, his grip like iron on my shoulders.

Not that Tommy H notices. The only thing he's seeing is red, and he advances on Gareth, closing in like an avenging demon. "He's hurt!" I shout. "You got him, okay, man? We're good, we're even—"

But Tommy just reaches down, grabbing Gareth by the collar again and hauling him up. I can see that Gareth's face is paper-pale and his wrist is twisted at an unnatural angle. He whimpers at the movement. All traces of his glowering defiance have evaporated, leaving behind exactly what Gareth is: a young kid in over his head, cringing back from the hammy fist that Tommy's got ready to let fly—

But it's not Gareth who takes the punch. It's Ronnie, shoving in front of him with a chewed-glass *"Hey."* And Tommy's never been the best player on the court, because his reflexes are too shitty to pull the punch at the last second—or maybe he doesn't want to. Either way, in the space of a blink, Ronnie's head is snapping sideways as Tommy's punch slams into her cheek.

In all the years of me getting my ass handed to me—of Hellfire catching shrapnel—it's never hit Ronnie. She's always danced above it, through no fault of her own. It's like the world all agreed that, no matter how close she was to the infection, she wasn't infected herself. She was Good, which meant she was safe. And now—

She whips her head back around. Her hand is still pressed to her face, but it doesn't obscure the absolute death glare she has leveled at Tommy H.

"Are you done?" she demands. "Or do you want to show off by beating up a freshman some more?"

Tommy's breathing hard, sweat standing out on his forehead. He looks like he's seriously considering the cons of taking another swing, another kick, maybe breaking Gareth's other arm, maybe taking Ronnie out with him—

"That's enough."

It's Higgins. He's planted right in the middle of the hall. And it doesn't take much imagining to see a storm cloud booming over his head.

He takes in the scene wordlessly, though the vein jumping in his temple does more than enough talking. But despite the chaos—Gareth on the floor, Tommy and his clenched fists, Ronnie and the budding bruise on her cheek—it's me his eyes lock on to.

Chapter Seventeen

There are more kids than chairs in the main office, to the point that Jeff is crouched on the floor, leaning back against the wall with his eyes closed. Ronnie accepts an ice pack from a thin-lipped Janice and presses it to her cheek with a wince. Dougie is glaring daggers at anyone unlucky enough to cross his field of vision.

On the other end of the spectrum, Tommy H and his buddies look extremely unbothered by where they are. As I watch, one of the guys balls up his detention slip and shoots it toward the wastepaper basket. A whoop of laughter goes up at his miss, and not even Janice is immune. She's smiling as she passes Tommy a Dixie cup of water.

"Sit down."

I tear myself away from the narrow window in the principal's office door.

Higgins is standing at his desk. Both arms are braced on

the tabletop, and he looks about two seconds away from com-
busting out of pure, unadulterated anger.

"After you," I say.

"Don't mess with me, Munson," he snaps. "Sit. Down."

I sit down. He does not. This was probably his plan all
along.

"How much money is it going to cost Mr. Hayes to bail
Tommy H out this time?" I ask him. "Three times the going
rate? Four? Maybe you need a new car. I've heard he's got a
great stock of new Volvos."

Higgins just stares down at me. "Are you finished?"

I fidget in my chair. His stony face is making me nervous.
"Whatever."

"Wonderful." Higgins straightens. "Now. I'd like to run
through the events of this afternoon with you, because you
seem to have an uncanny ability to ignore reality. Point one:
after the final bell, you led your . . . *club* in breaking into a
teacher's classroom without that teacher's knowledge or con-
sent. Point two: when Mr. Hayes and his friends discovered
your trespass, you goaded them into attacking—"

"That's *bullshit*—"

"—which leads me to point three: in the ensuing alterca-
tion, four students were injured, one badly enough to send him
to the hospital. Do I have that right?"

"No! We were minding our business and those guys *jumped
us.*"

Higgins shakes his head. "A child is in the hospital, and you
are sitting here whining and pointing fingers."

Finally he plunks down into his chair and pulls open the
top desk drawer. I catch a brief flash of something bright and
blue inside, something that rings a faint chime of recognition
in the back of my mind—

But then Higgins removes a piece of paper and slides it over to me, and whatever thread of recollection I'd been grasping at flies out of reach. "Read that," Higgins says. "If you would be so kind."

I eye it, uncertain. "What is it?"

"Read. It. Put your brain to work, for once in your life. Maybe you'll get your answer."

Feeling like I'm climbing the steps to the guillotine, I pick up the paper and start to read.

Dear Principal Higgins, it begins, and things only go downhill from there. It's a concerned letter from a Hawkins parent— Stan's mom, if the last name is anything to go off. She's disgusted by the breeding ground for Satanists and delinquents that the high school has decided to foster. *Surely an institution that purports to value morality and virtue cannot continue to support an organization called H—fire Club? Particularly when certain members of said "club" seek to exert their influence and inflict their values on more impressionable young students?*

She's taken Stan out of school. That's the message at the bottom of all of this. She found out what he'd really been up to every Wednesday afternoon, and she did what Stan was always afraid she'd do and shoved him into the Teen Frontier Program to—I don't know. Cleanse him?

"She can't do this," I mutter. "She can't make him leave Hawkins. He didn't want to—"

"I am well aware that Stanley did not want to leave Hawkins," Higgins says. "He tried pleading his case to me directly, once his mother made her intentions known. But there was, of course, nothing I could do. His involvement with your club concerned the family so deeply that they put two hundred miles between him and Hellfire.

"I want to make this very clear, Munson," he continues. "What happened to Stanley is your fault. So is every bruise on every student sitting out in that office. So is the child currently awaiting an orthopedic surgeon at Hawkins Memorial. *'Oblique displaced fracture.'* That's what the paramedics told me. *'Lucky if he avoids nerve damage.'* I'm not sure what that means, exactly, but I do know it means it will be at least eight weeks until he can use that arm again."

Crack. The sound of Gareth's wrist snapping ricochets through my head. So does his pained gasp.

"I see I have your attention now," Higgins says. "Then let me take the opportunity to spell one more thing out for you. *Hellfire is finished.*"

"No, it's not," I say, but it's an anemic protest even to my ears. "You can't just kick us out. We're a school club—"

"You are not. School clubs must be registered. They must have a faculty sponsor." His eyes narrow. "I've tolerated your— your *gathering's* presence on this campus as long as I have because there were teachers willing to give you the benefit of the doubt. But since the receipt of this letter"—he taps his finger against Stan's mom's perfect cursive—"those same faculty members have been persuaded that associating with your group will cause more harm than good."

That explains what happened with Mr. Vick. "So I'll find a sponsor. I'll register the club."

"I am asking you *not to.*"

I'm so used to Higgins *ordering* and not *asking* that this really takes the wind out of my sails. "What?"

Higgins clasps his hands in front of him. He's the image of the reasonable principal. I want to punch him in the face. "Let's talk about Veronica Ecker."

Somethings zings through me. I can't tell if it's fear or anger or a putrid, electric mix of both. But the world instantly becomes sharper, the hackles on the back of my neck going up.

"She doesn't have anything to do with this."

"She has something to do with you. Which means she absolutely has something to do with this." Higgins has no excoriat-
ing letter to slide across his desk this time, but he doesn't need
one. He knows he has my full and undivided attention. "This
afternoon, she was involved in a serious brawl on school property. This is the sort of act that universities find . . . shall we
say, significant? Or maybe the better word would be conse-
quential. Which is to say, there are often consequences." He
shakes his head. "We were all so proud of her for overcoming
her beginnings. NYU! A marvelous school. A terrific opportunity for a bright young woman. And to pile on a full scholarship on top of that achievement?"

Cold is working through me, starting at my fingertips and
moving toward my heart. "Ronnie didn't do anything wrong,"
I insist. "She was just trying to help me—"

Higgins cocks his head. "Then you see my point."

I open my mouth. I close it again.

The sick thing is . . . I do. I've been glimpsing the edges of it
for a while now—days, weeks, even months. It's been coming
through in glitches and gasps, but it had never popped into
focus until—

Crack. Again, behind my eyelids, Gareth's arm snaps. Out
in the office, Ronnie presses an ice pack to her bruised face.
Jeff slumps against the wall because nobody will get him a
chair. Tommy H and his friends laugh.

All of this happened because of me. That icy cold has settled
in so deep that it aches in my bones.

"We have an opportunity here," Higgins says from somewhere on the other side of the frigid fog, "to help one another."
I don't look up, but that doesn't seem to matter to him as he
plows forward. "You can help me appease all the concerned
parents at First Baptist. And I can help you to help your friends."

"How?" I ask. My fingertips are numb. My voice is scratchy.

"Drop out."

It's not a surprise. I barely blink in reaction, and maybe that irritates Higgins, because he leans across the desk toward me, speaking fast and quiet. "Drop. Out," he repeats in a low hiss. "Without you and your—organization haunting this school, Hawkins High will be able to move forward, untainted. As will Veronica and the rest of your friends. No notes on their school records. No letters to NYU. It will be as though today's unfortunate incident never occurred."

It's blackmail. Higgins is blackmailing me. *Accept being the pariah this town has made of you. Retreat. And in return—*

The bruise on Ronnie's cheek. The glint of happiness in her eyes as she'd told me about her scholarship. *"What are you doing?"* and *"Last time,"* and every life raft she's ever floated my way—

I meet Higgins's eyes. "Can I ask you a question?"

His mouth twists at the delay, but he gives one curt nod. "Fine."

"Why me?"

His jaw works. He doesn't know how to respond. "Why you what?"

"You're right. I'm number one on the shit list of everybody in this school. In this town. And I honestly don't know how I got there. I was hoping you did, since you've got such a clear picture of what I should be doing with my life."

Higgins sinks back in his chair. He's considering me— actually looking at me, studying me, and in a sort of distant, shocked way, I realize that this may be the first time he's ever done it. "Because," he says, and there's a long pause before he continues. "Because it's just who you are."

A freak. A fuckup. Junior. A rotting apple. Munson. The chorus screams louder and louder in my head, playing on a loop—

Barback turned front man—

Wait—

—*turned rock hero.*

I straighten in my chair. *That's right.* Just because everyone in this shitty town looks at me and thinks, *That's just who you are,* I don't have to be on the same page. I don't have to be the freak or the fuckup or Junior. Maybe I'm the guy a pretty, smart, fun girl looks at and sees a *rock hero.*

And maybe I've been holding every nerd in Hellfire back from having the same experience. Maybe I've been holding them back *with* Hellfire.

I can solve this. I can make it all right. I can protect Gareth's and Ronnie's futures and maybe even bring Stan home. And once I'm a goddamn rock star, I can give a big ol' middle finger to this shitty school and everyone in it.

"Then congratulations, Principal Higgins," I say, with my dad's best crooked smile. "You are looking at Hawkins High's newest dropout."

Chapter Eighteen

The Polaroids smack onto the bar, right in a puddle of something sticky. "This is the one," Dad says.

"Gross." I pluck up the pictures before they're ruined by
beer or vodka or God-only-knows-what.

"I'm telling you," Dad says, grabbing the photos back from
me and slapping them down again. "Topp's Twenty-Four-Hour
Auto. This is it. This piece of shit is where the magic is gonna
happen for us." He squints at me through the gloomy Hideout
lighting. Then, a second later, he's lunging across the bar to
poke at the corner of my mouth with his finger. "Could you
smile? This is good news! Act like it!"

It's a big ask, but I try to play along. Revelations aside, I'd
slumped my way out of Hawkins High and into my shift at the
Hideout still feeling like there was an elephant sitting on my
chest, and three hours of emptying chew spit out of pint glasses
and mopping spilled beer off the floor hasn't done much to
sweeten my mood. Then Dad had waltzed in with his handful

of photographs, talking a mile a minute about auto mechanics and logistics and ideas, ideas, ideas, and I haven't had a chance to get a word in edgewise much less let my brain catch up.

"Topp's Twenty-Four-Hour Auto," I say. "Cool."

"Damn right, it's cool. It's perfect. Two-man staff, open late, the only shop for thirty miles in any direction—"

"Cool."

"'Cool. Cool.' What's wrong with you? You look like someone took a hammer to your guitar and made you a necklace out of the pieces."

I take a deep breath. Let it out. "I dropped out of school."

Dad blinks at me. "Today?"

"Yeah."

He blinks again. And again. And then—

"Pop some goddamn champagne!"

For a second, I think he's gonna lunge across the bar to hug me. "What the hell—"

"It's about time!" Dad exclaims, loud enough to have the woozy Tuesday night drunks weave their heads up to look at us. "You've been killing yourself, wasting time in that hellhole when you could be out living your life!"

"Hey!" Bev stalks over, drawn by his outburst. "Keep the volume down. This isn't a goddamn rodeo."

But Dad just greets her stormy approach by flinging open his arms. "Bev! Get over here, gimme a kiss on the cheek!"

"You're out of your mind, Munson—"

"I'm not out of my mind, I'm *celebrating*! My son's a free man!"

"Shut *up*, Dad," I mutter.

"A pitcher of your finest ale, beautiful Beverly!" Dad braces both forearms against the bar so that Bev can experience the full force of his wink. And I can't be certain under the sickly neon lighting, but I'm pretty sure Bev *blushes*.

"Free man, huh?" she asks me. I shrug, and she blows out a sigh. "Well. I guess I can give you *one* pitcher on the house. Since you're celebrating."

Dad grins. "As gracious as you are lovely." I, on the other hand, say absolutely nothing. I'm pretty sure I'll never speak again, actually. I have worked in this bar for one full year, and I have never seen Bev comp anything for anybody, and the shock of witnessing it has altered me on a molecular level.

"I'm proud of you, kid," Dad says, as Bev turns to fill the pitcher with the cheapest Bud Light the Hideout has to offer. "Honestly. Dropping out might have been an easy decision for me, but I know it was different for you, so." He pats me on the arm with one firm hand.

"Thanks," I say, once I regain the power of speech. "But, uh. Let's just keep it quiet for now, okay? I don't know—when I'm gonna tell everybody else."

"You worried about Wayne? Don't be. He dropped out even earlier than I did."

"I'm worried about—" *what I'm gonna say when Ronnie asks me* why. "Yeah. Uncle Wayne."

"If he gives you any shit, just tell him to talk to me," Dad says and flashes another dazzling grin as Bev sets the pitcher down in front of him. "I can handle Wayne. You just enjoy your new freedom." He pours two beers and slides one toward me. "Cheers. To your future."

I clink my glass against his and take a sip. When I lower my beer, he's watching me with this assessing look that sets the hairs on the back of my neck standing up. "Why's your face doing that? What's going on?"

"Nothing," Dad says.

"Spit it out."

"I was just thinking. At the chop shop. You kept your head screwed on, you thought fast. You remembered what I taught you, even eight years after the fact. You ever considered—you could be good at this?"

"At—being a petty criminal?"

"That was grand theft auto, jackass, nothing petty about it. No—I'm asking if you've thought about saying *screw you* to society and its rules and doing what's best for you instead."

Behind Dad, the front door is opening, and someone is walking inside, and I don't even have to wait to see her face before I know it's Paige. She pauses, squinting in the dim light as she scans the bar. Looking for someone.

"Or were you planning on hanging around here?" Dad is still rambling. "Getting some crappy job in a factory like my brother, and waiting for life to grind the joy out of you?"

Paige's gaze lands on me, and her whole face brightens up. I feel it in my chest like a chemical reaction, bubbles rising as her expression sparks against the improbability that anyone could feel that way just at the sight of me. She waves, and I start to wave back, but—

"We could hit the road when this job is done," Dad says. "Keep the party going, you and me. We could be a team. Munson and Munson, like a law firm or some shit—"

She's coming over. She's coming over. The wave of panic swamps me all at once, burying those fizzy bubbles with an overwhelming, blaring alarm that sounds a lot like the words *DON'T LET HER FIND OUT.*

Because the thing is—everyone in Hawkins knows what to expect from Al Munson. And as Higgins has made abundantly clear, that's a reputation I've inherited as well. There's no dodging that bullet, not for Junior.

But Paige has somehow . . . missed that memo. To her, I'm *real*, someone to invest in, to go out on a limb for. I'm a rock star. Just seeing me makes her happy, and I want to keep being that person as long as possible. But if she meets Dad—

"I was hoping I'd find you here!" Paige says, sliding onto a barstool. Dad's reaction is almost comical, the seesaw of expressions zinging across his face as he realizes first that a) this girl is gorgeous, b) she's not talking to him, c) she's talking to *me,* and d) this means that we know each other. "How much longer is your shift tonight?"

"Uh," is about all I can manage, and even that's just a strangled scrap of a sound.

"Eddie," Dad says, amusement thick in his gaze as he glances from me to Paige and back again, "you gonna introduce me to your friend?"

Paige rocks back, a little embarrassed. "Sorry, did I interrupt something?"

"Nothing to interrupt," Dad says, swiveling on his stool to offer Paige a hand. "I'm Eddie's father, Al."

"This is Paige," I say from the other side of my total meltdown. I watch through telescoping tunnel vision as Paige takes Dad's hand and shakes it, convinced that as soon as they make contact, the veil is going to shred beyond repair, and she'll be left with no impression of me but mass-market Hawkins disgust.

But all that happens is that they shake hands twice and let go. "Lovely to meet you, Paige," Dad says. "How do you know Eddie?"

"From around," I blurt.

"I'm working with his band," says Paige at the exact same time, and then shoots me a quizzical look that questions my mental stability. It's warranted. It's all warranted. I've got to get out of here.

Dad's eyebrows shoot up toward his hairline. "His band, huh? Didn't realize Corroded Coffin had anything to work with."

I flick him with my dish towel. *"Hey."*

"You didn't tell your dad about the demo?" Paige asks me.

"I was—waiting for the right time."

The flicker of hurt that flares through Dad's eyes is bright, but he shuts it down almost as soon as it sparks, shaking his head in over-the-top paternal disapproval. "He's always been like this. You should have seen him with his comics when he was a kid. Stashing them everywhere he could—under the bed, behind the nightstand, under the rug. Like a little squirrel."

In a horrifying turn of events, Paige is absolutely delighted by this. "A little squirrel!"

"No—*Dad*, come on—"

"I even pulled a couple *X-Men* out of the refrigerator!"

It wasn't the fridge, it was the freezer, and Uncle Wayne was the one who found my Uncanny X-Men 98 *hiding in a stack of TV dinners because* you *weren't around.* But Paige is laughing, too bright and cheery for such a shitty dive bar, and so I bite my tongue against the protest and try to breathe through the mounting anxiety that's wrapped around my chest like a steel band.

"Can I get you a drink?" I ask Paige. Anything to end this interaction as soon as possible.

"On me," Dad says.

Paige flaps a hand. "That's sweet, but—"

"Do you have to get going?" I ask. "We can meet up later—"

"Now hold on," Dad says. "Before you go running all over the place. What's this Paige is saying about a demo and Corroded Coffin?" He leans sideways toward Paige, raising a hand over his mouth to stage-whisper, "You know, I was the one who taught him to play the guitar. He gets all his worst tricks from me."

Paige grins. "Glad I know who to blame."

"It was just a stupid tape," I tell Dad. "Paige works for WR Records—"

"Shit, really?"

"And I conned her into letting Corroded Coffin take a run at it—"

Paige pokes me. "There was no conning."

"—so that's the demo. That's all."

I shouldn't hate this. This is the kind of meet-the-parents moment that normal families have been having since the beginning of time. It's mundane in a way I thought meant I'd never get to experience it for myself. I should be excited, not riddled with anxiety, crawling out of my skin with the urge to shuffle Paige out the door as fast as possible, especially when she plucks one of Dad's Polaroids off the bar and asks "What's Topp's Auto?"

Dad doesn't miss a beat, doesn't fumble the change of subject, doesn't snatch the picture from her. He just cranes his head around to look at the photo with her. "I saw a HIRING sign in their window when I was passing," he says. "Snapped the photo so I wouldn't forget the name of the place when I got back. You ever been there?"

"Uh-uh."

"Damn. I wanna know if the owner's a bastard. The guys in the garage wouldn't tell me shit."

"Probably means he is," Paige says, handing the photo back to Dad. "Good luck."

"Thanks, sweetheart." I can't tell what he's thinking, even when he looks back over at me. Whatever it is, it's locked behind his smile as he says, "Music, huh?"

So no Munson and Munson? is what he's asking. I shrug. "It's an option."

He's quiet for a beat. I wonder if he's thinking about Mom's records next to the TV. The ones he drove up all the way from Tennessee. "Okay," he finally says, nodding just once. Then he whips the spotlight of his grin back on Paige. "Eddie was just wrapping up here."

"Huh?" Dad's working with a road map to this conversation that I can't keep up with. "No, Bev's got me on 'til close."

"Don't worry about Bev." Dad nudges my arm. "When a pretty lady asks what time your shift is over, your shift is *over.*"

"Your father's a smart man," Paige says.

"I'll handle Bev," Dad says. "You two get on out of here."

I shoot a dubious glance down the bar, where Bev is multitasking by glaring at me for procrastinating and cleaning a glass at the same time. "You sure?"

"Stop dragging your feet, jackass! Wouldn't you rather spend the night stargazing with Miss Paige than wiping up crusty beer stains?" He whips the dish towel off my shoulder.

The spike of irritation in my gut is milder this time, more of a gentle exasperation. *"Dad,"* I hiss, as Paige laughs.

"Go, kid," he says, nodding toward the door. "Do me a favor and celebrate."

Paige stands, smiling at me in the Hideout gloom. "Well?" she asks. Her dark eyes are still bright, the way they were when she first spotted me. All of a sudden those bubbles in my chest are back, and I'm ducking around the bar without realizing that I've done it.

"Don't say I never did anything for you," Dad says as I follow Paige toward the front door. And it's not a question, not a statement that demands a response, but as the door swings open and cool night air washes the dive bar cigarette smog from my lungs, I find myself whispering—

"Okay."

Chapter Nineteen

I open the van door for Paige. It's stupid, and I regret it as soon as I realize what I'm doing, but then Paige is putting her hand in mine, and I'm handing her up into the passenger's seat like some kind of gentleman.

She smiles at me. "Thanks."

"Uh-huh," I say. Not a gentleman's response, but I can kid myself only so far. I scurry around to the driver's side and slide in as fast as I can. I want to catch a glimpse of that smile from behind the steering wheel.

"Where to?" I ask.

She just leans back in her seat with a sigh. Her dark eyes are focused out the windshield, staring up at the full moon overhead. "Let's just drive."

So we drive. I hit the gas and the van putters out of the Hideout parking lot and onto the two-lane highway. We're not alone out here—it's not late enough for that—but the cars we pass are few and far between. I crank my window down and let the cool air whip the hair around my face.

"Your dad," she says.

"Yeah."

"Can I ask you something?"

I grit my teeth. "Sure."

"If his name is Al . . . bert?"

"Alan."

". . . and yours is Eddie . . . then why does Bev call you Junior?"

Not the question I was expecting. "She just does. Everyone does."

She hums, like she's turning this over in her mind. "He's nice," is what she finally says. "Funny too."

"Sure. When he wants to be."

"You didn't tell him about the demo."

"I . . ." I scramble for a way to say it that doesn't sound like *I didn't want you to know he existed.* "I didn't want to get his hopes up. Not until we heard anything back from WR." I shrug. "Dads. You know. They get excited."

"I get that," she says. "Managing expectations."

No two words have ever better summed up my relationship with Al Munson. "Yup."

We're tearing past the turnoff for Briggs Road, heading toward the eastern border of Hawkins, when Paige says, "I forget how many stars you can see out here." I steal a glance over toward her. She's got her feet on my dashboard, and I should be pissed about that, should bark at her about it like I do with Ronnie and Dad and everyone else who's ever sat in this van—

—but the sight of her with her knees tucked to her chest and her chin turned up toward the sky drowns that irritated flare right at the source.

"Thought you had plenty of stars out in L.A.," I say. "Stallone. Ford. Travolta."

"Big *Saturday Night Fever* fan?"

I strike a one-handed pose. "The biggest."

She laughs. "Turn here," she says, pointing off to the right. And because I've long since made peace with the fact that I will always be at this girl's service, I comply, wheeling the van onto the dirt road and into the woods.

"You're not gonna murder me, are you?" I ask.

"Not the plan tonight."

"What *is* the plan tonight?"

She just slides me a look, one that dries up any other words right on the tip of my tongue. I swallow, gripping the wheel with both hands, and focus on not crashing before we get to wherever she's got us going.

The van's headlights are struggling to pick out the road through the press of trees. Branches claw down at the roof, and if I gave half a shit about the paint job I'd be flipping out right now. We drive and drive, and the road gets narrower and narrower as we go, until—

"Here."

There's no warning before Paige says it, but I don't need one. The claustrophobic dirt road has suddenly opened up, spitting us into a grassy clearing large enough to park three vans side by side. She points, and I park smack in the middle, cranking the key until the rumbling of the van's engine quiets.

It's silent for a moment. Paige is still looking up at the sky, at the stars (maybe *Saturday Night Fever* is contagious). The moon is framed dead center above us. It's too perfect to be real.

"I heard back from Davey," she says.

I straighten up in my seat. My heart is suddenly going one billion miles an hour. "Are you gonna make me ask?"

"He said he'd never seen such a shitty recording studio in his life," she says. "He said, if that's what counts as a mix in Indiana, then the whole state should be wiped off the map."

I should be shrinking, deflating with every word. But there's something in Paige's tone that keeps my adrenaline pumping, my eyes pinned on her face. She's still looking at the moon. "What about our instruments? Maybe our clothes? He have any thoughts on them?"

"Yeah." Paige looks over at me. She's *glowing*, a smile biting deep into her cheeks. "He likes you."

I blink. "He—"

She moves all at once, surging across the gear shift to grab my arm. "He *likes you*. All that bullshit with the studio and the demo—he *likes* that it's shitty. It's *real*, that's what he said. You're *real*."

I can't breathe. I can't look away. If I do, I'll be shaken out of this moment. I'll have to move on with my life, which would *suck* because right now, someone thinks I'm worth a damn. Someone in *Los Angeles* has seen me and my ripped jeans and my dad's T-shirt and thought, *Yeah, that's what I'm looking for.*

"He wants to see you play," Paige is saying, and her wonderful words only spiral me higher. I'm holding her hand, I realize, clamping down on the grip she's got on my arm. When did that happen? "He wants you to come out to Los Angeles to audition for him, and for the other label guys. Eddie, this is *it*."

"This is it," I echo, very faint. "Jesus Christ. This is *it*." All those late nights scheming with Dad, every time Higgins scraped me off the bottom of his shoe. Every order Bev ever barked at me and every sad frown from Uncle Wayne. It's all brought me here, made me *real* or whatever. And I get to leave it behind me when I go.

"You did it." She squeezes my arm, just once, but it's enough to snap me out of my stupor. I reach out toward her. My hand is trembling. I don't give a shit. All I notice is that she's not moving away as I slide my fingers along her cheek, into her hair. Her eyelashes flutter, which is something I didn't think happened outside of romance novels.

"Well?" she asks, but what she really means is *What are you waiting for?*

There's nothing to wait for. There's nothing but wide open road ahead of me right now—wide open road and Paige's dark eyes, and so I lean in and kiss her.

She wraps her arms around my neck, clinging to the shoulders of my jacket. It's zero to sixty, zero to sixty-fucking-million, all in one single instant. I feel drunk. I feel *high*, the combination of Paige's news and Paige's lips and *Paige* all swirling together. I can see the edges of the universe. I'm real, and somebody likes that. Paige is trying to climb across the center console into my lap. *I* definitely like *that*, but—

"Waitwaitwait—" I haul back. Paige overbalances with a squeak, and I have to catch her shoulders to steady her. "The band—"

"Eddie."

"I have to tell Ronnie, she's gonna flip—"

Paige plants her hand over my mouth, shutting me up. "Eddie," she says again. Her lipstick is smeared. It's probably all over my mouth. "I said Davey liked you."

"I know," I try to say through her palm.

"He liked *you*. Not Corroded Coffin. *You*."

Whatever the opposite of that flying-soaring-racing feeling is? That's what's souring my stomach right now. I gingerly take her wrist and move her hand away from my mouth. "The demo was for all of us."

"But you were what he responded to. He thinks the rest of the band is . . . I don't know."

"Garage." I can still hear it in Ronnie's voice. Her hopeless matter-of-factness.

"Hometown. In a way you're not."

"So when you say he wants me to come out to audition . . ."

"He only wants you. Davey thinks you could be a star, Eddie.

Stallone. Ford. Travolta. Munson." She mimics my *Saturday Night Fever* pose.

But I can't bring myself to smile. "But without Corroded Coffin . . . I can't."

"Can't you?"

Can't you? She asks like it's obvious. *Can't you go it alone? Can't you risk it? You wanted to leave all the bad shit in Hawkins behind—did you forget there was good shit you might be leaving too?*

The van walls are closing in around me. Paige's perfume is turning my brain into a dizzy mush. "I need—" I manage, and then I'm yanking the car door open and stumbling out onto the grass. The warm May air hits my face, and I take a few massive breaths, feeling the damp humidity fill my chest.

"I know this is a lot." Paige has followed me out of the van. She's leaning against the front bumper, arms crossed across her chest. Giving me space. "But I promise. I wouldn't have told you if I didn't think you could do it."

Dad watches me across a stack of pancakes in a terrible diner. *I wouldn't come to you with this job if I didn't think it was something you can handle.*

There're a lot of people out there who think they know more about me than I do, it turns out. "It's just—going out there alone is—"

"Not alone." Paige's glare is fierce, warming me from the inside. "You and me. We're in this together."

That's right—finally getting something through Davey means this is her victory too. And I've been so wrapped up in my own bullshit that I hadn't even registered it. "Yeah?" I ask, trying not to wince at how pathetic it sounds.

"Yeah," she says. "I'm gonna get cheesy for a second here. Don't puke on me, but—you've got something. I saw it that night at the Hideout. I think—I saw it years ago, at the stupid talent show. You get up there and whatever you play, it's raw. It's life-or-death. And people can feel it. I think that's why it makes some people—"

"Hate my guts?"

She gives a sideways nod and takes a careful step forward, approaching like I'm some kind of wounded animal. I let her. "You could be a *legend*. I really believe that. You could be a goddamn hero, but this town won't let you."

She's right. As long as I'm in Hawkins, I'll always be Junior, another Munson fuckup. Everyone around me will count down the hours until I'm dead in a ditch or shipped off to prison. And when that does happen, the only thing they'll talk about is how they're not surprised.

I have a shot here—a chance to get away from all of it. To make a new name for myself. And if my friends are *really* my friends . . . they'll understand.

They *have* to.

Paige is in front of me now, looking up at me with a question in those dark eyes. "Are we doing this?" she asks.

I take a deep breath and let my shoulders loosen. "We're doing this."

"Thank *God*," she breathes, and then she's jumping into my arms, arms and legs wrapping around me like a tree. It's all I can do to barely catch her before she's barreling me off-balance. We land in the grass together, Paige's weight knocking the air out of me, and I don't have a chance to catch my breath before she's kissing me, destroying her lipstick beyond repair.

"Oh," I mutter as her hands start to wander. "Are we doing this too?"

"Shut up and take your pants off," she says, and then that's all she says for a while.

Chapter Twenty

I fly.

That's how the next week feels, anyway. I've left the take-off ramp, and now I'm soaring through the wide blue sky, and there's nothing to do but keep spiraling up, up, up—

Between dropping out of school, hearing back about the audition, and the fact that Charlie Greene's truck will be making its way across Indiana next Sunday night, the screws are being turned on every corner of my life. It's all do-or-die right now, make-or-break, sink-or-swim . . .

I should be waking up in the middle of the night in stress sweats. I should have a panic attack whenever I think about anything more complicated than what I'm gonna eat for lunch. But instead—

Up, up, up.

Now that I'm not trapped in the prison of Hawkins High, I spend my days with Dad. For the most part, we're hammering out the details of our scheme. But we're also, I don't know. Just talking. It's the most time I've spent with him since I can remember, and it's . . . nice. Getting to know him as a person.

I spend my nights with Paige.

"I'm sorry we can't go to my house," Paige had told me, whispering through the close darkness in the back of the van. The mountain range of Ronnie's drum kit had been pressing in around us, pressing us together. Not that we minded. If I had the choice, I'd have picked life imprisonment by snares and stands if it meant I could stay in this moment.

"I never liked sneaking out of windows anyway," I'd said, shifting around to look at her.

"We could try your place?" Paige had said carefully. *"Does your dad care if you have . . . friends over?"*

"No, but—" The vivid image of leading Paige through the living room and into my bedroom in front of my dad had flashed horrifically through my mind. *"I think that's worse, somehow."*

I think Paige had been having a similar vision, because she'd snorted, loud enough to shake the van. *"Maybe we just stay here."*

I'd raised an eyebrow. It was dark in the back of the van, but I could still make out the shape of her mischievous smile, the moonlight limning the curve of her bare shoulder. *"Here's good."*

Up, up, up. I've caught a column of warm air, and it's floating me toward the clouds.

There're only two downsides to any of this. The first is that my sleep schedule is completely screwed. I usually don't creep back in the front door until well after two, and then Dad's waking me up by seven to tackle the next leg of this job. *"Grab the walkies, we gotta test the range." "Grab your keys, we're flyering for Topp's." "Grab your work gloves—show me how to work that hitch."*

The second is that I haven't had time to break the news about—about anything to Ronnie or to the Corroded Coffin guys or to Hellfire.

You mean you're avoiding it, whispers a voice in my head. I quickly shut it up. There'll be time to talk to everyone after this weekend. After I've got my future set. After I touch back down.

I'm running on bargain basement coffee and adrenaline and fumes by the time the final Saturday rolls around. And when Dad wakes me up that morning, he takes one look at my fuzzy eyes and *tsks*.

"You're gonna be no use to anyone tomorrow like this," he tells me as I blink up at him from the nest of my rumpled blankets.

"Hm?" I grunt.

He shakes his head. "Go back to sleep. I'll call you if I need anything." Then the light is flicking off, and the room is dark, and that's all I remember for the next ten hours.

It's not Dad's exasperated shaking that draws me back to consciousness the next time. It's this smell, rich and *wonderful*, wafting in through the crack beneath my bedroom door. I squint through the fuzzy gloom—*Jesus, it must be six p.m., how long did I sleep?*—trying to place it. I know it's familiar . . . just not in this context, in my shitty house on my shitty street.

It's not until I've stumbled into the kitchen, hair sticking up every which way and sleep hanging heavy in my eyes, that everything clicks into place. "Are those . . . onions?"

Dad is fiddling around at the ancient range top. He smacks a spatula at me as I reach over his shoulder, leaving a smear of grease on the back of my hand. "You wanna burn yourself?"

"I can't believe you're cooking."

"I said I would, didn't I? And what's a better occasion than this? We can't go off into battle with stomachs full of Beefaroni and warm beer. Get the plates."

It takes me a second to follow his orders. I'm too busy wondering where the hell Dad got a spatula, because I am 90 percent sure I have never owned one before. But the mystery utensil whips through the air again in my direction, and I scurry back with a yelp. "I'm doing it!"

Throwing open the cabinet, I take out our two least-chipped plates and watch as Dad attempts to re-create the Himalayas out of spaghetti on each of them, topping one peak with three meatballs and going for a fourth before I yank the plate away from him. "You're gonna have to roll me onto that truck."

We move to the table (carefully, to avoid meatball casualties). I settle in on one of the chairs, but Dad hovers. There's something working at the back of his gaze. Something considering. "I got one last thing," he says.

I look from my heaping plate to Dad and back again. "I don't think I'm gonna have enough room left over for my lungs, let alone whatever—"

But those words evaporate when Dad sets a bottle of wine on the table. It's dusty, the paper wrapper peeling. But I'd recognize it anywhere. "Are you serious?"

He shrugs, trying for nonchalance. "Your mom would want us to drink it together."

I pick the bottle up, handling it as carefully as I would a kitten. One finger traces the edges of the yellowing label, picking out the fading printed words. ALAN MUNSON & ELIZABETH FRANKLIN, MARCH 12, 1966.

"What, uh." I swallow past the lump in my throat. "What kind of wine is it?"

Dad snorts. There's a watery shine to his eyes. "We didn't have 'kind of wine' money. We had 'do you want red or white' money. Here." He thumps two plastic tumblers down. "Forgot to pick up real glasses when I was at the store."

"I knew that spatula was new." I pour two healthy glugs into the tumblers. The wine is rich red even through the foggy plastic. I hand one to Dad. "Should we—do we toast?"

He's studying his drink, like maybe if he stares into the

glassy, dark surface of this wine for long enough, he'll catch a glimpse of Mom's face. "Yeah," is all he says.

Okay. Then—I lift my cup. "To us. To tomorrow. And to everything going perfectly."

That considering look in Dad's eye has only deepened since we sat down, and now it's so overwhelming that it spills across his entire face. He lifts his own cup, and I expect him to lead us in a *"Cheers!"* or a *"Quit yapping and let's eat."*

But instead, all he says is, "To you, kid. And all you've managed to become, despite everything. I'm—I'm proud of you."

That lump in my throat is expanding. "Thanks," I croak. We both battle back our welling feelings by drowning them in big swigs of wine. It singes along my palate, harsher than beer and smoother than whiskey, lighting my taste buds in a way I could get used to. I lick my lips before I realize I'm doing it, and catch Dad's amused smirk. "It's good," I say, embarrassed.

"I know," he says. "What are you just staring at me for, huh? Eat. It's gonna get cold."

There it is. I grin and dig in, shoveling my fork through curls of spaghetti and into my face at a breakneck pace. Dad chuckles and follows suit, and soon the kitchen is full of nothing but the sounds of two men with born-in-a-barn manners chewing with their mouths open.

"I've been thinking," Dad says, after a few masticating minutes, "about—what we were talking about. A few nights ago."

"Huh?" I wipe spaghetti sauce off my chin with my sleeve.

"I asked you, you know. How you felt about Munson and Munson."

The spaghetti comes to life in my stomach, wriggling around, twisting with guilt. "Dad—"

But he barrels on, cutting whatever weak apology I was about to offer off at the knees. "I get it. It's not what you want for yourself, and honestly, I shouldn't want you to want it." Dad stabs his fork into a meatball and leaves it there, standing on its end like a rock at Stonehenge. "You're done with Hawkins. You're on to bigger and better things. And I think . . . I should be too."

Something cold crashes through my chest. "So this is it? You're disappearing again?"

"What? No—no, no, no, not like that—" He pushes back from the table, getting his thoughts together. "Listen. After to-morrow, you're getting out of this town, you're escaping to California. Hopefully you're never coming back. Right?"

I just look at him. I don't want to give him any more of my-self, in case he takes it and vanishes with it too.

"Well. If you leave, then there's—really nothing else keeping me here. Your grandparents are long gone, your mom—well. And Wayne'd be happy if he never had to lay eyes on me ever again. So what if I . . . came with you?"

"To Los Angeles."

"Yeah."

"I—" I honestly don't know what to say. In one million years, I'd never have thought Al Munson would uproot his life for anything but the promise of a payout, and now he's offering to move across the country with me?

"I'm sure you don't want your old man hanging around, and that's all right with me," Dad hurries on, talking fast. He's twirling his fork in his fingers, watching the meatball spin, not meeting my eye. "We could get separate places—you gotta have your space, and I don't wanna move in on that, obviously. But there's plenty of work in L.A., even for somebody like me, so . . . what do you say?" He taps the edge of his plate with a fingernail. "Wanna make this a tradition? Spaghetti Satur-days?"

I raise a wry eyebrow, hoping that my rabbiting heartbeat isn't too obvious. "Like a real family?"

He nods. "Like the fucking Cleavers. Munson and Munson."

"Yes." It's out of my mouth almost before he finishes talking, tripping over his last words. "Yeah, I mean. That would be—cool. If you wanted to come."

"Yeah?" His grin is wider than any Munson Magic bullshit. This is the real deal, goofy and wide, not designed to be anything but a smile. "Well, all right then."

"But you're serious about the not-living-together thing, right?"

"Hell yeah, kid. I've seen the way you look after a bathroom, I'm not putting myself through that if I can help it. Nah, I'll get a little studio. Somewhere on the west side, close to the beach."

"Isn't all of L.A. close to the beach?"

The incredulous laugh that busts out of him is loud enough to rattle the windows. "Oh, *man*. That's what your girl's been letting you believe? It's a good thing I'm coming with you."

I can feel myself flushing, and I can't tell whether it's due to the wine, the embarrassment, or the bubbly sense of happiness fluttering in my guts. But before I can throw a meatball at him to shut his gleeful cackling up—

—someone knocks on the front door.

Dad wipes at his eyes, his laughter calming. "You got friends coming around tonight?"

"Not that I know of. Might be Wayne?"

There's another knock. "Well, tell him to come in here and get himself a plate or get lost," Dad says. "We've got a big day tomorrow. We'll need to be sharp." He's already clearing up our plates as I stand.

Dusk is already slipping into night by the time I open the door, ready to fend off a round of well-intentioned and exasperating concern from my uncle. But it's not Wayne's gruff, lined face that watches me from beneath the flickering porch light.

"Hey," Ronnie says, serious as a heart attack. "You got a second to talk?"

Chapter Twenty-One

I shouldn't be dismayed to see my best friend. But I shouldn't have spent the last week steadily avoiding her, either, so here we are. I grin, like that'll make a dent in the concerned frown she's got pasted on her face, and try to edge the front door shut with my sneaker. "I didn't know you'd be coming by."

"I would have asked. But I haven't seen you around." She cocks her head, studying every sleep-rumpled inch of me. "You been sick?"

"No, I, uh—I've just been helping my dad with some stuff."

"Always nice to see you, Ronnie," Dad calls from the kitchen. "Don't worry about cleanup, kid, I got this."

He's giving us space. But right now, staring down the barrel of whatever the hell *this* interaction is about to be, I'm tempted to run back inside the house and slam the door, to hop in my van and take off, to retreat to the dark drum-kit cave, to hide somewhere Ronnie can't find me.

Instead, I force myself to choose maturity. Stepping out onto the front steps, I close the door behind me and face my fate.

"What's going on with you?" Ronnie asks, once the latch clicks into place. "You dropped off the face of the earth. You missed Hellfire."

I know. Of course I know. "I told you, I had to help Dad with—"

"You *never* miss Hellfire. Dougie thought you vanished like that Byers kid. Gareth was two seconds away from forming a search party."

I shrug. "Here I am. No search party needed."

"Hey." Ronnie slams her fist into my shoulder, right where she always does. I wince. "Cut the shit. What's going *on* with you?"

There are so many ways to answer that question, and I've been putting off every single one of them. But Ronnie is right in front of me now, glaring from a meter away, close enough so that I can make out the edges of the fading yellow bruise on her cheek. I can't keep playing limbo with reality.

"I dropped out of school."

I can actually see the breath catch in Ronnie's chest. "You did *what?*"

"It's fine, it doesn't matter." Maybe if I'm dismissive enough, she'll actually believe me.

"I wasn't going to graduate this year anyway—"

"You don't know that!"

"Higgins told me."

"Higgins." She spits the name, and I live in that surge of gratified warmth for a second. "That guy has it out for you, you know that."

"Doesn't mean he's wrong. Anyway, it wasn't about grades."

"Why the hell would you drop out of school if it wasn't about your grades?"

We have an opportunity here, to help one another.

The deal I made with Higgins (and when does a deal become blackmail? When does that chemical reaction kick off?) itches under my skin. My absence for Ronnie's future. It's a fair trade, and there's still no doubt in my mind about that. I square my shoulders. "You think I was doing anybody any favors by staying there?"

Ronnie stares at me, like she honestly doesn't know what to say to that. "What are you talking about?"

"I'm talking about—how Gareth gets the shit kicked out of him every day by Tommy H and his idiots. And how Stan had to lie to his parents about playing D and D every week because the second they found out what he was doing, they shipped him off to get *exorcised.* These kids—deserve better than the *freak* label I'm giving them. Without me around—without Hellfire—"

"Without Hellfire?!"

"—they'll be better off. And you—"

Ronnie goes still. "What about me?"

You're leverage. You're my weak spot. You're the broken link in my chain mail.

I can't tell her. If I come right out and tell her, she'll flip out. She'll bring this whole mess back to Higgins's doorstep. She'll set her chances on fire, and then we'll both be the ones going up in smoke.

No. The blackmail stays with me. But the rest of it—well. It's common knowledge. Which means all I have to do is huff a quiet laugh and say, "You can't pretend you don't know."

She does. It's blazing out of her eyes, bright as a lighthouse beacon. But she'd never admit it aloud, which is why I have to be the one to say it for both of us.

"I'm holding you back. Everyone in this town sees you like Cinderella—rags to riches, clawing your way out of the trailer park—"

"Granny's not *rags*—"

"*I know.* But that doesn't matter to the rest of these people. They've got their story set for you, and it's a good story, and I don't fit into it. I'm the thing that could shove the whole narrative off the rails."

Something in Ronnie's face has hollowed out. "What if I don't care about that shit?"

"What if I do?" I try to shrug and realize that I'm not so much crossing my arms across my chest as clutching myself around the middle. Protecting my soft underbelly. Not that it's doing me much good. "You've spent ten years bending over backwards to make me feel like I'm worth something. There've been times when I think you're the only person out there with anything good to say about me. You saw me wandering around like a lost little sheep and you, you guided me home. Is it crazy if I want to pay you back for that?" I force a smile. "You're my best friend. You're gonna do amazing things. You're gonna be the best lawyer in the entire world. How do you think I'd feel if I was the one who got in your way?"

"So—so you just stay in Hawkins forever?" Ronnie asks. She looks drained. Every part of her is slumped. But if she didn't think I was right, then she'd still be arguing with me. "You spend the rest of your life—waiting for your dad to come home or, or waiting for the next shitty factory job like your uncle? Can you seriously tell me you'd be happy living like that?"

"No." I shake my arms loose and square my shoulders. "That's why I'm moving to California."

There's a beat as Ronnie's eyebrows furrow. "Is—did Corroded Coffin—"

"No. But, uh. I did." My ribs expand with a shaky breath. "Paige's boss listened to our demo and he—he wants me to audition for him. Out in L.A. Only me."

Maybe I'd been expecting a more explosive reaction to this, but this information just seems to sink into Ronnie like a sponge. She's standing as still as a statue, and for a moment I have the crazy idea that if I reached out and touched her, I'd find frozen marble where human flesh should be.

"Okay . . ." Ronnie says, as slow as molasses. "Okay . . ."

"Are you mad?"

"No . . . I . . ." She shakes her head, like she's trying to jostle her thoughts loose. "I'm just trying to make things make sense. You're going to Los Angeles. To audition for WR."

"In, like, two weeks. Paige thinks I have a shot."

"Uh-huh."

"Her boss liked—my energy, or whatever. I'm exactly the kind of small-town dirtbag the world is craving. So if the audition goes well, they'll be figuring out, like, how to market me?" I laugh, because it seems like somebody should, and Ronnie is definitely not rising to the bait. "I might even get a makeover. Me. Who'd have thought there was anything worth making over?" Ronnie doesn't say anything. This schtick is getting old. "Don't get too excited now. I don't want to bother the neighbors."

"Sorry," she says. She's worrying her bottom lip, the way she always does when there's something on her mind. "I'm just—thinking."

"I just told you I've got a shot at a *record deal*. Think less. Celebrate more."

The smile she gives me is watery at best. "Congratulations."

O-kay. "Listen, I'm sorry Corroded Coffin didn't get through. But you're headed to NYU anyway, and Dougie's got that job waiting for him with his dad, and Jeff's still got a few years at school—"

"Yeah."

"You'll all be fine."

"I know."

"So . . . you said you weren't mad."

"I—"

"But it kind of seems like you are."

"Of course I'm mad, Eddie!" Ronnie snaps. "Did you seriously think I wouldn't be?"

"Well—yeah! This is a huge deal for me—" Her derisive snort stings. I glare at her. "I said I was sorry about Corroded Coffin. But I have to do this. I thought we were good enough friends that you wouldn't get pissed at me for taking the one chance anybody's ever given me."

"Jesus Christ, I'm not mad because our stupid band didn't get a stupid audition!" There's a dangerous glint in Ronnie's eyes. "You're ditching Hellfire. You're letting it die, actually, which is worse than just ditching it—"

"Because it's only making things worse." *Because it was my only choice.*

"No, it isn't!" she shouts. "Yeah, sure, Tommy H gives Gareth shit for his Hellfire shirt. But if Gareth wasn't wearing that shirt, do you think he'd just skate by? He's a freak, whether he's with you or not. And the only thing that makes things better for him is the fact that he's got somewhere to go to hang out with *other freaks.*" She advances on me, and despite the brave face I'm trying to put on, I press back, feeling the railing dig into my spine. "If you blow Hellfire up and walk away, where does that leave those kids? Who's gonna look out for them? Because it's sure as hell not Higgins."

"Then *am* I supposed to stay in Hawkins forever?" I fire back. "I thought you were telling me that I should be trying to do more with my life."

"I didn't think you'd be erasing half of yourself trying to be some dumbass *rock star.*"

"Who says I'm erasing anything? They liked me at WR. *Me.* They think I'm real, and they think that's a good thing."

"They like the story they're telling themselves about you," Ronnie says. "You like that story too. That's why you're tripping over yourself to run out the door."

"So? If I have to choose between being a rock star and being the town fuckup, I know what I'm picking. Damn it, Ronnie, this is why I didn't want to tell you. I knew you wouldn't understand."

"So help me understand!"

"I *can't.*" I'm angry. I've never been angry at Ronnie before, not even when she rejected me all those years ago. "I can't teach you what—what it feels like, years of people throwing you out with the trash. Especially not since you're standing there telling me I should let them keep doing it."

"That's not what I'm saying—"

"It is, though."

"*No.*" She actually stamps her foot, like we're eight years old again and she's trying to get her way. "I'm saying—you're trading one story for another. Rock star, fuckup. It's all stories, none of it's the whole truth. The whole Eddie. You're running from one, toward the other, and they're both fairy tales. Not real."

I feel this like a knife to the lung. "You don't think I can do it. You think I'm gonna go out to California and fall flat on my face."

"I think—I'm worried about what happens when the illusion shatters. Where does that leave you?"

"Well then, what's your amazing advice? Since you know everything. Stay here and rot in Hawkins? Lie down and play doormat for everyone who wants to scrape their boots off on me?"

"Stop playing the victim. I'm just telling you not to pull the ladder up with you when you leave! Find a way to make sure Hellfire continues. It's too important to the kids—"

"I'm doing them a favor by ending Hellfire. They'll figure

out what to do without it. I did. We all have to, one way or another. Look at you—you made it to the ball, *Cinderella*. You're out of here, and you never have to think about us talking mice ever again."

The low blow rocks Ronnie back on her heels. "That's what you really think, huh." It's wounded, quiet, not at all a question. She's looking at me with wide eyes, like she's seeing me for the first time. Like she's hurt by what she finds.

This is my last shot, I realize. Last chance to explain myself— to tell her about *we have an opportunity here* and everything that Higgins is holding over me. She'd forgive me, if she knew. We could move past all of this—move on—

But I'd meant what I'd said about ending Hellfire. And if this is how I stop the next generation of Hawkins weirdos from getting tarred with the same Munson brush . . . then I've got to be okay with that.

I nod. "Yeah."

And after a beat, Ronnie nods too. "I guess we're done, then," she says. "Don't worry about breaking the news to the guys. I'll do it. The fewer people who hear your little speech, the better." She picks up her bike and slings a leg over the seat.

"Ronnie," I start, but there's nowhere to go from there. I click my jaw shut against the *wait,* and *I'm sorry,* and *don't go* that bubble up in my throat, and try to ignore the pitying look she throws back over her shoulder. And then she's pedaling down the gravel drive and out of sight, and I've never felt more like all the things Higgins has said I am than in this moment.

"Kid."

I don't notice how long I've been standing on the stairs, staring after Ronnie, until I hear Dad's voice. He's framed in the open doorway, a dish towel thrown over his threadbare Stooges tee, looking like a parody of domesticity.

How much has he heard? The walls of this house are like paper.

"You good." It should be a question. He doesn't say it like one. And I realize, in that moment, that it's because I don't have another option. Everything Dad and I have prepared for—everything we'd pie-in-the-sky'd about over dinner—every scrap of future we were fighting for—it all comes down to tomorrow night. And unless I'm good, it all goes up in smoke.

"Yeah," I say, whipping the towel off his shoulder and stomping back inside. "Let's get this done."

Chapter Twenty-Two

It isn't hard, clocking the truck as it crosses the state line into Indiana. The logo emblazoned on the side—FARRIS FARMS, with a little straw-hatted cartoon farmer—is a dead giveaway, even whipping past on the highway at sixty-five miles per hour.

The hard part is how in movies, they make tailing someone look so *easy. Keep a few cars between you. Don't use your turn signals. Never let them out of your sight.* But none of those stupid movies takes place in rural Indiana, and they *definitely* don't take place at, like, eleven p.m. Which means that me and the Farris Farms box truck are basically the only two vehicles on this dark stretch of road, which *also* means that any I'm-following-you moves I could pull would be that much more obvious.

"Just hang back," had been the last words I'd heard from Dad through the walkie, just before I'd driven out of range. *"You should be able to see their taillights from a ways away. And don't forget to breathe, kid."*

"Hang back," I mutter to myself now, glancing over at the walkie clipped to the dashboard like Dad can still hear me. My sweaty hands are wrapped tight around the steering wheel. "Okay."

I breathe. And I drive. Miles of Indiana highway flick by beneath my wheels. My heart thunders loud in the quiet of the tow truck, but I don't want to put the radio on, not if it means there's a chance that I'll get distracted and miss a cue from up ahead.

It was a long haul from Oregon to Maryland. We'd mapped it out more times than I could count, tracing the route along the flimsy gas station map, and that was the biggest thing I'd taken away. It was a long haul from Oregon to Maryland, and it was an even longer haul behind the wheel of a refrigerated box truck. The things had to stop for gas every two hundred, three hundred miles or so, which, if I was thinking about becoming a truck driver, would be a real deal breaker.

I'm not trying to be a truck driver, though. I'm trying to *rob* a truck driver. And in that situation, the truck's frequent gas breaks were going to work in my favor.

It feels like forever that I float in the wake of the Farris Farms truck. It's probably only like forty-five minutes. But then—

"They're pulling off." I'm still narrating to the unhearing walkie. "They're pulling off. They're pulling off."

Don't forget to breathe, kid, whispers Dad's voice in my ear.

I bully myself into not hammering the gas to catch up, and casually ease off the road a minute behind the truck. *Slow and steady.*

It's a gas stop, sure enough. I watch the cartoon FARRIS FARMS farmer roll toward a glowing Shell sign. Still forcing that relaxed pace, I wheel myself down a side street, tracing the edges of the Shell station without entering the parking lot. Soon, I've left the anemic circles of light from the flickering streetlamps. I park, turn off the ignition, and—

—and nothing. I sit. I root my ass to the driver's seat and just sit. *Get up,* I tell myself. *You're wasting time. Get* up.

But the bullying that had helped me keep it together through the last tense hour is hitting a wall here—a wall that doesn't make *sense.* Because at the end of the day, this stupid gamble was *my dumb idea.*

Of all the impossible angles to this job, there was one that was even more precarious than the rest. Because it didn't matter how well guarded the truck was, or how tricky the locks were, or even how much weed was actually on board. What mattered was the fact that the truck was barreling across the country at seventy miles an hour, and if we wanted to take a run at it, then that would have to change. And more than that, it would have to change without the presumably well-armed men inside being any the wiser.

"Spike strips, nails, razor wire . . ." Dad ticked them off on his fingers one by one, like he was making a grocery list. *"They're easy, but they're obvious. And anyway, a blown tire on the side of the road is something a person could fix for themselves."*

We'd been hunched over the kitchen table together, a spiral-bound notebook open between us. I'd just come off a late shift at the Hideout, and I'd been feeling every minute of the late hour in the bags beneath my eyes. It was only the second can of Coke I'd chugged that was keeping me upright, and I watched, impressed, as Dad make his way through his second glass of bottom-shelf whiskey without one single dozy blink.

"What we need," Dad had continued, *"is a way to fuck up their truck just enough so that they need outside help . . . but not enough to total it."*

"That's a pretty fine needle to thread."

"That's the job." Dad had leaned back in his chair, hands braced on top of his head. *"Any thoughts?"*

I'd tapped a finger against my pop can, listening to the *tink-tink-tink* of my ring on the aluminum. *"If it's not the tires . . ."* I'd said, thinking aloud, *"then . . . the engine?"*

"Hard to get under the hood of a speeding truck."

"You don't have to get under the hood," I'd shot back. I could feel the thrum of my heart in my throat, the way that I always could during a Hellfire battle when I *knew* I had the upper hand on my players. *"We didn't when we hot-wired the tow truck, and we won't now."*

Dad's gaze had been level, serious. There had been no playful spark. It was the same look he'd had at the chop shop, the look I was starting to realize was reserved for Junior and Junior alone. *"Don't leave me in suspense, kid."*

Suspense had been the least of our worries. It had all seemed so easy, in the warm light of the kitchen. Now, with the river of sweat running from my hairline down my back, I think I'd like to find the version of myself who came up with this idea and punch him in the face. My tongue is sticking to the roof of my mouth. Maybe this sudden paralysis is my body giving me one last chance to back out. Because this is it—the moment of truth. Once I pull this trigger, I can't un-pull it.

But I made my decision weeks ago—over a pool table at Reefer Rick's house, over a stack of pancakes at a shitty diner, over a Jack-and-Croak at the Hideout. All that's left is to see it through.

"Wish me luck," I tell the walkie. And I don't need a signal to hear Dad's response, clear as day.

Munsons don't do luck.

Then I'm slamming the door shut and setting off to get this party started.

Chapter Twenty-Three

T he line for the diesel pump had been two trucks deep
when the Farris Farms truck arrived, which means they're
just pulling up by the time I creep around the back of the gas
station, keeping to the darkness as best as I can. I wish I could
have brought Dad's broken binoculars with me, but I need my
hands for the five-gallon jug of water I've hauled out of the
backseat.

Unlike the deserted highway, the Shell station is halfway
busy—only to be expected, since it's the only gas station for
miles. I sneak sweatily around the corner of the convenience
store and peer out into the lot beyond, at the scattering of cars
posted up at the four available pumps. Lugging the water jug
this far has already left my shoulders burning, and I readjust
my grip on the handle as I take stock, planning out my next
move.

It's about five yards between my hiding spot and the Farris
Farms truck—close enough that, even with *my* athletic ability,

I could probably ding the logo with a tossed pebble. I'm staring at the rear doors; they've parked facing away from me. As I watch, a pair of men clamber down from either side of the cab and slam the doors shut behind them.

The thing that I'm surprised to be surprised by is how short these two guys are. I've been telling myself a story about how this whole adventure is going to go—me and Dad versus a couple of hulking bruisers, Davids versus Goliaths. But the men that emerge from the truck both top out at five-seven, max, and there's not an ounce of muscle to spare between them— they're whipcord-skinny, drowning in their oversize canvas jackets. If anyone's Goliath in this matchup, I'm starting to worry that it's me.

It's chilly this late at night, so I don't blame the driver for shivering and yanking a knit cap low around his ears. I can't hear what he mumbles to his partner from this distance, but from the stabbing of his thumb toward the convenience store, I'm betting that he's headed inside to pay for gas and probably take a leak. Sure enough, a moment later, he's stomping toward the plexiglass station door with the unmistakable hurried stride of a man who's about two seconds away from pissing himself.

But I keep my eyes pinned on his partner. Because this is the moment of truth: if he caves to the elements and retreats into the cab of the truck, then I'm screwed, and this plan is finished before it even gets off the ground. If he doesn't . . .

The man stretches, flexing his spine with a satisfying *crack-pop*. Then, ignoring the forbidding signs on all the pumps, he shoves a cigarette into his mouth . . . and lights it.

The cherry-red glow of the lighter is practically a green light. So, keeping the truck between me and the smoking man, I clutch my water jug as close to my body as I can and slink toward the far side of the cab.

Toward the gas cap.

"About . . . ten months ago," I'd told Dad, leaning over the kitchen table, *"we had two solid weeks of rain. It poured down, just* sheeted *down, nonstop. There was water coming in through the roof, there were mudslides, roads were closed. And then—it started to flood. South Hawkins, just down the road, they got the worst of it. I heard the Baker twins blew up a raft and floated all the way down Persimmon Street. But once it stopped pissing down rain, everything seemed like it was normal, right?"*

It had been a call-and-response cue, and Dad had played his part. *"Right."*

"Wrong. *'Cuz after I filled up the van at the 7-Eleven, I only made it about two miles before she died on me. And I wasn't the only person that happened to—almost everybody who grabbed gas at that station wound up conked out on the side of the highway."* I'd leaned across the table. *"The flooded water had leaked into the 7-Eleven's gas tanks, and we'd gone right ahead and pumped it into our cars. I had to grab a tow to the mechanic's, and they flushed the gas tank and the fuel lines to get all the water out. It took five minutes, that was all. And afterwards— she ran as good as she ever had."*

"Water in the gas tank," Dad had mused. *"It's pretty simple. But how do we pull it off?"*

"I'm not the only person planning this job, am I?" I'd drained the last sip of my pop. *"The floor's yours, old man."*

Probably I should have taken the reins on that part of the planning process as well. Because without that little step figured out, the order of operations we'd landed on had been 1) sneak up on truck in gas station, and 2) pour water into gas compartment. "Pretty simple," like Dad had said. But now that I'm close enough to this guy to smell his cigarettes and see the outlines of the tattoos creeping up his neck, I think that maybe a little complexity isn't such a bad thing.

He's paced away toward the edges of the lot as I've been

sneaking closer, keeping as low to the ground as possible. From here, I have a clear view of the man's work boots through the gap beneath the truck, and I keep one nervous eye on them as I scuttle closer and closer to the gas cap. I'm so close—it's five feet away—four feet—three—

—but maybe I should have been paying less attention to the smoking guy's feet and more to my own, because I don't see the curb of the diesel pump until I'm smacking into it. Overbalanced as I am with this stupid goddamn water jug, I topple sideways, only barely managing to catch myself before I can go sprawling onto the ground. Still, I'm not smooth enough to entirely muffle the *thunk* of my shoulder against the pump, and—

Chrrrk.

I know that sound. It's the scrape of shoes on asphalt.

And knowing what I'm going to see before I see it, I peer beneath the truck—just in time to see the man's work boots turn in my direction.

Chapter Twenty-Four

For a second, all I can do is panic. *Maybe he didn't hear.* There're still a few people milling around this lot, murmuring to one another in tired, late-night road trip voices, crinkling open bags of Doritos and packets of Slim Jims. With a little luck, I'll be okay. With a little luck—

Munsons don't wait on luck.

But the boots haven't moved any closer. I'm watching them closely, ready to bolt. My eyes are starting to water because they've been posted open for so long. I hold my breath. I wait.

And after a lifetime of a few seconds, a still-glowing cigarette butt lands on the asphalt next to the guy's heel. He grinds it out at the same time as the unmistakable *thwick* of a lighter sparks up his next smoke.

Remember to breathe. I exhale—quietly. Inhale. Exhale. And maybe it's the adrenaline lighting up my nerves, but the second that fresh, cool air hits my lungs, I feel like someone's pumped liquid fire into me. I'm awake, I'm alive—and most importantly, I'm motivated.

You'll never get to California if you don't stop wasting time, I hiss to myself. *So stop messing around and do it.*

Three feet to the gas cap. *Three feet.* I cross the space with a single step. The cap screws loose with a few quick twists. Another twist pops the top on my water jug, and I lift it, tipping it toward the open fuel filler with careful hands.

This is the tricky part—trickier than tailing a truck full of illegal drugs from the state line, trickier even than sneaking up on a couple of dealers in a remote gas station in the middle of the night. Too much water in the tank and the truck will crap out before it gets where we want it to go. Too little? It'll overshoot by a matter of miles. And either way, I'll have blown it.

If it's the Standard Oil in Russiaville: one liter. I run through the list Dad and I had made together. *Marathon in Pine Village, four liters. But this is the Shell in Chalmers. How much water for the Shell in Chalmers?*

On the other side of the truck, I hear the tinkle of a bell as a set of rusty door hinges creak open. A moment later, footsteps are crunching across the lot—in the direction of the truck.

"Took you long enough," the smoking guy grumbles.

"The shitter's a goddamn nightmare," the driver replies. "You'd be better taking a piss out here."

I'm out of time. The smoking guy is stomping out his second cigarette and I'm out of time. *If it's the Shell in Chalmers—if it's the Shell in Chalmers—*

Recollection hits me in a rush, and I nearly fumble the water jug in my hurry to tip it into the gas tank. *If it's the Shell in Chalmers . . . two liters.* My breath comes in bated pants as I watch the waterline glug down. I'd practiced this at home, channeling every late night pouring drinks at the Hideout into eyeballing the volume. *Two liters.* Two bottles of Jack, Smirnoff, SoCo, spilling empty like it's Drunk Sam's birthday.

I'm moving the second the final drop drains into the truck. There's no missteps now, no scuffling or tripping. The two men are circling around the cab, and so I beeline in the opposite direction, racing around the cargo hold. I duck behind the rear doors just as I hear the driver tromp up to the diesel pump.

"CJ!" he calls. "You unscrew the gas cap already?"

Fear doesn't even have time to swamp me before the tattooed CJ is grunting back, "Huh?"

"Whatever," the driver mumbles, wrestling the gas nozzle out of the holster. "Fucking moron." Then he's clunking the nozzle into the truck, and as the hum of the pump kicks up, I scurry toward the shadows behind the convenience store like a couple of drug smugglers are on my heels.

I'm about ready to puke by the time the lights on the Farris Farms truck finally ignite once again. I watch, certain with every second that passes that the drivers will notice something off, something wrong, turn the truck off, and come striding over to put a bullet in the middle of my forehead. But instead, the truck rumbles out of the lot, making for the reflective green highway signs. On the road again.

It's a quick scurry over to the gas station pay phone, and even quicker when I abandon the sloshing water jug. I carefully refuse to think about whatever might be growing on the receiver as I snatch it up and press it to my ear, plugging my change into the slot and hammering in the phone number.

It barely rings once before Dad picks up. "Eddie?"

Something in my shoulders unwinds. I didn't realize how much I needed to hear his voice. "I'm here." It comes out in a stressed, hoarse rasp.

"Are you okay?"

"I'm good, I'm good." I let out a slow breath, trying to get myself back under control. Out in the flat darkness of the Indiana night, I watch the Farris Farms truck turn up the on-ramp to the highway. "I did it."

"Did they see you?"

"I don't think so," I say, and then reconsider. "No. They didn't." If they'd seen me, I'd be bleeding out in the parking lot.

"Thank God," Dad says, and his relief is tangible—more pronounced than I'd expected, and I register just how worried he'd been about me. Part of me is comforted by this, and part of me prickles with the realization that this job is dangerous enough to throw even Dad out of whack.

"They're on their way," I say. "Ball's in your court, Dad."

"Then you better stop yammering and let me hit it," he says, and I laugh and hang up on him, listening to the *clink-clink* of the pay phone eating my dime.

The plan's in motion. My truck's still lurking in the gloom at the edge of the gas station, still undisturbed. And I don't have any time to waste.

Somewhere at the end of this long night, California is waiting.

Chapter Twenty-Five

Topp's 24-Hour Auto. Dad had waved the grainy Polaroids of that grungy garage around the Hideout like they were first-class tickets to Bali. *"This piece of shit is where the magic's gonna happen."*

Magic or not, Topp's 24-Hour Auto is where the phone should have rung a few minutes ago—cued by my own call to Dad from the gas station pay phone. On the other end of the line, the mechanics would have heard from a desperate man in a broken-down F-150. And because it was so late and the customer was stranded so far away, both on-duty mechanics should have piled into their tow truck and driven *way* the hell out across the fields of rural Indiana. And if they hadn't been careful and hadn't watched where they were driving, then they should have slammed across a couple spike strips laid out across the road, right around their destination. Maybe they'd get super unlucky and veer into the ditch someone had dug along the side of the road, the perfect size to trap a truck tire.

And then, miles from the nearest pay phone—the nearest shred of civilization—the mechanics should have to spend *hours* struggling to get themselves up and moving again. Hours in which their auto shop should be standing empty and unwatched. Open for anybody to move in, take it over . . . use it for their own ends.

There were a lot of *shoulds* rattling around in that plan. Too many to be comfortable, and no way to know if they've gone from hypothetical to, like, *real life* until I got within range of Dad's walkie.

"Once we make contact," Dad had said, breath coming heavy as he'd heaved another shovelful of dirt aside, *"you'll sit tight. Wait for my signal."*

We'd parked at the side of a dirt road that ran between two cow pastures, and for once, I hadn't gotten the short end of the stick when it came to jobs. Dad had picked up the shovel without even *trying* to pawn it off, and since I hadn't been about to look any horse in the mouth, much less a gift one, I'd shoved my hands into work gloves and grabbed the spike strips without questioning it.

"Be hard to get a signal if I'm anything over thirty miles out," I'd told him, laying one end of the spike strip in the dirt and starting to unroll the rest.

Shunk. Dad's shovel had bit into the dirt on a violent punch. *"If that truck goes down where we want it to go, then Topp's should be their first call,"* he'd said.

Another *should.* Topp's was the only auto shop inside a pretty substantial radius—one of the little details that had made Dad so starry-eyed when he'd stumbled across it—and the tedious day of flyering every roadhouse, gas station, and telephone pole with Topp's ads was some added insurance on top of that. But even so . . . that wasn't a guarantee that Topp's would be the place Charlie Greene's guys would be calling. There *was* no guarantee. There were only *shoulds.*

Not that Dad let that discourage him. He'd just gestured at the trench, at the spikes, at the wide, wide fields of nothing. *"And if all this shit works out? Then the person answering that phone is gonna be me. Which means that if you're not in range, then you've gotta get your ass in range."*

"We don't know where they'll be stopping for gas," I'd protested, stomping an iron stake through the end of the spike strip to hold it in place. *"I could be on the other side of the state."*

"Doesn't matter," Dad had responded. *"The clock starts ticking when it starts ticking. And after that, it's all up to us."*

We'd mapped it out—drawn a circle around Topp's Auto, a border between connection-land and the nothing-but-static wilderness, and of *course,* because nothing in this world is easy, that border is a forty-mile hike from Chalmers. I take the journey at a moderate sprint, leaning my head against the doorframe and trying to maximize how much of my face is catching the breeze that rushes in through the open windows. It's eerily quiet in here, so I turn on the radio, scrubbing through the dial to find something to listen to that isn't the buzz of static.

"It's all stories."

I shake my head, trying to dislodge the whisper of Ronnie's voice. But it's no use. Ever since our blowout, her words have been popping into my head at the worst possible moments. *Rock star, fuckup. It's all stories, none of it's the whole truth.*

I scan to the next station, and I'm rewarded with even more static. "Barback turned front man turned rock hero," I whisper to myself like a mantra. "Barback turned front man turned—"

My fingers freeze on the dial. Because somewhere in the barren stretch of rural Indiana static, the truck antenna has managed to pluck out the fuzzy traces of—

"One-and-two-and-one—"

It's Muddy Waters's voice filtering through the shitty truck speakers, rasping out the words to "Rollin' Stone." But it's also his voice echoing from a distant memory, ringing out of my mom's old record player, summoned from the spinning black disc like some magic spell.

"One-and-two-and-one-and-two—now you're gettin' it!"

Mom had laughed, dancing me across the threadbare carpet. I'd been standing on her feet so that she could whirl me faster and faster, and I had laughed with her, because when Elizabeth Munson was happy, then the whole entire world was happy.

But Elizabeth Munson isn't here in this truck. Maybe that's why there are tears stinging suddenly at my eyes. I inhale a giant sniff, bracing myself against the steering wheel, and concentrating on the feeling of whipping wind against my face.

I like this music because it's real. That's what I'd told Paige all those weeks ago, whispering through the microphone at Live Mike Studios.

Something real, Paige whispers in response, her voice echoing back from that first night at the Hideout.

It's all stories, the Ronnie in my head says again, wounded and angry and on the edge of walking out of my life. *You're just running from one, toward the other.*

So what? I think back at her. At least I'm able to *choose* now. At least I have options. And what's the alternative, anyway? Something in between? What would that even look like? Who would that even be?

As far as I'm concerned, you're only as good as the story people tell about you. And I'm going to choose the story that doesn't put me on the shit list of everybody in Hawkins.

With a jab of my finger, I turn off the radio, cutting Muddy Waters off mid-riff. In the silence that follows, I shake my shoulders loose and take a deep breath, clearing the fuzzy cobwebs and confusing voices out of my head. *Focus, Junior,* I tell myself.

I focus.

And that is when I hear the police sirens bearing down behind me.

Chapter Twenty-Six

My heart is so far up in my throat that if I bite down right now, I think I'll find myself chewing through coppery muscle, chomping through a thumping aorta. The flashing lights are closer every time I glance in the rearview, and the whitened knuckles of my hands on the steering wheel flash red-blue-red in quick succession.

This is it, I think, fuzzy with panic and distance. I know how this goes. I've been through this situation with Moore too many times to count. Even if this guy is only pulling me over for a routine sobriety check, even if I start at peak Miss Manners politeness . . . I'm a Munson. Which means I'm done for. The cop'll shine his flashlight in my eyes and get me to hand over my ID and hammer me with nonsense questions until he decides he's got enough of an excuse to search the car, which he'll take his sweet time doing. I'll miss my shot at fifteen thousand dollars because one asshole decided he wanted to waste some time before the end of his shift.

A fantasy of leading this guy on a high-speed chase flashes through my head, but only for a split second. For one thing, I'd never be able to outrun him, not in this oversize monster of a truck. For another, what would be the point? Another couple years on my sentence? No thanks.

I force myself to tap the brakes, to hit my turn signal, to ease over to the side of the road. And then all there is to do is grit my teeth and listen to the siren grow louder and louder and wait for the hammer to fall.

And then I keep waiting.

And then—I realize that the squad car isn't slowing down. It's not even drifting in my direction. It just keeps barreling on down the road, full speed ahead. The only sign that the cops inside have even registered my existence is a brief flash of the headlights as they zoom past, thanking me for letting them through.

I stare after them for a solid thirty seconds, watching until they round a bend in the road and disappear behind a stand of trees. And once they're out of sight—

I laugh. Hysterically. Maniacally, even. All that fierce adrenaline that has been pounding through me since the gas station bubbles over and out like a fountain, and I laugh and laugh until it's all gone and I'm nothing but a sack of bones slumped in the driver's seat of a double-stolen tow truck.

Of course those cops didn't give a shit about me. They don't know I'm Munson Junior. To them, I'm just some guy who's been stuck with the midnight shift, same as them. And I'd been so busy spinning out about shit that doesn't matter that this fact didn't even occur to me.

Focus, I order myself, sitting up and shaking my shoulders back. There's no space in tonight for Ronnie, or Hellfire, or even Paige. Just the job. Everything else will have to wait. And willing my thoughts into clarity, I shove the truck into gear and ease back onto the road.

Five miles. Five miles until I'm within Dad's walkie range.

If I pretend I don't know what speed limits are, I can make it inside of four minutes. And I'm going to have to, because my cross with that cop has messed up my schedule. If I drag behind any longer . . .

I punch the gas to the floor and keep it there, tearing through the dark like every single one of Ozzy's bats is on my heels, not letting up until every single one of those five mile-markers has flashed past outside my window.

Finally, I see a sign loom out of the night, green and glowing as a UFO. CREEKSIDE RD. It's just a dinky little cross street, but if my map is right, it's also the boundary for Dad's walkie range. I gun it, already snatching the walkie up and hammering the talk button as I zoom by. "Dad? Dad!"

But there's only static on the other end. "Can you hear me?" I try again. "Dad?"

Another staticky silence follows, long enough for me to flash through every horrible thing that might have happened to him. Maybe there was a third mechanic on duty, someone left behind to watch the shop—someone who'd caught Dad trying to sneak in. Maybe the mechanics hadn't left at all. Maybe a neighbor had spotted Dad trying to break in and called the police—maybe that's where the cop who'd zoomed past me had been headed—maybe—

I'm right on the verge of abandoning the plan and driving straight to Topp's Auto (to help Dad fight off an army of looming mechanics? To scoop up his bullet-riddled body?) when the walkie in my sweaty hand *finally* fizzles to life. "—ddie—"

"Dad!"

"—ve you bee—"

It's Dad, no question. But his voice keeps dipping in and out, crashing through waves of interference. "I can't hear you," I say, shouting into the walkie, like that'll somehow help me hear Dad better.

"Outside the old Kenney farmstead."

I blink. That wasn't Dad. I don't have a single goddamn clue who that person was. "Huh?"

"Tree came down two hours ago." It's the same voice, much clearer and less crackly than Dad's had been. A burst of static fills the airwaves as whoever this signal pirate is takes a breath, and buried in the static I make out one lone word.

"—call—"

But then the guy is *talking again,* erasing whatever Dad was trying to say. "But I think the crew should have it cleared by the morning."

What the hell is going on? But I've barely put a question mark at the end of that sentence when a turn in the road answers it for me. Up ahead, I see the telltale eye-searing spotlights of a roadwork crew, and as I get closer, I also make out the red and blue flashing lights of a squad car. This is what had that cop hauling ass past me: a downed tree that's taken out a vulnerable power line.

The road crew, the cops—their walkies are all *way* more powerful than the shitty ones Dad and I picked up at Radio Shack. It's no wonder that they're dominating the channel.

"It's gonna be a late night," the cop is saying. "Can you ask Jessie to send along—"

Dad's voice breaks through, just for a second. "—they called—"

But then the cop is talking over him. "—a couple pies from Reggie's—hang on. I think we're getting some interference on the channel."

The channel is quiet for a second—long enough for us to get a word through. But if we can hear them, then they can hear us. I'm going to have to play this smart. I clear my throat and press the talk button. "Tow to shop," I say. "Could you repeat that?"

There's another beat of blessed silence. Then I hear Dad's voice, intact and uninterrupted. "Hey, Matty," he says. "Got a call—box truck conked out at Taylor's Late-Nite Diner, over on Madison. Think you could bring it in?"

Madison. I'll have to look it up, but—

"Copy that, Jerome," I reply, trying to sound as official as possible. "I'm on my way." And as I pass the work site and the parked cop car, I return the headlight flash. *Thanks for that, officer. These are not the droids you're looking for. Carry on.*

The truck is impossible to miss. It's parked diagonally across like five parking spots, sulking in the light of the neon TAYLOR'S LATE-NITE sign. And so that's where I park too, rolling to a stop on the nearest available scrap of asphalt.

Inside the Farris Farms truck, two sets of eyes slam up to look at me over their Styrofoam cups of take-out coffee. Both watch me with varying levels of mistrust and hostility. I greet them both with the friendliest, most open Al Munson smile I can muster and roll down my window.

"Hey, fellas," I chirp. "Heard you needed a tow."

Chapter Twenty-Seven

It's a tight squeeze in the cab of the tow truck—this bench seat is really not meant for three full-grown men. "Lucky you guys crapped out so close to the shop!" I say, because we're all crammed so tightly, shoulder-to-shoulder, that I can feel the hard knob of something that is *definitely* a gun tucked into the waistband of the jeans of the guy next to me.

This is CJ—the smoker I'd snuck past in order to douse the Farris Farms gas tank—and he is not a talker. But when he'd first loaded into the tow truck, he'd made a point of shoving that gun into me hard enough to leave a bruise. As far as silent warnings go, I don't think I've ever met a more effective one.

Even with CJ contributing nothing more to the conversation than the occasional grunt, his partner, Toby, carries his weight and then some. The guy chatters, like, *nonstop*, and in the fifteen-minute drive from the diner, I don't think I see him pause to take a breath more than twice. ". . . which is why you never tell your girl your route, because if she gets all worked up about checking in, you don't want her to actually be able to find you—" It's not until we're approaching the weather-beaten TOPP'S 24-HOUR AUTO sign that I realize why. *He's trying to keep me from asking any questions.*

Works for me, man. I don't want to know any more about these guys than I have to.

"All righty," I eke out in the space between two of Toby's sentences, wheeling into the lot. Topp's 24-Hour Auto is set back in the dark woods, a couple yards off the main road. Its grungy exterior doesn't exactly inspire confidence, and as close as CJ is, I can feel the disapproval radiating off him. But there are lights on inside, blazing from every window and out of the open garage door, lighting the place up like a jack-o'-lantern. And that, mixed with the fact that this is the only mechanic's shop open for *miles* at this time of night, is enough to keep CJ from grumbling a protest as I pull to a stop in front of the garage doors.

"I'll let you fellas get out here," I say. All the way in the back of the garage, I can see a slim figure puttering around. It's Dad, in his War Zone coveralls, grease and oil already staining his hands up to the wrist. With a ball cap pulled down low over his eyes, it's easy to see the resemblance to Uncle Wayne. "There's a waiting room right though that front door, with a TV and all of that. Not much on this time of night, but there should be fresh coffee."

"Well, that is some customer service," Toby says. He's leaning forward, grinning his shiny, pleasant smile around the glowering DMZ of CJ. I think I can count every single one of his teeth, even out here in the dark. "How about that customer service, CJ?"

CJ grunts. This is as much as a monologue, coming from him, as I am starting to understand. "We try our best here at

Topp's 24-Hour Auto," I say. "I'll just pull up right here to let you get out and—"

"Great customer service," Toby says again. The dude's like a broken record. "But CJ and I aren't fancy. We don't need any cushy waiting room. We're just trying to get back on the road as soon as possible."

He's making me nervous. I try a laugh. "I bet you are. We'll get your rig up and running in no time—"

"Wonderful. Then you don't mind if we hang out in the garage while you work."

Dad is watching. He's still lingering at the back of the shop, so I can't see his face, but the rag twisting between his hands tells me all I need to know about his anxiety level. I'm starting to wish I had a rag of my own—something to fidget with, to wring out some of my nerves. Because getting into their trailer isn't something that'll go unnoticed, not if these two are standing ten feet away.

"Precious cargo," Toby says, and I realize that, even through my long moment of silent panic, Toby hasn't budged a centimeter. He's still smiling at me, and it's not just that I can see his teeth in the dark, it's that they're the *only* thing I can see. The rest of Toby is just a pitch-black silhouette, shading out the stars through the window behind him.

CJ shifts on the bench next to me, and again, I feel the grip of his gun pressing into my hip. And then—

It's not so much that I make an executive decision as that one has been made for me. "Cool," I croak, and then I tap the gas, inching the tow truck into the garage and angling the truck behind me over the scuffed yellow scale pads that frame the open pit.

By the time I shut off the engine and climb out of the tow truck, Dad is nowhere to be seen. Only the sound of a muffled *thump-thump* from beneath my feet tells me that he's already in the pit. "Hey, Jerome," I call down to him. "We got company."

"No customers allowed on the floor," is the response that floats back from somewhere under the truck tires. "Company policy."

I cast an apologetic grimace back over my shoulder toward CJ and Toby, who are making themselves comfortable at a workbench on the side of the garage. Toby gives me a friendly wave. CJ just lights another cigarette. "Looks like we're gonna have to make an exception."

Something taps the toe of my boot. I glance down to find a sliver of Dad's face staring at me from beneath the truck. As casually as I can manage, given the circumstances, I kneel down so that we're in whispering distance.

"What the hell, kid?" he hisses at me, once I'm within range.

"They won't leave," I whisper back.

"Make them."

"They've got guns, *Jerome*."

"Then you're gonna have to figure something out," Dad says. "We didn't bust our asses putting this together just to screw it up now."

He's right. I know he's right. But that doesn't mean I don't want to grab the nearest socket wrench and throw it at his face.

I stand, trying to ignore the river of anxious flop-sweat coursing from my armpits. Thank God for these dumbass coveralls. "Jerome's saying there might be a problem with your fuel line," I say. "But it's never just one thing with these old reefers. You fellas mind if I take a lap?"

"Whatever gets us up and running," says Toby.

"That's the plan, boss," I tell him. Then, because I'm out of other ideas, I start to pace a circuit around the truck.

Think. I try to bully my brain into functioning, into looking at this like a Hellfire session, like a castle I'm laying under siege. *Think.* The front gates are guarded. The archers are in position. They've pulled up the drawbridge, they've unleashed the crocodiles in the moat . . .

The long side of the cargo trailer telescopes out in front of me. It feels like it goes on forever, an eternal, unbroken stretch of flat steel. No way in. Not unless it's through the reinforced double doors that Toby and CJ are watching like a couple of gargoyles.

Finally, I reach the end of the trailer. In the space where it connects to the cab, the reefer cooling unit hulks outward, thrusting over the hitch like a pimple. It's still running—I can hear the hum of the air conditioner as I circle closer and closer, and the metal is warm to the touch.

And if I knew anything about mechanics or HVAC repair, maybe this could have even helped me. But all I see, staring up at this huge, lumpish sore of an AC compartment, is yet another thing standing between me and California. Another obstacle. Another full stop.

Castles, moats, drawbridges. I give myself a shake. *This isn't a game. You're not some kind of* noble paladin. *You're a criminal. This is a goddamn reefer truck. And it's not crocodiles making sure nobody gets inside. It's a couple of cold-blooded killers.*

Beneath the truck, something *clangs.* Dad is doing his best to draw out the work, to take as much time as possible to flush out the fuel lines and get the truck going again. But he can't keep it up forever, and Toby and CJ aren't morons. Sooner or later, they're going to start getting suspicious.

I give myself a few mental slaps, running my hand along the smooth metal of the cab as I pace around the side. The cartoon Farris Farms farmer grins at me from the door panel. I look away, avoiding eye contact—

And freeze.

That's right. Toby and CJ can crawl all over the front doors as much as they want. But this is a reefer truck, not a castle. And reefers aren't designed to have just one entrance.

I find what I'm looking for just as I edge around the cab, circling back to the other side of the cargo trailer. It's no wonder I hadn't noticed it before now; it's nestled in next to the bulk of the cooling unit so tightly that it almost disappears in the shadow.

They keep the air circulating. That's what Dad had told me over a stack of pancakes and Dot the waitress's obvious advances. *Keep everything fresh.*

Well, if you're going to circulate the air *in*—through the main doors—you'll need a way to circulate it *out*. To vent it.

And sure enough, that's exactly what I see set in the front of the cargo container. A small hatch, about as big as a sheet of paper. *A vent.*

I peer around the truck toward the back of the garage. Toby and CJ are right where I left them, slouched on the workbench. They're talking, quiet, so I can't make out their words. But from CJ's tight nodding and Toby's frown, they look stressed— like this delay is the last thing in the world they need.

And maybe I can use that to my advantage. I tramp toward them, my steps shaking the scale pads underfoot. *Wake up, Dad, I've got an idea.* "I think we found everything we need, fellas."

"What was the problem?" To my surprise, it's CJ that asks, the most I've heard from him all evening.

"Like we thought. Fuel line," I say, as nonchalant as I can muster. "Simple enough, we just want to make sure we get it done right. You don't want to have to make any more stops before you get to . . . ?"

Toby doesn't fill in the blank with anything but his unnerving smile. "Good," he says.

"Good," I echo. "Hey, you guys mind if we turn on the radio? Working in silence this late at night's a little—"

"Yeah, sure, whatever," Toby says. He's already crossing his arms over his belly and leaning back against the wall. His eyes slide to half-mast, but I can still feel him watching me as I reach over to the portable AM radio hanging off a hook on the wall and flick it on. The staticky crooning of a saxophone fills the air. Apparently, the mechanics at Topp's 24-Hour Auto are fans of smooth jazz. Not my first choice for covering up the sounds of a break-in, but beggars can't be choosers.

"We'll have you back on the road in no time," I say, grabbing up the black nylon tool bag slouched on the floor under the radio. "Trust me."

Chapter Twenty-Eight

In the surge of excitement that races through me, my fingers are already on the latch by the time my thoughts catch up with my actions. *Careful, Junior,* I tell myself. *Don't blow it now.* I force myself to lower my hands, to consider my next steps before driving forward and maybe making a lethal mistake.

An image flickers through my mind: Dad, crouching outside the chop shop garage, carefully oiling the hinges so that the creak of the door wouldn't give us away. Fighting back another rush of adrenaline, I reach down and unzip the tool bag.

What I'm looking for is rolling around near the bottom, buried under screwdrivers and hammers and drill bits. I lift out the can of WD-40, thanking whoever's up there that it's not empty yet. And trusting in the power of Grover Washington Jr. and his sick-ass saxophone solo to cover up the sound, I spray the hatch hinges.

The latch pops open soundlessly, gliding against the bolt that keeps it in place. Then, all there is left for me to do is to hold my breath . . . and open the hatch.

It swings back raggedly, juddering on its hinges in a way that tells me that, if I hadn't gone nuts with the WD-40, everyone in this garage would have just been treated to the whine of jagged metal. But in the heart-pounding seconds that follow, I hear nothing but the murmur of continued conversation from Toby and CJ.

I'm clear. I'm clear, but the clock is ticking. And so I lean forward, peering into the darkness inside the reefer. The AC unit just above my shoulder is doing a phenomenal job of keeping this truck and its contents fresh and cool, and as I get closer, I can feel the spill of chilled air against my skin. At first, the truck's hold is impenetrably dark. But then, as my eyes start to adjust to the low light, I start to make out vague shapes—wooden crates and boxes, their open tops covered with shiny blue tarps, tied with nylon straps and fastened to the walls and the floor to keep them from sliding.

"Can I use your phone?"

It's Toby, calling out across the garage floor. I nearly slip and fall off the hitch in surprise. "Uh," I shout back, once I'm balanced again. "Sure thing. Phone is—"

"Thanks," Toby says, before I can panic about the fact that I don't know where the phone is. Turns out I didn't have anything to worry about, because it's literally two steps away, on the wall next to the workbench, and Toby is already shuffling over, picking up the receiver, and dialing without any more fumbled directions from me.

Once his back is turned again, I set back to work. There's a crate lashed to the wall just beneath the hatch, and the tarp is easily within reach. Ignoring the awkward stretch in my shoulder, I pretzel my arm through the hole, grasping at the edge of the tarp. A flick of the wrist pulls it aside, giving me a direct line of sight on my goal, which is:

Carrots.

A mound of carrots, jumbled on top of themselves, heaping past the rim of the crate in an earthy-smelly pile. But when I reach down to grab one, digging as deep into the crate as I can, I don't feel the firm, rough of fresh produce—or at least, not *just* fresh produce.

Because just beneath the top layer, my fingers close around something *else*. It's about the same size as a carrot, but it gives just a little in my grip, crunching like a dense sandbag. And when I pull it out into the bright fluorescent garage light, I can see why.

The thing resting in my hand might look like a carrot. But anything more in-depth than a cursory glance immediately reveals what it truly is: a cone-shaped bundle, folded in orange plastic and fastened closed with clear packing tape. I bring it to my nose and take a deep whiff. Sure enough, even through the layers of wrapping, I pick up the unmistakable pungent smell of weed.

Twenty pounds of Golden Ambrosia. That's what we'd promised Reefer Rick back in his shambling lake house, an entire lifetime ago. *Twenty pounds for fifteen thousand dollars.* I stare down at the package in my hand. How much weed equals one fake carrot? How much cash? This isn't the kind of arithmetic they taught us at Hawkins High.

"What's the ETA, Matty?" Toby calls over. He's still on the phone, but he's peering in my direction now, glancing back over his shoulder.

"Not long," I tell him in a voice that doesn't crack. "What do you think, Jerome?"

"Not long," echoes Dad's muffled voice.

"They're saying not long, boss," Toby says into the phone,

and then he's turning his back again, cradling the receiver between his shoulder and his ear as he scrabbles for a pencil and paper on the workbench. "I'm thinking we shave off half an hour or so by taking I-70 through Ohio instead of sticking to the back roads—"

CJ makes some comment to his partner that I can't quite make out, and there's no time for me to waste trying to unravel it. I stash the plastic carrot into the tool bag, immediately reaching in to dig around for the next. It's weirdly a tough workout, maneuvering my arm in such a cramped space, and I have to be easy with my digging. If I move too quickly or too roughly, I run the risk of jostling some of the real carrots out of the crate and sending them clattering to the reefer floor, and not even melodious Topp's 24-Hour Auto smooth jazz would be enough to mask that sound.

I retrieve another two carrots. Then another three more. The stash in my tool bag grows until there're two dozen piled up inside, each one about two inches in diameter. And the next time I reach back through the hatch and into the produce crate, my fingers come up empty. There's no more in this box, at least not within reach.

I eye the tool bag. *Is that twenty pounds? What does twenty pounds even feel like?* Maybe if I go a little less carefully, root a little harder, I'll be able to dig down deeper and find another package—

"Understood," I hear Toby say, somewhere beyond the bulk of the reefer. "We'll be there. Thanks, boss." And then there's the click of the receiver and the murmur of voices as Toby and CJ compare notes about something—

—and then footsteps.

One of them is coming over here.

Shit. I'm out of time. Moving as quickly as I can, I jam my hand back into the reefer, grabbing the edge of the tarp and yanking it haphazardly back over the crate. As soon as my arm is free again, I swing the hatch door shut, wincing at the whine of the latch as I jam it back into place. The orange of the plastic carrots blazes bright against the black nylon of the tool bag. It's practically a homing beacon, unmissable even when I squat down on the hitch and start piling tools on top of it. Hammers and wrenches and drill bits and screwdrivers land in layers, and still, all I can see are the bits of orange poking through in the spaces between.

The footsteps come to a stop behind me, but I can't look around to see who it is, not when there's a signal fire still blazing away in front of me. I struggle with the zip on the tool bag, my fingers trembling as they try to force the overstuffed bag shut, to squish all evidence down, to hide it out of sight—

Finally—*finally*—the zipper gives way and the bag closes. Only then do I stand, slinging the bag over my shoulder and trying not to sag under the added weight.

CJ is planted a few paces away, watching me with his cold, level glare. *Did he see anything?* I can't tell, and he's not about to let me know. "All finished," I tell him. "Jerome?"

"Yup," is all I hear from Dad, who's been through flushing the fuel lines for at least twenty minutes.

"How much?" CJ asks. I thought I didn't mind a man of few words, but I'm learning that maybe that applies only to Uncle Wayne. Whatever energy CJ has going on is freaking terrifying.

I fight through my sudden dry mouth and hitch the bag of stolen already-illegal weed higher onto my shoulder. "Let's call it an even hundred," I say.

"Cash okay?" Toby calls over from the workbench.

Who knows what Topp's payment policy is, but it's not like they wasted any man hours on this particular caper. "It's always okay," I say, hopping off the hitch and back onto solid ground. "You just can leave it on the bench while I back the truck out of the garage for you—"

"Wait."

It's a whip crack of a word, lashing out from just behind my left shoulder. I freeze in place, knuckles whitening around the strap of the tool bag, as the ice bath of CJ's command dunks my nervous system all at once.

I don't want to turn around. There are so many things that could have gone wrong in those last few moments, more than I can count. Did the hatch swing open again? Did my shitty attempt to replace the tarp knock a bunch of produce out of the crate? Or—and my blood dips impossibly colder at this thought—did one of the carrots roll out of my tool bag when I was rushing to shove everything back inside? A series of nightmares tumbles through my head, each chasing on the tail of the next—

Something raps against my shoulder. It's long and metal and it's got enough weight to actually kind of hurt. "You left this," says CJ, and when I force myself to twist back around, it's to find him dangling a stray wrench in my face.

"Thanks," I say, and it doesn't come out as strangled as I feel. I take the wrench from him and shove it into my back pocket. "You fellas ready to head out?"

He nods, and I sidle around him, clambering into the tow truck. Somehow, between the numbness thrumming through my bones and the static in my brain, I manage to back the Farris Farms truck out of the garage and back into the lot. And since Dad is still nowhere to be seen, I handle unhitching it by myself too.

"You guys really saved our asses," Toby says, clapping a heavy hand on my shoulder.

The image of the tool bag burns in front of my eyes. In my mind, it's like it's got a neon sign safety-pinned to the strap.

Your Shit (Stolen). And yet Toby and CJ are clambering up into their truck like nothing's happened, like this hasn't been the single most stressful night in the history of humanity, like the last six hours haven't shaved ten years off my life.

"No problem," I say. "You guys take care."

"Tell your buddy to come up from his gopher hole some-time," Toby calls down to me, twisting the key in the ignition. I take a few steps back to give them space. "Or does he live down there?"

"Hah," is all I say, and Toby probably wasn't really looking for a response, because he just gives me a little wave. CJ glowers, the engine revs, and then the truck is moving, rolling out of the lot and down the drive—

Dad doesn't reappear until the truck's taillights are red pin-pricks in the distance. Then he's tromping up, wiping his grease-stained hands on a scrap of terry cloth. We stand side by side for a long moment, saying nothing, just watching the road until the Farris Farms truck has disappeared somewhere down the two-lane highway.

"Well?" he asks me, the question floating out in the quiet night air.

I open the tool bag. The orange rubber tumbled inside glows under the garage floodlights. Munson Magic.

And this time, I beat him to the crooked smile. It spills across my face and onto his, twisting both our mouths in crooked mirrors of each other. "Abracadabra," I say.

He laughs. I laugh. And then we're just two idiots, falling over ourselves outside an auto shop at two in the morning be-cause our future looks like a bunch of carrots in a tool bag and we did it and—most importantly of all—

—it's finally, *finally* done.

Chapter Twenty-Nine

Fifteen. Thousand. Dollars. It's more money than I've ever seen in my life—more money than I ever thought I *would* see. And it's just sitting in the paper grocery bag on the floor of the van between me and Dad, rustling with every bump in the asphalt as I drive.

"Eyes on the road, kid," Dad tells me, laughing as I guiltily tear my attention back to the windshield.

"Do I wanna know?" Reefer Rick had asked, eyebrows raised clear to his hairline as I'd upended the bag of rubber carrots onto the pool table in front of him.

Dad had shaken his head. *"Uh-uh."*

Rick had scanned us over, squinting in the morning sunlight. *"All fingers and toes accounted for?"*

Did you run into any trouble, is what he's really asking. And the incredible answer to that question is: *No.* Two days after that anxiety-inducing night at Topp's 24-Hour Auto, and we haven't heard a single whisper about it. No sight of a Farris Farms truck, no Charlie Greene, no Toby, and definitely no CJ. Against all odds, it looks like we've gotten off scot-free.

Dad had waggled his fingers for Rick's inspection, and when he'd kicked me, I'd done the same. *"Ten little piggies."*

"Right on," Rick had said, after a long, long pause. *"Let's trade some green for some green."*

I don't think I'll ever get sick of the sight of money. It's why I keep getting distracted—why Dad finally resorts to folding the top of the grocery bag over itself and tucking it under his leg to hold it shut.

There's no question where my cut of Reefer Rick's payout is going. As soon as I drop Dad off at the house, I'm making a beeline for Uncle Wayne's mechanic buddy, battling Topp's Auto flashbacks as I watch Greg poke around under the hood of the van.

"How many miles?" he asks me once he resurfaces.

"Like . . . two thousand. Plus some."

He whistles low, shoving his wrench into the loop on his belt. "You know this is a piece of shit, right?"

"But can she make the drive?"

"With some R and R, yeah." He slams the hood shut. "But that kind of spa treatment's not cheap."

I meet his gaze, steadied by the wad of bills stuffed into my back pocket. "Cheap's relative," I tell him. "How about you let me be the judge?"

A week ago, the number he quotes me would have given me a stroke. Now I just nod, hand over a small stack of twenties, and let Greg get to work. I have only about a week until I'm supposed to be on the road to California—better let him have as much time as he needs.

The next couple of days are a shot of frenetic activity as I allow myself to contemplate, for the first time, what the practicalities of leaving Hawkins actually look like. And one of the first items I check off my list is swinging by the Hideout.

"I didn't schedule you today," is how Bev greets me when she finds me loitering in the back, waiting on her arrival before the bar opens for the evening.

"Yeah." I rock back on my heels. "You, uh. Don't have to. Anymore."

Bev's gaze is level under her teased bangs. "You saying what I think you're saying?"

"Pretty sure."

"Hm." She stomps her cigarette out and slips a key into the back door lock. "This to do with your old man? Or the girl with the earrings?"

I shrug. "Yes."

"Well." She inspects me for a long moment. Then she nods. "Be safe out there, Junior."

"Thanks, Bev."

It's a long trudge to the front of the Hideout and across the gravel parking lot when your wheels are in the shop. I'm almost around the side of the building when I hear Bev say, "Tell that band of yours I miss their music."

But when I turn around to double-check that my ears aren't playing tricks on me, the door is banging shut and Bev is out of sight.

I'd thought packing would be easier than quitting my job. Actually, I'd thought it would be the easiest part of this whole process. I'm no stranger to loading up my life and shuffling it to another place, but there's a difference between moving to Uncle Wayne's trailer for a few weeks and moving across the country for . . . forever? For one thing, garbage bags don't really cut it. For another—I hadn't really considered myself a pack rat, but it turns out that a lot of stuff just kind of naturally builds up over eighteen years living in a place, and I lose a full twenty-four hours just sorting through a stash of old school projects I hadn't even known I still had.

"But have you found any dead cats yet?" Paige asks me over the phone late one night. I'm neck-deep in the tumble of knock-off Tupperware I'd discovered in the back of my closet, sitting on the floor with the phone cradled between my shoulder and my ear.

"Only a matter of time," I tell her, tossing a cracked lid over my shoulder. "Hey, so when I get to L.A., I wanted to ask—where should I start looking for motels? Like what part of town?"

"What neighborhoods were you thinking?"

"I don't know any neighborhoods, Warner. That's why I'm asking you."

"Well if you're asking *me*," Paige says, "then I would say . . . forget the motels. Stay at my place."

I'm glad, in this moment, that we're not face-to-face. I don't want her seeing the dumbass, walleyed expression I must be wearing right now. ". . . with you?"

"I mean—" It's a stammer. She's stammering. Somehow I have made Paige Warner nervous enough to stammer. "I've just—got this place in West Hollywood. It's really nice, and there's, like, an orange tree in the courtyard and—and I'm not saying, like, *move in* with me. That would be crazy. But I have an extra bedroom—"

"You want me to be your . . . roommate?" All thoughts of Tupperware have fled my head. I'm just turning this old Pyrex bowl over and over in my hands, staring blankly into it like a crystal ball.

"Maybe."

"Your roommate who you sleep with."

"Jesus, Eddie—" She laughs, and just like that, the uncertainty of the moment is broken. "It's an option. Unless you *want* to brave the roach motels on the Sunset Strip."

"I don't want to brave the roach motels," I say, all in a rush.

"Well. Good."

"Good."

"Um." There's some rustling on the other end of the line as Paige shifts position. "So. My parents are having this, like, goodbye dinner. To send me back off to California. Tomorrow. Would you—do you want to come?"

I look around my room, at the rumpled sheets on my bed and the water stain on the ceiling and the unending yards of broken Tupperware. I've never been to Paige's house, but it's got to be a goddamn mansion compared to this. "Come to— meet your parents?"

"Yeah."

"As your roommate."

"I will hang up on you."

I hold my breath. *This is the moment,* I think to myself. *This is the Rubicon.* For eighteen years, I've been living the life of a perpetual screwup. But I'm leaving all of that behind now. This is the birth of the new Eddie Munson—the guy who's got a future, the guy people expect things from. That's the Eddie that's going to California. That's the Eddie those record producers at WR want to meet.

Maybe that's the Eddie that can impress Paige's parents. I just have to make sure he shows up.

"Just tell me when," I say, braver than I feel. "And I'll be there."

———— **Chapter Thirty** ————

I don't know what it says about me, that I'd conjured the image of some sprawling estate whenever Paige talked about her family or her home. But the door I approach the following evening is attached to a modest split-level ranch off Cherry Street, with two well-worn old Fords parked in the drive and a rambling attempt at a garden lining the front walk. It's not fancy, not extravagant. It's just . . . comfortable.

Remember, I tell myself as I climb the brick front steps, bouquet of flowers in one hand and box of overpriced chocolates in the other. *It starts tonight. No more Junior. No more rotting apple. Paige signed up for a rock hero, and that is what she is going to get.*

I square my shoulders. I straighten my spine. I knock.

Paige yanks the door open before I can lower my hand, and, worryingly, the first thing out of her mouth is "I'm sorry."

Not a promising start. "Huh?"

She just opens the door wider, and this is when I see that

she is not alone. And the man and woman hovering just behind her can only be her parents.

Mrs. Warner, the source of Paige's freckles, might be five-
foot-nothing, but her smile hits me with the force of a sunlit
battering ram. She's *beaming* around Paige's shoulder, the puff
of her permed hair held in check by an oversize tortoiseshell
barrette.

Her husband stands half a pace back. As soon as the door
opens, I can tell that he's inspecting me—not with mistrust
but with genuine interest. Like his wife, Mr. Warner isn't a tall
man—he'd probably be stretching credulity to claim five-foot-
eight—but he's sturdy in his well-worn denim shirt and jeans.
Something about him rings some familiar bell in the back of
my head.

No more rotting apple, I remind myself. So I clear my throat
and say, as brightly as possible, "Hello. I'm Eddie Munson."

"Eddie!" Mrs. Warner says from somewhere behind Paige.
"*So* nice to meet you. I'm Julia, this is my husband, Hank—"

"Munson, huh?" Mr. Warner's eyes have narrowed in that
chillingly recognizable way people's eyes always do when they
hear that name. "Any relation to"—*oh no*—"Wayne Munson?"

I practically sag in relief. That's what was so familiar about
him—he's exactly the kind of guy I've seen Wayne drinking
with down at the Attic on some Friday nights. "He's my uncle."

Mr. Warner nods, satisfied. "Good man, Wayne."

"Yes, sir."

Paige widens her eyes at me. *Help.* I do not widen mine back
because somehow I've got a good thing tenuously going with
her folks, and I am absolutely not going to screw that up if I
can help it.

Mrs. Warner swats at her husband's shoulder. "What are we
standing around in the doorway for? Come in, come in—" As
a unit, the Warner clan shuffles aside enough for me to sidle
into what turns out to be the den.

Like the outside of the house, the word to describe this space is *comfortable*. A couple of squashy, beaten-in couches face the TV, and the coffee table between them has been scuffed and nicked with years of use. Boxes fill every unoccupied square inch, stacked on top of one another, teetering toward the ceiling. Some have words scrawled on them in thick black marker—BOOKS; PANS; SWEATERS—but most are blank.

"Thank you for having me for dinner," I recite, just how I practiced on my way over. Like an automaton, my arms hinge out, shoving the flowers and the chocolates toward Mrs. Warner.

I'm a little surprised by the enthusiasm with which she snatches the bouquet out of my hands. "Daffodils!"

"Mom *loves* daffodils," Paige says with an affectionate eye roll.

Mrs. Warner just flicks her fingers at her daughter, brushing aside the words. "Go get me a vase. One of the *nice* ones."

"Where are the nice ones?"

"In the pantry."

"I thought Gran's stuff was in the pantry?"

Mrs. Warner huffs an annoyed breath and flounces toward what I'm assuming, from the wafting aroma of roasting chicken, is the kitchen. She does not, I'm kind of happy to see, put the daffodils down.

"I'm sorry to say, that's kind of the status quo for this entire house at the moment," says Mr. Warner, watching his wife bustle out. "My mother passed about two months ago—"

"Paige told me," I say. "I'm very sorry to hear that."

He nods. He's got the same dark eyes as Paige, which is maybe what makes it easier to pick out the sadness still lingering there. "Thank you," he says. "Anyway, we've become the storage unit for all her things, and since we weren't swimming in square footage to begin with—" He waves a hand at the mountains of boxes that heap every corner. "It's a goddamn mess."

"Language," Paige singsongs, but her tone says that this is an inside joke.

"Shit, I'm sorry." Mr. Warner bumps her shoulder with his.

"Language!" Mrs. Warner sticks her head back into the den, ignoring the amused looks her husband and daughter share. "Come on in here and eat before it gets cold."

Dinner is as much of a curveball as the house—a no-frills home-cooked meal that Mrs. Warner ferries from the oven to the kitchen table in a few short trips. And as the crispy-skinned roast chicken plunks down in front of me, I can finally put my finger on what's had me so unbalanced since I first pulled up out front.

It's the same thing I felt on the job a few nights ago, when that cop car zoomed past me. I'd been bracing for a fight, for things to go the most difficult route possible. And then they hadn't. I'd imagined Paige and her family living in some upper-crust Maple Street minimansion, prepared to prove myself, to defend myself every step of the way. But they're spooning green beans onto my plate, pouring the same off-brand pop into my glass that Wayne gets at the Big Buy, asking me about my life, and joking with one another over chicken drumsticks.

I'd thought things are never easy. But now that I've left Junior behind—maybe they can be.

Mrs. Warner is in the middle of showing off the vase she's put the daffodils in (covered in hand-painted gray blotches that are apparently elephants; Paige made it in sixth grade art class) when the kitchen door swings open. A boy in a dirt-smudged baseball uniform trudges inside, backpack slung over one shoulder and baseball glove dangling from his hand. *Paige's baseball-playing little brother.*

"Mark!" Mrs. Warner exclaims. "You said today was late practice—we would have waited for you."

"Gabe sprained his ankle," Mark says, tossing his bag onto the linoleum tiles. He nods at me. "Who's that?"

"You wanna remember your manners?" Mr. Warner remarks mildly.

Mark sighs. "Who's that, *please?*"

"This is Eddie," Paige says.

"He's sitting in my chair."

"You weren't supposed to be here, shrimp," Paige retorts.

"I can move," I offer.

"Mark can get himself another chair," Mr. Warner says as his wife springs to her feet to dig another plate out of one of the kitchen cabinets.

"How did you get home?" she asks over the *clink-clank* of ceramic. "And it better not have been one of your teammates, you know I don't trust their driving."

"It was Simon's mom. You can ask her if you don't believe me," Mark says. He's in the corner, shifting a stack of boxes off what turns out to be another chair, the sibling of the ones we're already sitting on. "But I wouldn't. She was *super* teed-off today."

Paige leans over toward me as her brother keeps talking. "You okay?"

I grin. "When the food's this good? I'm great."

"She wants me to tell you," Mark's saying, dragging his chair over to the table, "they're having a meeting over at First Baptist on, uh, Thursday, I think? Something about devils and demons running around, after all that weird stuff back in November."

"The poor Hollands," Mrs. Warner murmurs, putting the plate down in front of her son. "They still haven't heard a peep from Barbara."

First Baptist. Isn't that the church Stan's parents belong to? Isn't that the church that had them pulling Stan out of school because—

"Simon's mom says it's because there's a *Satanic cult* at Hawkins High," Mark says, with obvious enjoyment.

All of a sudden, this meal isn't tasting nearly as good as it had two seconds ago. Because I can see the direction this conversation is about to take, clear as day. I choke down a bite of potatoes that have turned to sawdust in my mouth.

"Don't be stupid," Paige tells her brother. "There're no *cults* in Hawkins."

"How would you know?" Mark shoots back. "You don't even live here anymore, you're a California surfer-chick."

"I am *not a*—"

"And even if there're no *cults*," Mark cuts in, "there's a club for Dungeons and Dragons. An official one. That's what Simon was saying—that's what set his mom off. They meet each week and everything."

I put my fork down.

Mr. and Mrs. Warner are exchanging looks. "I'm not sure I like that," Mrs. Warner says.

"At school?" Mr. Warner says. "On campus?"

Paige is shooting me some significant looks right now, but I can't meet her eyes. "It's a club," she tells her parents. "For nerds. They sit around, they roll dice. They're not doing ritualistic sacrifice."

"I'm not saying they are," her dad says. He's put his fork down as well, and he's leaning back in his chair, arms crossed over his stomach. "I'm just not sure I like the fact that the school is signing off on the spread of those kinds of . . . ideas."

I open my mouth to say that the most controversial thing that's ever happened at Hellfire was when Stan's fireball almost flambéed Jeff into the next life. That the closest thing to Satanism during our sessions is the string of curse words Dougie sometimes unleashes when he misses an attack.

But Paige is jumping in before I can marshal these thoughts into some kind of order. "It's harmless, Dad, I swear. Right, Eddie?"

She's trying to support me. It's no secret that a ton of Corroded Coffin's songs are filled with references to D & D—the first song of ours that Paige ever heard is named after one of the spells. And Hellfire has been a huge part of my life ever since I got to Hawkins High as a freshman.

But that was the old Eddie. The guy who stuck around school, spreading his rot to everyone who got close. And I'd told myself that I was leaving him in the past, starting tonight.

"I wouldn't know," I say with a careless shrug. "I don't really mess with that stuff. Can you pass the beans?"

Again, Paige is looking at me, a little uncertain. Again, I don't meet her eyes. Instead, I just watch Mrs. Warner's face break out in a relieved smile as the tension is broken, and she presses the serving dish into my hands. "Take as much as you'd like," she tells me, and I do. Maybe if I eat enough, I'll be able to fill the deep hole I can feel gnawing in the pit of my stomach.

"Now," Mrs. Warner says, "does everyone have room for dessert?"

Chapter Thirty-One

I have just enough time to get my van from Greg the next morning before I pick Paige up to drive her to the airport. The long miles between Hawkins and Indianapolis pass in a blink of not-enough-time, blurring under wheels that shake and judder a lot less than they had when I'd first dropped the van off. Before I know it, I'm parked in a long line of cars as planes zoom in and out overhead and Paige hustles her two giant bags out the back doors.

"I'll call when I get in," she tells me through the open window. "And here—" She presses a scrap of paper into my hand. "That's for my place in L.A. Our place."

It's a phone number, and it immediately sears itself into my brain. *Our place.*

"I'm gonna miss you," she tells me, and her laugh is a little thick. "Is that stupid?"

"I'll be there soon." But that doesn't change the fact that "I'll miss you too."

"Good." She leans in the window, and I'm once again shrouded in the fall of her dark hair as she kisses me. I close my eyes and do my best to memorize this feeling—her lips on mine, her fingers tracing my cheek.

Someone honks. Paige pulls back, just a few centimeters—just far enough to echo "Soon" into the warm space between us.

It's the fading reverb of that kiss that gets me through the last few days. I finish packing, shoving everything I own into two duffel bags. I obsessively tune and retune my guitar, practicing until Dad tells me I'm going to lose my voice before I even get to California. I organize the van, trying to make enough room for my shit as well as Dad's. I cross off every item on my to-do list. I get it all done.

Well. I get most of it done. But there're one or two loose ends . . .

I'd gotten as far as picking up the phone. I'd gotten that far three times, actually. But each time, I'd hit a wall, staring at the stupid mustard-yellow receiver in my hand and debating whether this was harder or easier than having this conversation in person.

And each time, I'd chickened out. Hung up and just twiddled my thumbs, mostly because not making the call in that moment meant that I could put it off for—just a few hours, a day on the outside.

One day had become two, had become four, had become oh-shit-I-leave-for-Los-Angeles-tomorrow-morning. Which meant that if I wanted to have this conversation at all, I'd run smack into do-or-die time.

And still, I'm procrastinating. Sitting in my van, idling between the Ecker trailer and Uncle Wayne's, lurking like a creep.

Fuck it. The clock is ticking, and I've already wasted gas driving over here, so. *Get your ass up, Junior.*

Ronnie's screen door rattles beneath my knuckles, short and staccato. I'm only able to bring myself to knock twice, and then I'm shoving my hands into the pockets of my coat, studying the sky, the dirt, anything except the door in front of me.

There's a long beat before anyone answers, longer than I've ever had to spend on this doorstep in the decade that I've known Ronnie. I'd think that there was nobody home, but Granny Ecker's rusted-out Chevy is drooling oil in front. And if I listen very closely, I can hear someone whispering somewhere inside.

Finally, the door opens. Granny Ecker squints out at me from beneath the paisley kerchief she's got tied over her wild white curls. "Mr. Munson," she says, the words plinking out like ice chips.

"Hi, Granny." She's made no move to shove open the screen door, and so I keep my hands in my pockets and don't try to open it myself. "Is Ronnie here?"

"Mm." She hasn't blinked, not since she opened the door. "No, she ain't."

This is a lie, and not even a good one. I can see Ronnie's bag on the floor next to the sofa, and those had been two voices I'd heard murmuring just before the door had opened. "Granny—"

But the protest dies in my throat as soon as she shakes her head. "She ain't here, Eddie. Not right now." *Not for you.*

And unless I'm going to bust through the door and fight my way past Granny and her wooden spoon to see somebody who doesn't want to see me—

I mutter something inaudible and polite. Then I leave. I stomp past my van and down the gravel path toward the second stop on the grand Munson farewell tour of 1984.

There's not nearly as much trouble getting into Wayne's trailer. As usual, the front door is unlocked. Now that I'm fresh off my debut into the criminal world, I feel like I should maybe talk to him about that. Drive down to Melvald's and grab a bolt lock. *Something.* But it's past five, so the store's closing, and if I won't be around in the morning . . .

There's a lump in my throat, which hardens as Wayne looks

up at my arrival. I swallow past it and step through the front door. "Hey."

"Hey, Eddie." He puts down the magazine he'd been paging through, and I catch a glimpse of the glossy flowers printed on the cover. *Gardener's Weekly.* Wayne's always had a green thumb. "You all good?"

"Yeah. Just stopping by to say hi."

He nods, stoic as ever, but I can tell there's a pleased micro-smile somewhere under that beard. "Well, I already ate, but there's some dinners in the freezer if you're hungry."

"No, uh." I cough, trying to shift that stubborn lump in my throat. I'm starting to realize that it wasn't so much that I didn't want to have this conversation on the phone as it is that I don't want to have it at all. "I wanted to. Uh."

"Eddie?" There's a concerned line digging between his eyebrows. "Something wrong?"

"I wanted," I start again, because if I'm going to spit this out then I'm going to need a full runway to get to it, "to thank you. For everything you've done for me."

"Thank me?" That concern isn't shifting, it's just etching deeper.

"You know. Taking me in when Dad wasn't around. Making sure I don't starve, or get scurvy from only eating Cheerios."

"Well, sure." He's watching me like he knows there's another shoe, and if I don't drop it soon, he'll drag it out of me.

No sense in putting him through all that effort. "I said I came by to say hi," I say. "But actually—I came by to say bye."

"You going on a trip?"

"I'm—moving."

"Out of Hawkins?"

"Yeah."

That's enough of a second shoe for him. He sinks back into the couch. The *Gardener's Weekly* slides to the floor, and he doesn't try to catch it. There's no reply chewing in the tension of his jaw, nothing he's even trying to put into words.

I clear my throat again. "I'm going to California. I've got—an audition, actually. At WR Records. In a week. It's a pretty big deal." He's just looking at me. "Anyway. I wanted to. Tell you. Before I was gone."

"California," is all he says.

"Yeah."

"How are you getting there?"

"I'm driving out tomorrow morning." *With Dad*, is on the tip of my tongue, but I bite it back. God knows what kind of reaction *that* tidbit'll unleash.

But even with my tactical lying-by-omission, there's something ticking behind Wayne's eyes. "Congratulations."

"Gee, thanks."

"I mean it," he says, and I can tell he does. "You're talented. I always thought so. Anybody'd have to be blind not to see it."

I blink at him. Of all the things I'd anticipated, this hadn't even made the list. And faced with my silence, Wayne keeps talking. "But California. That's expensive."

Again—not even on the list. "I'll make it work."

"Your old man told me you dropped out."

"Just keeping up the family tradition." I've got my Munson grin on, inviting Wayne to laugh along with me, to laugh at all of us. *Just a family of fuckups, nothing to see here—*

"So you been using that extra time to pick up shifts at the Hideout?" Wayne asks. That look behind his eyes is intensifying. "Saving your paychecks?"

"Like you said. California's expensive." It's not an answer, but at least it's not a lie. "I'm eighteen. I'm an adult, Wayne. I'm gonna be fine."

"Then promise me there's nothing to worry about, and I won't worry."

I want to. I try to. But the words catch around the lump in my throat and die there. I'm left with my mouth flapping open like a suffocating fish. And all of a sudden, that intensity in Wayne's eyes clarifies, coming together in the space between seconds.

What was it he'd said, the last time I'd stood in this trailer and listened to his cautions? *You can't blame me for putting some pieces together.*

"What did you do?" he asks. Resignation is engraved deep into every movement as he stands, crossing his arms over his chest. And in his voice, I can hear the echoes of every time he's asked that question—not to me, but to Dad, ranging back however many decades to their childhood.

And now he gets to ask Junior. *What did you do?*

"I got myself a chance," I say, "to be something better."

"Better than what?"

"Than—than—you know what I mean."

"I don't. Better than what, Eddie. Better than you?"

I throw up my hands. This conversation is going nowhere. "I shouldn't have come here. I just wanted to say goodbye, make sure we parted ways with a clean slate. But if you want to break out the third degree—"

"This is a big choice. I just want you to be sure you're doing it for the right reasons."

It's so close to what Ronnie had said that I very suddenly cannot be in this trailer anymore. "Whatever," I say, already stomping toward the front door.

"Eddie—"

"Maybe the next magazine you buy'll have my face on the cover."

"I hope that's the case." Just like when he congratulated me, I can tell that he means that.

Somehow that just ticks me off even more. I snatch the door

open, hard enough to slam it into the paneled wall. "Have a nice life," I mutter.

I feel the impact of his "Be safe" in my teeth, all the way back to the house. I drive like a monster; if Officer Moore had caught sight of me, he might actually have had grounds to do something beyond turning my van inside out in a meaningless search. I drive like I'm trying to shake the trailer park, and every uncomfortable memory it holds, off my heels.

It doesn't work. If anything, tearing down the road only stokes my irritation, and by the time I grind to a stop in front of the house, I'm gripping the steering wheel hard enough to dent the pleather.

Promise me there's nothing to worry about.

Nobody asked him to worry. Nobody asked him to do anything. If he's going to get himself all twisted into knots over me, then that's on him. And it just means he'll feel like that much more of an asshole when I sign a three-album deal with Davey Fitzroy.

But I'm still fighting through anger as I swing out of the van and down onto the drive, my vision all hazed over with red.

Which is probably why I don't notice the two figures that materialize out of the darkness on the edges of the porch lights until they're practically standing on top of me. And once that happens—it's too late.

"Hey there, Matty," says Toby. CJ lurks at his side like a sleep paralysis demon. "Mind if we come in?"

Chapter Thirty-Two

I open my mouth to shout—to warn Dad, to call for help, I'm not sure. But it doesn't matter anyway, because CJ grabs me by the collar, and every scrap of voice I ever thought I had dries up in that split second.

"Inside," he growls and doesn't wait for a response. Once again, I feel the knobby outline of a gun's grip as I'm shoved ahead of them, up the front steps and, once I fumble my key into the lock, through the door.

"Dad!" I shout, the second the door opens, like maybe that'll give him enough runway to jump out a window, to escape. But this time, Toby and CJ don't try to shut me up. That's enough to let me know—they've got us where they want us. And no matter what I try, that's not going to change.

They barely glance in my direction as the door locks behind us. Their attention is on the kitchen, where Dad is slowly stepping back from the sink.

Toby shakes his head, all oversize disappointment. "I knew you were behind this," he says.

"Can I help you boys?" Dad asks. He's wiping his hands on a kitchen towel, like these two crewcuts aren't anything more than a couple of inconsiderate guests. But I know better than to watch his hands—I keep my eyes pinned to his face. And I can tell he's doing his best to bury a deep well of terror.

"Yeah," CJ says. "You can tell us where you put the shit you took."

"'Fraid you've got the wrong guy," Dad says. "I'm just heating up some leftovers here. If you like, I can fix you a couple of plates for the road."

Toby's hands are balled into fists. "Cut the shit, *Jerome.*"

Dad doesn't seem to have heard him. "Eddie, go grab a couple paper plates out of the hall closet—"

CJ moves fast, and between blinks he's at my side. His fingers clamp around the collar of my shirt so tight that I can hear the stitching strain. "Uh-uh," he says.

"The kid stays here," Toby says, "so that you stay here. And if you're quick about telling us where you put the weed, we might even let one of you live when all this is over."

I want to say that these words don't spiral me into a tornado of panic. I want to be like the action heroes in the movies Ronnie and I always sneak into down at the Hawk—Snake Plisskin, Han Solo, Conan the Barbarian, guys that can keep their cool.

But there're no helpful thoughts spinning around in my skull in this moment. Not when I know for sure that CJ has a gun on him, not when I can see dread written all over Dad's face. Actually, the only thing I *can* think in this exact moment is *this house is way too small for this shit.* It's hysteria, I know that in the last microscopic logical corner of my brain, but that's not enough to keep me from circling the same idea over and over. *This house is too small. Even if we moved into the liv-*

ing room, we'd all be smooshed together with Dad's stuff. Should we take this outside? How the hell do you do a good standoff with dirty dishes sitting in the sink?

"Okay." Dad holds his hands up, just high enough to show that they're empty. "The kid stays. Fine. Just do me a favor and get your hands off him."

CJ is doing no such thing. If anything, his grip on me just gets tighter. "Where's the *shit*, Munson?"

Munson.

Dad doesn't look at me. "I've got good news and bad news for you."

Munson. They know his name.

"I'm gonna start with the bad news. My pops always used to say that was the only way to do it, because you always want to end with dessert, right?"

If they know his name . . . then they know him.

"The bad news is, the weed is gone."

Toby shakes his head. "That's the wrong answer."

Maybe they looked him up in, like, the white pages before they came by.

Dad raises his hands a little higher. "You didn't let me get to the good news yet! See, this is why you wanna eat dessert last. Takes the bitter taste right out of your mouth."

Maybe they asked around. Maybe that's how they learned his name.

"We already went through the trouble of moving it all for you. So you can wipe all those risky deals and late-night meetings right off your to-do list."

CJ's frown might as well be carved from marble, for the amount I've seen it move. "You got the cash?"

"I've got—some of the cash. Most of the cash."

CJ practically growls. "More wrong answers, Al."

I can't keep kidding myself. Not here, in this tiny house,

with this cement block of a man ripping the collar out of my good shirt. Nobody here looked Dad up. Nobody here asked around. CJ and Toby turned up on our doorstep because they knew who they were searching for. Because—

"You know these guys."

It's not a question, and I don't say it like one. But Dad's still got his gaze pinned on Toby, and I realize now that it's because he's actively avoiding me. Because if I look him in the eye, I'll know what he's thinking. And that's the last thing in the world he wants right now.

"Listen," Dad says. He's talking fast and low, like his words are meant for Toby and Toby alone. "It doesn't have to be like this. How about I give you what I've got, and you tell Charlie you couldn't find me. We all walk away from this, we're all winners, and best of all, we don't ever have to see each other again."

"Wait, wait, wait—" Toby flaps a hand at Dad's muttering, brushing through the words like so much smoke. "Hold on a sec. Kid." A yank on the shirt from CJ brings me front and center, and now I'm framed in the kitchen doorway, looking straight at Dad.

"Leave him out of this—" Dad says.

But Toby just blazes past him. "Your old man hit you up for this job, and he didn't tell you why?"

"He doesn't have anything to do with—"

But if Dad is going to ignore me, then I'll return the favor. "He said he owed money," I say. "He said some bad guys were after him."

Toby sucks his front teeth with a dismissive *tsk*. "Well that's definitely the case *now*. Let me clue you in on a little secret about your daddy, okay, Junior? Up until, oh—three months ago, was it?"

"Three months," CJ echoes.

"Al had it *made*. He wasn't some down-on-his-luck ex-con. He wasn't a struggling thief. He wasn't a good guy trying to make it in an unfair world, no matter what he's told you." The edge of a vindictive smile twists Toby's mouth. "He was Charlie Greene's right-hand man. He was one of *us*. Or at least he was until he disappeared off the face of the planet."

I don't want to believe it, but this all makes too much sense to be a lie. I keep compulsively scrubbing back through the last few weeks, my brain scrabbling for puzzle pieces that just keep clicking seamlessly together no matter how much I beg for ragged edges. Dad's insistence that I play the face man on the job, despite the fact that he had far more experience. The way he'd known exactly where the truck would be and when and how to get inside. The bitten-off warnings from Reefer Rick.

"Why?" It's the only question left unanswered, the only question with any hope of redeeming this situation. Maybe Dad had been disillusioned by working with these people— maybe there was some secret, beneficent reason he had to loop me into this—to lie to me—

"Why do you think?" CJ is a solid presence at my back, his bulk blocking my path to the front door.

Dad takes a step closer. "That's enough."

Toby's grin just widens. "He thought—"

"That's *enough*," Dad snaps, and then—

—the world is spinning, just like my thoughts, because CJ has shoved me to the side, and I'm slamming into the wall and it takes me a solid few seconds to get my bearings again. And when I do, it's because two gunshots have gone off, and they have gone off only a few feet away from my head and now my ears are ringing and there are two holes in the plaster just past Dad's shoulder. And Dad himself has frozen in his tracks, his arms still outstretched, ready to tackle Toby.

"That is *not* how this goes," Toby says, loud enough for me to hear even through the muffled buzzing of my eardrums. "You got that?"

Mutely, Dad nods. He's finally looking at me, like the gunshots have finally drawn his attention to the fact that I am here in this kitchen and that the next bullet hole could be in either one of us.

"He thought," Toby goes on, "that his slice of the pie wasn't big enough. He thought he could go ahead and bake a pie of his own. And he thought he'd do it by *stealing from us*. Do I have that about right?"

It shouldn't sting. It shouldn't. It's not as though I'd thought we'd been embarking on some noble quest together—Sam and Frodo ascending Mount Doom to save the world. The plan had been to break into a drug smuggler's truck, steal some of their cargo, and sell it. But I'd thought—I'd thought I'd been helping my dad out of a tight spot. I thought I'd been doing a good thing in a roundabout way. But now—

Now I see this was just another con. Another ploy to grab what he could for himself and use anyone he could along the way. I hadn't been his son in all of this. I hadn't even been a fellow grifter. I'd never been working *with* Al Munson. He'd been using me, the way he's always used everyone dumb enough to trust him.

It's gotta be you. That's what he'd said the first night he'd come crashing back into my life. I'd thought it meant he'd wanted me for the job specifically. But in reality, I'm starting to realize, I was the only person left in the world who was stupid enough to work with him.

"Where's the money?" CJ demands. He's still got his gun out. In the back of my mind, I vaguely register that the barrel is pointed toward me.

Defeat is inscribed in every line of Dad's body, from his

slumped shoulders to the flicker of his eyelashes. "Living room. There's a paper bag behind the sofa."

At Toby's nod, CJ disappears, stomping in the direction of the living room. Dad doesn't say anything at the sounds of CJ's destructive search. Neither do I. We just look at each other across a kitchen that suddenly feels much bigger than before. Maybe there's enough room here for a standoff after all.

"See, this?" Toby waves a hand between the two of us. "This is why I never work with family. It's too damn messy."

"I was going to tell you," Dad says.

I snort. "Yeah? When?"

"When we got to California."

Bullshit. It's bullshit, and I know it's bullshit, and even *though* I know it's bullshit, there's still some shitty, tiny part of me that wants to believe him.

I stamp it out.

"Why?" I ask.

"Why California? Or—"

"Why were you going to tell me? At all?" I cross my arms and watch the look of consternation dawn across my dad's face. "Tell me," I say. "Tell me one reason why you were going to let me in on how you were conning me."

"I thought—I was going to—"

"You weren't." I squeeze my arms tighter, hugging my rib cage, willing away the ache in my heart. "You were never going to tell me. You were just going to keep lying and lying as long as it got you what you wanted."

Toby snorts. "He's got you pinned, Al."

Dad shakes his head. "That's not true—"

"You're still doing it!" I laugh. "It's incredible. You know, I don't think you've said one true thing since you've been back here. Maybe you haven't said one true thing my entire god-damn life."

"Now you're the liar."

I cock my head. "How do you figure?"

"I said I'm proud of you."

It's a low blow, and it has my breath catching in my chest. Before I can figure out how to reply in a way that won't come out strangled, CJ is stomping back into the kitchen, paper sack in hand.

"Got it," he says.

"Good," Dad says. He's got his game face back on as he turns away from me. "There should be about eight grand in there. It'll be more than enough to cover me with Charlie, or to pad your pockets and look the other way. The choice is yours. And in the meantime, you can get the fuck out of my house."

"I'm definitely gonna be doing that," CJ says, grinning wide enough to show off his ragged graveyard of teeth.

This is about when I start to smell the smoke.

"What—" I say, and then the rest is lost in a coughing fit. This, more than the growing haze in the air, is what clues Dad in, and his head whips around to stare at CJ, all color draining from his face.

"You psychotic—"

"It's only fair," Toby says. "A little payback."

"You have the money!"

"And you *embarrassed us*, Munson," Toby spits. "You cost us respect. You know how long it's going to take for Charlie to trust us again? This is a drop in the bucket."

Maybe Dad shouts something back at him, but I'm already shoving past CJ, racing toward the living room. Surprise vaguely registers in the back of my mind when CJ lets me go without putting a bullet between my shoulder blades, but then again what trouble am I to him? It's pretty clear at this point that I'm way more of a clueless pawn than a criminal mastermind.

CJ has turned the tiny living room upside down in his search for Dad's cash. The TV stand is tipped over, and our shitty fifteen-inch TV is lying faceup on the threadbare carpeting, a thick crack running diagonally across the screen. Dad's belongings, all packed up to leave for California, have been piled up on the sofa, which has been tilted forward on its front two legs . . .

And set on fire.

I barely feel the heat. The temperature must have been rising gradually while Dad and I glared at each other across the kitchen. It's been cooking me alive like a frog in a stockpot.

My first instinct is to step forward, to do something about the fact that the fire is catching the walls now, spreading up toward the ceiling. I watch the blackened spots grow and think *my house my house my house* on a helpless loop. But if there was anything in this room that might have been able to smother the blaze, CJ has used it as kindling.

Just like he's used Mom's records.

I'd missed them at first glance. My shocked stare had skipped over the scattered sleeves that CJ must have dumped onto the rug before he'd gone to town on the furniture. Now they're all I can look at—the faces of Muddy Waters and Bob Dylan and Jimi Hendrix crackling and blistering in the flames—every album Mom had carried from Tennessee to Indiana, every song she'd shared with me during the lonely late hours waiting for Dad, every memory—

No, no, no—

If I can make it across the living room, maybe I can save one—maybe I can save this house—maybe I can stop this—

But someone grabs the back of my jacket just as I'm about to lurch into the smoke, and I stumble backward. One half second later, something in the depths of the couch creaks and groans and snaps, and then there's a shower of sparks, a spray of flaming couch stuffing that spits across the room—peppering the spot where I would have been standing if Dad hadn't snatched me back in that exact moment.

"Let go of me—" The words scrape raw with smoke in my throat. "Get some water or something—"

Something in the living room gives another *snap-pop,* and this time the sound goes on and on and on. It's the cheap insulation in the wall, and it all goes up at once, a tidal wave of flames that race across the whitewash in the space between blinks.

"We have to go," Dad shouts into my ear, and this time I have to admit that he's right. There's no saving the living room, and the fire is starting to creep across the polyester carpeting, licking toward the kitchen. "Eddie—"

But it's not his hand that clamps down on my shoulder and shoves me toward the front door; it's CJ's. And when I finally tear my gaze away from the blazing inferno in the heart of what was my home, I see that Dad is getting the same treatment from Toby. We're both being marched out of the house side by side.

"I thought we were done," Dad protests over his shoulder, trying to catch Toby's eye. "You got your money, you burned my house down—that's not enough?"

But Toby doesn't reply. There's a muscle ticking in his jaw. He looks stressed. And it's not until Dad and I are shoved down the front steps that I can see why.

There's a squad car parked diagonally across the drive, red and blue lights still flashing. And crouched behind one open door, gun drawn and aimed squarely at us . . .

"Munson and Munson," says Officer Moore. "Why am I not surprised?"

Chapter Thirty-Three

"Evening, officer," Dad says. He's smiling like maybe that'll distract Moore from the fact that Dad and I are both being used as meat shields.

To his credit, Moore doesn't rise to the bait. He squints past us, trying to get a glimpse of Toby and CJ. "We got a report of shots fired inside. These friends of yours?"

CJ's gun is shoved deep into the small of my back. "Definitely not," I mumble.

"Anybody else left in the house?"

I shake my head. "We don't want any trouble," Toby shouts over Dad's shoulder. "Just stand down and let us pass, and we can all walk away from this."

Moore glances between me and Dad. "You taking them with you?"

"You want us to? This town'd be better for a couple fewer Munsons, don't you think?"

I can see Moore chewing this over. The son of a bitch is actually considering it, actually considering standing back to let CJ and Toby drag us away to whatever deep ditch they've got dug for us, somewhere on the edge of town.

"Backup's on the way" is what he eventually says. It's not the fervent denial I'd love to hear, but at least he's not rolling out the red carpet for our execution. "This property'll be knee-deep in cops in a few minutes, and if you want things to go your way, you'd better start making things easy on yourselves now. Drop your weapons." Out of the corner of my eye, I see Toby and CJ exchange sidelong looks. Moore tightens his grip on his gun. *"Drop them. Now."*

The house windows explode.

"Fuck!" Moore shouts. I hit the ground in something between a controlled dive and a rag-doll toss. Glass rains down around me. I can definitely feel the heat of the flames *now.* They reach out toward us, gobbling up the night air, charring the peeling clapboard of the walls.

"He's up."

I can barely hear Toby's mutter over the crackling of the fire, but the words send a chill through me. Carefully, I lift my head, feeling slivers of the broken windows slip through my hair and hoping that I won't see what I think I'm about to.

Sure enough, Moore is on his feet, one hand on the roof of his squad car and the other planted on top of his head. He's staring at the burning house in shock, the firelight making his shocked expression dance. And most importantly—he's broken cover.

"Do it," Toby says, and if I'm having trouble hearing, then Moore is definitely out of earshot because he doesn't move. He doesn't even flinch, and I'm only halfway through a shouted *"Get down!"* when CJ's trigger-happy finger squeezes and—

It's not the first time I've heard a gun go off, not even tonight. But it is the first time I've seen a bullet strike a human being. It arrows straight through the open car window and plunges deep into Moore's side. A spray of something wet goes up, but the blood looks black, caught between the moonlight and the blazing fire. Moore spins and staggers and goes down, his scream more of punched-out surprise than animal pain.

Not that this has any impact on our unwelcome visitors. Toby just claps CJ on the shoulder. "Come on."

There's a growing puddle of blood on the ground. I can't look away. "You're just gonna leave him here?"

"Just be grateful it wasn't your dad, Junior," CJ says. "Or you."

Is it just shock ringing in my ears? Or are those police sirens? My money's on the latter, because CJ and Toby are exchanging slightly panicked looks. "Come *on*," Toby says again, and then he and CJ are sprinting up the drive, arrowing for the vague outline of a shitty old Mustang that I can just pick out in the nighttime shadows of an overgrown maple tree.

Moore isn't moving so much anymore. I take a fumbling step toward him—

"What are you doing?" Dad hisses, grabbing my arm. I yank myself free and stumble to Moore's side, tumbling to my knees next to him. There's a huge dark stain spreading across his right side, and his breath is coming in little hitches. His eyes are open, staring up at the stars, and even in this gloom I can tell that his pupils are blown wide. *Panic? Shock?* Who knows. This isn't the kind of thing they teach you in health class.

"Officer Moore? Hey, can you hear me?" I pat at his shoulder, feeling more than a little useless.

"Eddie," Dad says. "Don't be stupid. We have to get out of here."

At my shaking, Moore groans. "Munson?"

"Hey—hey—you're gonna be okay—"

"Did someone fucking shoot me?"

"Eddie," Dad hisses. He's hauling at my arm now, strong enough to pull me back to my feet, and he won't let go no matter how hard I resist. "There are more cops on their way. Get in the van."

"I can't just leave him here."

"Yes, you can."

"Are you serious? He got shot because of us—"

"He got shot because CJ shot him, that's all. But how do you think that's gonna play out for us if we're still here when those squad cars pull up?"

I stare at him, at his soot-smudged face and wide eyes. I'm still staring at him when the corner of Dad's mouth pulls up in that crooked smile. "Come on, kid," he says, radiating that Munson Magic. "Think about your lady. Your audition. You want to make it to California, don't you?"

Something heavy sinks in the pit of my stomach. *California.* He's right. There's no way I can explain this to Paige, not if I stick around. Not if I absorb the ball of shit that's headed my way with those flashing red and blue lights.

At my feet, Moore groans again.

I pull my arm free of Dad's grip and kneel beside Moore. Tentatively, because I'm literally only going off what I've seen in movies, I press my hands to the part of Moore's torso that looks the wettest. He hisses a pained gasp.

Dad's smile flattens into a grim line. "Didn't think you were that much of a fool."

"Stay," I urge him. "We can explain it to the cops—it'll be easier if there're two of us."

"That's not how this works." He's already backing away from me. I can see something glinting in his hand—my van keys. He must have lifted them when he was dragging me away from Moore. I hadn't even noticed. *Guitar picks, lock picks. Pickpock-*

eting. You figure out one, you figure out the other. "Nothing we say'll make a difference to them."

"Then stay because—because I need you." I try my own crooked smile, but there's something stinging at my eyes, ruining the effect. I tell myself it's just the smoke from the burning house. "It'd be pretty shitty if you ditched me again right now. Not after we made all those plans."

The firelight dancing across Dad's face makes him look like a marble statue. He watches me for a long moment as those sirens grow nearer and nearer. Beneath my hands, Moore twitches and curses.

"You're the one changing the plan, Eddie," Dad finally says. "And I didn't sign up for the new one." He nods. Decisive. Tosses the keys once and catches them again. "I'll leave her somewhere near Hawkins. Good luck, kid."

"Munsons don't do luck."

"Yeah, well—I think you're gonna need it."

And then all I can see is his back, retreating—my van's taillights, retreating—my father, retreating. And just like every time he walks out of my life, I'm left in the dirt to pick up the pieces.

Chapter Thirty-Four

I should probably be surprised that it's taken me eighteen years to land in lockup for the first time. It sure as hell surprises everyone else. But as I stare at the lock in the barred door, listening to the buzz of activity out in the police bull pen, all I feel is numb.

"Officer down—"

"That's right, the Munson place—"

"Ambulance on the way—"

"We'll need the fire department on the scene—"

Chaos had unfolded as soon as the pair of squad cars had zoomed to a stop in my front yard. I don't know how many cops had been present at the scene—it could have been any number between two and twenty for all I could process. The only thing that existed to me was the press of Moore's stomach beneath my hands and the memory of Dad's retreating back behind my eyelids.

It had taken two cops to haul me away from Moore, one holding on to each of my arms. *"Is he gonna be okay?"* I'd asked them, a little dazed, a little out of it. *"It's his stomach, I think—is he gonna be—"*

"We've got a suspect," one of the cops barked into a shoulder walkie. *"It's the Munson kid. We'll bring him in now."*

I hadn't protested, not when they handcuffed me, not when they shoved me into the back of the squad car. What would have been the point? I'd known this would happen—Dad had known this would happen. But I'd stayed anyway, and so all there was left to do was to drown in the consequences.

They hadn't given me a chance to wash my hands before they'd trotted me into the police station. Moore's blood is still under my fingernails, crusted onto the knees of my jeans. And since Hawkins isn't big enough for more than a drunk tank, there's no toilet or sink in the cell. Drunks get to sit in the messes they make.

I scrub my hands over my eyes. Screw crusted-on blood, all I want to do is tear my face off. If a new one grows in its place, maybe it'll make me a different person. Someone who isn't such a complete fuckup.

"Hey. Junior."

Chief Hopper looms into the frame of my blank stare. He's huge as ever, nearly blotting out the light. And his face is impassive as he watches me through the bars.

For once, I don't feel the urge to correct him on the nickname.

"The guys been hassling you?" he asks, nodding back toward the burning fluorescent lights of the bull pen.

"No." My voice is a smoke-singed croak. I realize in that moment how thirsty I am.

He nods. A moment later, he's reaching through the bars. It takes me a second to figure why, my eyes struggling to focus through dim light and shock. He's got a paper cup of water, holding it out to me.

"Thought you might need it," he says. "Come on, my arm's tired."

I slouch toward him, taking the cup. One sip runs down my scorched throat, and suddenly this is the best thing I've ever tasted. I gulp down the rest before remembering that I wanted to save some to clean my hands, and that the chief of police is watching me drink like a dehydrated Labrador. I wipe my mouth on my sleeve. Maybe I can save whatever shreds of my dignity are left by glaring at him. Maybe it'll seem like defiance.

Maybe not, though, because there's a twist of something almost like pity on Hopper's face. "Moore's out of surgery," he says.

"Is he—"

"Docs say the bullet missed anything major, against all odds. Blood loss wasn't even that bad." I tuck my hands under my thighs. "He'll hobble out of the hospital with a scar to show the ladies and not much else. He's fine, kid." He pauses, like he's searching for the next words. "He says you tried to help him."

I shrug. I'm not sure if anything more will be digging this hole deeper for myself.

"He also says there was another man who didn't stick around. A man who looked a lot like you."

I shrug again. This one I'm *definitely* not chipping in on.

"I knew your old man at school." Hopper says it like it's a non sequitur, though we both know it's not. "A few years behind me, but I knew him. Everyone knew him. If there was a shitstorm kicking off, Al Munson was always the furthest person from the center." He leans a shoulder against the wall, crossing his arms over his chest. "Funny thing was, if you looked hard enough, you started to notice he was usually the person who kicked it off in the first place."

I don't need another reminder of what a dumbass I was to trust my Dad, so I just clunk my cup down on the bench. "Am I free to go?" It comes out hollow. I know the answer before I see the twist of Hopper's mouth. I know before I even ask the question.

"Not without bail," he says. "Your house burned down, Junior. Someone *burned* your house down. That's arson, and until we can dig into it—"

For a second, the fog dulling my mind parts, and a flash of angry protests pile up inside my skull. *Why would I burn down my own house? Did you miss the two guys at the scene who shot one of your cops? Isn't it obvious I'm the victim here?*

But just as quickly as the clouds had rolled away, they roll back in again. All I can do is listen as he continues. "No one's pressing charges, not 'til we figure out what's going on. Which means we're gonna be asking questions." He's watching me closely through the bars. "It's in your best interest if you're here to answer them. I can't keep you in Hawkins. I'm not gonna try. But I will tell you that if you disappear, you'll be making a universe of trouble for yourself. You'll only be doing what your dad would've done." *What he* did *do.* "And I don't have you pegged like that. Not yet." He straightens up, shaking out his shoulders with a sigh. "Of course, you've got a lifetime to prove me wrong."

I just look at him, my gaze dull. The edges have been sanded off the world, sanded off me.

"Do I get a phone call?" I ask.

There's a tinge of pity in his eyes as he reaches for the keys on his belt. "Sure," he says. "Follow me."

Maybe Hopper takes pity on me, because he doesn't lead me into the bull pen. Instead, I trail him the long way through the police station, squinting in the light that filters through the windows. Sometime between my house burning down and now, the sun's come up and a new, terrible day has begun.

Hopper stops outside a door. POLICE CHIEF is inscribed in the frosted glass. He's letting me use his office.

"Don't try to steal anything," he says, pushing the door open for me. "I'll know."

"Yes, sir."

"You go over fifteen minutes, I'm pulling the plug."

"Yes, sir."

"Phone book's on the desk. Wayne's number's in there, I checked."

I just nod. He studies my face, looking for . . . something. I don't care what he finds.

"Okay," he finally says, stepping aside. I sidle around him and pace toward his desk. I don't need to look back over my shoulder to know that he's still there, the door still wide open. He's keeping an eye on me. Why wouldn't he? Nobody in their right mind would let a criminal loose in their office without supervision.

I keep my back to him as I pick up the phone and dial. No phone book necessary. I know this number by heart.

"Hello?"

Paige's voice is rusty with sleep when she picks up, and I add yet another tick to the tally of fuckups in my roster. It's three hours earlier for her out in Los Angeles, practically the middle of the night—I must have woken her up.

"Paige. Hey. It's Eddie."

"Eddie?" I hear a rustle through the receiver as she sits up in bed. I've never seen her apartment, but I imagine it now—open and airy. Big windows, with the first rays of golden California sunshine peeking through. Paige's dark hair, tousled around her pretty freckled face. An orange tree in the courtyard outside. Paradise. "Are you on the road already? What time is it?"

"No, I—"

"Oh, my God, it's four in the morning. Why did you call me at four in the morning, you psycho?" She's laughing through the insult. "You excited to see me? It's barely been a week."

"I know." I swallow hard. This is gonna hurt. "Listen. Paige. I have to tell you something."

"Are you okay?" That laughter is gone now, drained away. I did that to her. "What's wrong?"

"I'm okay. But I—I'm not going to make the audition."

The silence that stretches over the line after that is heavy. It sits on my chest, suffocating me. "Run that past me again," she finally says, flat.

"I can't come to California. Not right now."

Hopper's words had only confirmed what I'd already realized watching Dad run away from Moore's bleeding body in the drive outside our burning house. When Toby and CJ had shown up on our doorstep, they'd brought Junior with them. There was no escaping that shadow now, not even all the way out on the West Coast. If I'd run with Dad, I'd never have been able to stop. I'd have had to spend my life dodging the law the way that Dad spends his. The way everybody in this town already thinks I do.

"Are you serious?" Paige says. "This is a bad joke—"

"It's not a joke."

"For fuck's sake, Eddie!" I wince, flinching back from the receiver. Behind me, I hear Hopper clear his throat uncomfortably. Paige's voice *carries*. "This isn't something we can just *reschedule*. You know how important this is!"

"I know," I fumble, but she blows right past me.

"This is your shot. You *wanted* this."

"I know."

"This was *my* shot." Oh, God. Are there tears in her voice? "I stuck my neck out to get you this audition. This was going to make both of us. You and me. In it together."

"I know." It's all I can say, like a stupid broken record.

"Then where are you? What was more important than coming to L.A.?"

I can already hear it. The way she thinks about me—it's changing. Even if I had the best excuse in the world, now I'm the guy who screwed her over. And it's only going to get worse from here.

I grit my teeth. "I'm at the police station."

Another moment of nauseating quiet on the other end of the line. "What did you do?"

And there it is. Not "What happened?" or another "Are you okay?" *What did you do.* "Does it matter?" I snap.

"Yeah, it *matters*," she bites back.

"Right, because this isn't the story you sold Davey Fitzroy."

"Don't—"

But I'm on a roll, so I plow through her and keep going. *"Barback turned rock hero.* No room in there for a little tarnish, huh? You're telling me there's no one on WR's roster who's seen the inside of a jail cell?"

"Don't be an asshole," she says, but it's too late. I'm already an asshole. I've been an asshole all along. I'm just the last person in all of Hawkins to accept it.

"No, sure, you've only got a place for delinquent musicians after they've started making you money."

"Fuck you." Then there's just a dial tone, and I'm glaring at the receiver in my hand hoping that somewhere, out in sunny, golden California, Paige can feel it.

"You finished?" Hopper asks, and *shit*, I forgot he was here, listening in on that entire train wreck.

"Yeah," I say, slamming the phone back into the cradle. "I'm finished."

Chapter Thirty-Five

I don't sleep. I don't even doze. I just toss and turn on the bench, counting the cracks in the ceiling and trying not to touch the lacerations in my soul that Paige's *fuck you* left.

I have no clue how long I lay in the dark hating myself. For some reason, it's not the cops' top priority to put a clock in the drunk tank. But after some murky amount of time, the cell door swings open again. I swing my legs over the side of the bench and sit up.

It's not Hopper, not this time. A deputy frowns at me from the open door—Powell, I think. Pretty sure he's arrested my dad at least once. Good for him, collecting the whole Munson set.

"You're good to go," he says. It's absolutely the last thing I expected to hear from him, so I just stare. He frowns even harder at me, his mustache dipping with the corners of his mouth. "You deaf, son? Get out of here."

"But—" For some reason my first impulse is to protest. I deserve to be in here, don't I? I fucked up. Fuckups go to prison. This is where I belong.

Then my brain catches up with reality, and I surge to my feet. "Thanks," I mutter and scramble out the barred door before he can change his mind and slam it shut on me again.

It's not until I step into the hallway that I realize how truly screwed I am. My house is burned to a crisp. My dad's in the wind. I have no money, no job, no place to go. Maybe I could live in my van for a few months, but that would mean I have to figure out where Dad left it . . .

"Hey."

Uncle Wayne is standing in the police bull pen. He's got his ball cap clutched in both hands, like he's at church or something, and he's pressed his shoulder blades to the wall, keeping as far out of the way of the bustling cops as possible.

"Hey," I say. What the hell else is there to say?

Nothing, apparently, because Wayne just turns around and starts walking toward the front door. I watch him go for a moment, confused, before he glances back at me over his shoulder. "You coming or staying?"

I follow him out of the station.

Wayne's pickup has been on its last legs for more than ten years. The ancient Ford's chugging and clanking are the only sounds to be heard as Wayne navigates out of downtown Hawkins. I rest my head against the window and stare at the air vent in the dashboard. I don't want to risk a glance outside, not when it might mean making eye contact with some Hawkins busybody. How many people saw me get hustled into the police station last night? How many people saw me leave just now?

It's not until we pull off Pine that I realize where we're going. Wayne is taking me back to the trailer park. Frowning,

I twist in my seat to glance out the back window. There, half-covered by a tarp, I can see a pile of bags. The smoke-blotted flannel sleeve poking out the mouth of one tells me they're full of clothes. My clothes.

"I got what I could," Wayne says. He's still watching the road.

"Did you"—I almost don't want to ask, but—"Did you see any of Mom's records?"

His mouth thins. "Fire took out the front of the house. Kitchen, living room. There was—nothing left."

Nothing left. All Mom's music—her plane tickets—*gone.* The next breath I take feels like a stiletto in my lungs. I power through anyway, willing away the sting in my eyes. "Dad was staying in the living room. That's where his stuff was."

Wayne shakes his head. "Al'll be fine. Always is."

"Have you heard from him since last night?"

Wayne slides me a sideways look. It's sad but not pitying. I straighten up a little in my seat. "No," he says.

I nod. It's not a surprise, but it still hurts—dull and aching, somewhere behind my ribs. Wayne nods too, and I get the impression that he's got that same hurt in the same place. A bruise where a brother should be, decades older than mine.

He pulls to a stop on the dirt patch outside his trailer and turns off the truck. Moments later, I'm clambering slowly out, looking around like an astronaut on Mars or something. I can't count the number of times I've been to this trailer park, but this feels different, somehow.

The hinges on the Ford's gate groan a protest as Wayne flips it down. He steps back, considering the lumpy tarp for a second. There's a frown working somewhere under his beard. Finally, he looks back at me, a little uncertain.

"I'm not saying you have to stay here," he says. "I don't want you to think I'm—forcing it. But—" He breaks off, jaw working. "Shit, Eddie. You know what I'm trying to say."

I do and I don't, at the same time. "You still want me to stay with you? You just had to bail me out of jail."

He leans back against the truck, arms crossed across his chest. His shrug is tired, and I realize that he's just come off the night shift. He must have driven straight to the police station from work. "Chief told me what happened," he says. "He said you tried to help one of his guys."

"Yeah, but that cop got hurt because of me."

"He got hurt because Al is too dumb to know when his smart plans circle around to being dumb-shit stupid again."

"No one cares," I snap. It's loud—too loud for the quiet sunlight, for the chirping birds and rustling wind. But none of that matters right now, because the sullen dullness of last night has started to fade and now I'm starting to *feel it.* The knowing smirks of the cops as they loaded me into the squad car. The sight of Dad's back retreating into the dark as he skipped away from every single problem he'd created. The cop's blood under my fingernails—*Christ,* it's *still* under my fingernails, I haven't had a chance to wash it off.

Ronnie's face, hardening to stone as I blow a chasm in our friendship with my insecurity.

Paige's voice, right before she'd hung up on me. Right before that dream had burned up like my house. Like my life.

"It doesn't matter whose fault it is," I grit out. "It just matters that I was there. That's all anyone needs to know—Eddie Munson was there. *No shit he was there, he's the fuckup of Hawkins.* I could have pulled the trigger or I could been handing out cotton candy, it doesn't make a difference. No matter what, to everyone in this *goddamn town,* I'm guilty."

Wayne is just watching me levelly, letting me make a scene. Somehow that just makes this all worse. "I have tried *so. Hard.* To make these people see me like something else. But whatever I do, I just end up right back here. Public enemy number one, worth *nothing.* I can't even disappoint them anymore.

They expect me to fail. And they're *right*. Any chance I get, I'm just gonna screw it up for myself. After all this, I'm just like Dad. Actually, I'm worse than Dad. I'm *Junior*."

"You ain't Junior." Wayne says it quietly. I have to shut up to hear him, and maybe that was the point. "Al didn't name you for himself. Might be the only smart decision he ever made."

All at once, my chest tightens. If I try to talk, or even take a breath, I know it's going to come out in a shuddering mess, so I just clench my jaw and let my teeth grind together.

"You listen to me now, Eddie, 'cuz I've been trying to get you to hear this for a while," Wayne continues. "Al Munson is a fuckup, and I'm not gonna argue with you on that. It's why he didn't stick around to clean up his own mess last night. It's why he never does. You, though—you did. You did the right thing. That's not what a fuckup does."

"They still think I'm—"

"To hell with what *they* think!" It's the loudest I've ever heard Wayne speak. "You can't walk through life shaking yourself to pieces over how other people think you should be. They'll always try to fit you in some box—angel, devil. Hero, villain. Fuckup, saint. But we ain't meant for boxes, not 'til we're dead in the ground. You're the only person who knows who you are. So stop trying to fit yourself into one of their boxes and just let yourself be you."

"It's not that easy."

"You think I don't know?" Wayne snorts, ripping the tarp out of the truck. "I've been around a lot longer than you, fighting this fight the whole while. But what I can tell you is, even if it's hard, it's worth it. Here."

He hauls something long, wrapped in my old, sooty sheets, out of the truck bed, and hands it to me. I wrestle to push the wrappings aside—and find myself staring down at the glossy body of my guitar.

That tightness in my chest has traveled up to my throat. "I thought this was gone."

"Fire didn't touch it," Wayne says. "Thought you'd want to have it back."

"Thanks," I whisper. My knuckles are white around the fretboard. I don't think I'll ever let go of this guitar again.

"I'm gonna start some coffee," Wayne says, hauling a bag of clothes out of the truck. "You want some?"

His words are still swirling through my head, ping-ponging off the nooks and crannies of my brain. I'm not sure what to make of them—if I'll ever know what to make of them. But for now—

"Yeah," I say, grabbing another bag with my free hand. He nods, and I can see an edge of relief in his face.

"Oh," he says, as we start to trudge toward the trailer. "You were wrong about one more thing, you know."

"What's that?"

"I didn't bail you out," he says. "You think I got that kinda money? Chief told me it was already paid by the time I showed up."

I frown. "By who?"

"Some girl," Wayne says. "Wired the cash. All the way from California."

What did you do? Paige had asked, and *It matters.*

It matters, when you need to know how much to pony up for bail money.

"Sounds like not everyone thinks you're guilty," Wayne says, pushing in the front door. "Maybe there's hope for the Munson name yet."

Chapter Thirty-Six

It's weird and easy at the same time, settling in to the trailer. It's not like Wayne is strict—he hasn't laid out a single rule since I off-loaded all my shit out of his truck. But having someone around all the time is strange. When I'd been living on my own, I'd gotten used to silence, to being able to do whatever I wanted whenever I wanted. When Dad was there, things weren't that much different. I'm starting to realize that he'd never seen me as a kid. He'd seen me as a buddy. And you don't have to keep an eye on your buddies.

It's obvious, though, that Wayne feels a kind of responsibility toward me. For the first few days after I move in, he even makes an effort to stock *vegetables* in the refrigerator. This stops pretty quickly, after the first bundle of carrots wilts, untouched. But my surprise at the sight of leafy greens under the yellow fridge light still hasn't faded.

I spend the first week kind of . . . drifting. I'm so used to having somewhere I've gotta be every minute of every day—

school, work, Hellfire, rehearsal. Now I'm at loose ends. Chief Hopper comes by twice, once with Officer Powell and once by himself. He tosses me the keys to my van and tells me that he'd found it behind the Turnbow Tractors billboard at the edge of town. I answer his questions like an automaton, reciting my responses from ten miles away until Hopper gives Wayne a firm handshake, me a somber nod, and stomps down the front steps. I spend as much time as I can stand playing around on my guitar and paging through the Gormenghast paperbacks Wayne had salvaged from the old house. But claustrophobia is a bitch, and soon it feels like the walls are closing in. Sleep becomes something that exists only for other people. I haunt the trailer at night, watching the sky through the windows as I pace a circuit around the tiny living room.

Saturday Night Fever, Paige had said, pointing at the stars. I push her voice out of my mind. She hasn't returned any of my calls, and I can't keep trying her without turning the corner into megacreepdom. If she wants to talk, she knows where to reach me.

It's at the tail end of one of these sleepless nights when it happens. I've had a productive evening of lying flat on my back on the bedroom floor, trying to count backward from one million in my head. Out in the living room, I hear the trailer's front door open. Wayne stomps inside, and a moment later there's a squeak-thump as he slouches into a kitchen chair. The silence that follows is broken only by a deep sigh.

I flip over onto my belly and army crawl toward the bedroom door, sliding it open a crack. Peering through, I catch a glimpse of my uncle slouched over the table. There's something pinched between his fingers—a piece of paper. In the warm light from the rising sun, I can make out the word OVERDUE stamped in red across the top.

I flop back down, letting my chin rest against my stacked fists. Wayne took me in. He's trying to stand by me, when no one else will. I can't just spin my wheels while he runs himself into bankruptcy. And even if no one in this stupid town will hire me, I know someone who will.

Rick answers the door at my first knock. He's still in his bathrobe, and he's carrying a mug of something hot that's spiraling steam up into his face. He grins at the sight of me, which throws me a for a loop. "Munson Junior!" he exclaims, loud enough to send ducks flapping off the lake in the distance.

"It's just Eddie," I say. "Do you have a sec?"

"For sure, absolutely." He steps aside. "D'you want tea? It's Darjeeling."

I do. Which is how I find myself leaning against the counter in Rick's kitchen as he putters around, boiling water in a saucepan on the stovetop and pouring it into a mug. It's not entirely clean, but who's got the time to care about shit like that.

"What brings you to my neck of the woods?" Rick asks. His slippers are bunnies, but there's an ear torn off the right one. "I heard you skipped town with your old man."

"Nah," I say. "I'm sticking around. That's actually why I'm here."

"You need a place to stay?"

I blink in surprise. It sounds like he's actually offering. "I need—you said to look you up. If I needed cash."

"Oh, right on." He nods, opening up a cupboard. The jumble of pots and pans inside is chaos, but Rick seems to know where to look. He hauls down a stack of colanders. "Yeah, you can start today, even."

"How does this work?"

"Oh, it's easy, dude. Basically, I get weed and other shit and bring it here. Then you buy off me whatever you think you can turn around, and you get to sell it for however much you want. You don't owe me a cut or anything—whatever you make is all yours."

"I buy it off you."

"Well, yeah. This isn't pizza delivery. I'm not paying you to run weed all over town." He peers at me over his stack of colanders. Maybe his bloodshot eyes can tell just how empty my pockets are, because he gives a little laugh. "Tell you what. First ounce is on me, all right?" The last two colanders separate, and Rick fishes a plastic sandwich bag out from between them. He tosses this over to me, and I catch it with both hands. "You can pay me back after you move it. Call it thirty bucks? And then we can talk about branching out."

There's something on the counter just past Rick's elbow—another one of those bright blue pill bottles that Dad had clocked on our first visit. "Branching out, like—"

Rick sees what's grabbed my attention and laughs. "For sure, dude," he says. "Those are good movers too. Plenty of folks in this town like a little pep in their step."

A little puzzle piece of memory slots into place, for all the good that it does me. But until I figure out what to do with it—

I'm in. Thirty dollars for an ounce is an insane deal, and we both know it. I pocket the baggie.

"Pleasure doing business with you, Eddie," Rick says.

I grin. "Pleasure *is* the business, man."

"He gets it." Rick toasts me with his tea. "Glad to have you on the team."

The sun feels friendlier when I leave Rick's house. I take a second to turn my face up to it, letting the light warm my skin. *I could stay here,* I think. Just for a bit. *Wander toward the water.* There's a boathouse or something down there; I can see it through the trees. I should take a moment and—listen to the birds. Isn't that the kind of thing people do when they're out of prison? When they've got a new lease on life? Commune with nature?

But I don't want nature right now. I want normal. And for

the first time in over a week, I know exactly what kind of normal I'm craving. So instead of going all mountain-man, I climb back into my van and drive into town.

The bell on Main Street Vinyl's front door jingles as I push inside. It's blissfully dark in here, and Jerry barely glances up as I enter. He's got some old-school Ray Charles playing, just loud enough to muffle the sound of my sneakers on the old carpet as I shuffle toward the back of the shop.

I should feel good. I know that, in my head. Intellectually. I should be climbing out of the dark hole I'd put myself into. I've got a roof over my head. Soon I'll have money coming in. I'll be able to help my uncle out. I'm on my way.

But that storm cloud still dangles heavy over me, so dense that even the familiarity of the record shop can't disperse it. And I think I know why.

I might be on my way. But toward *what,* I have no idea. I'm not catching the express train to San Quentin like Dad. I'm not gonna be some golden rock god out in California. So where does that leave Eddie Munson? Small-town, second-string drug dealer until *forever*? That doesn't feel right either.

Let yourself be you. That's what Uncle Wayne said. But how am I supposed to know what that is?

The front door bell jingles, and I glance back over my shoulder to see who's come in. If it's someone who's gonna give me trouble, I might as well leave before Jerry decides I'm not worth the hassle and bans me for life.

But the two boys who slink inside look like they've come from my side of the street. The older one I place immediately. His sad eyes and shaggy hair—I saw him earlier this year, putting *Have You Seen Me* flyers up around school. Jonathan Byers. He'd been looking for his missing little brother. From what I'd heard, despite there being a freaking *funeral* for the kid, he'd somehow found him again.

The small kid trailing in Jonathan's footsteps is the smiling boy from those photocopied flyers. He's got a twitchy look to him, and he keeps his head on a swivel, always looking over his shoulder. Scanning the shop, he locks eyes with me for a second. The color drains from his already pale face, and he looks down, keeping even closer to his brother.

"Mr. Byers," Jerry says as the boys approach. "Hoped you'd be in sooner."

"I've had to help my mom the last few nights," Jonathan says. "Sorry."

Jerry stands, his stool creaking beneath him. "It's in the back. Come on."

"Thanks." Jonathan and Will begin to follow as Jerry ambles toward the beaded curtain at the back of the shop— toward me. I quickly look back at my bin, flipping through records without registering title or artist.

"Hold on—" I hear Jerry say. "No kids behind the curtain."

"He's fine," Jonathan says, "I promise.

"No kids," Jerry says again. "I can't sell scratched records. Even the smudged ones are hard to shift."

"He won't even touch anything. Right, Will?"

But Jerry is not having it. "You want this album or not?"

Jonathan does. I can hear it in his voice. I watch out of the corner of my eye as he leans in close to his brother to mutter, "Are you okay out here?"

Will rolls his eyes. "It'll be like two minutes."

"I know, but—" Jonathan breaks off at the warning look Will gives him. "Just don't tell Mom."

"I'm not *crazy*."

Jonathan laughs at that and squeezes his brother's shoulder. Then he's following Jerry through the clacking, beaded curtain, and into the back.

Will sidles back around to the bins at the side of the room, paging idly through Jerry's pitiful funk and soul collection. I do the same, and we continue in silence for a few long seconds as "I Got a Woman" starts up.

Ray's just halfway through the first chorus when the bell over the door jingles again, louder than it had for the Byers boys. A split second later, the door slams into the opposite wall as two kids in Hawkins High JV jackets bust inside, shoving at each other to be the first one through.

This is the kind of trouble I was hoping to avoid. From the way I can see Will's shoulders tense, all the way across the store, he feels the same way. But while I'm lurking in the shadows at the back of the record shop, Will is squarely out in the open. Which means that he's the first one in the jocks' crosshairs as the door swings shut behind them.

"Holy shit," says the kid at the front. He's tall, a good amount of baby fat still clinging to his cheeks. His jacket practically drowns him. "Is that Zombie Boy?"

Will doesn't say anything. He keeps his gaze pinned to the record bin in front of him, but he's gripping the sides of it, no longer sifting through titles. I've seen that stance before, usually before one of my Hellfire kids gets dumped into a trash can. He's bracing for impact. And I—

I'm frozen, standing in the shadows, listening to the jocks blunder their way into the store. My fingers are glued to the album I'd just revealed, and I can't seem to tear my eyes away from the cover.

Muddy Waters stares back at me, guitar clutched to his chest. And from some distant past I hear—

One-and-two-and-

"Zombie Boy!" the second jock is saying. "Hey, Zombie Boy!" But Will's not turning around, and that's just working these guys up.

"You deaf?" the first jock demands.

"His ears are full of grave dirt."

"Maybe maggots." The first jock shoves Will's shoulder. The kid staggers, catching himself against the record bin. "You got maggots in your head, Zombie Boy?"

"N-no," Will stammers. He's shaking.

"You need a head shot to take out a zombie," the second jock says. He's got something in his hand, tossing it up and down. A baseball. "Watch this."

He's drawing back his arm to throw, to smack Will right in the bowl cut with a quarter pound of solid rubber and rawhide, and—

Now you're gettin' it, says Mom, dancing me across the carpet.

—this, I suddenly realize, is the end of my particular rope.

"Oh, damn," I say, shoving one hand into my pocket. The other is gripped tight around that Muddy Waters album, which I may never let out of my sight again. I saunter out of the shadows, up the aisle toward the bullies, and relish the unsettled twist on both their faces. "I knew you jocks were stupid, but I thought you at least knew what a baseball diamond looked like. This—" I talk gentle, like they're a couple of dumbass children "—is what grown-ups call a *store*. What you're looking for is *outside*." The jocks are still closed in around Will, but it's me they're glaring at now, and I count that as forward momentum. "I'll give you a couple hints, okay? Think . . . sky. Clouds. Big ol' trees— those are the wood things, with the leaves and the branches."

"You friends with this freak, Zombie Boy?" the first jock asks.

Freak. The word smacks me between my eyes, and I wait for the sting to come. But it's just a muted echo that ripples through me, without the heated anger that typically follows.

To hell with what they think. I hear Wayne's voice in the back of my head, clear as the bell over the record shop door. And for the first time, those words seep into my bones. They're injected into my bloodstream. They light me up from the inside.

I grin. It's manic. Or maybe that's not the right way to say it. It's *fiendish*, with an edge that actually makes these assholes take a step back. Will is watching me from between their shoulders, his eyes huge.

"You want to throw that thing at someone?" I say. "Throw it at me."

They just look at me.

"*Throw it.*" I spread my arms at my sides, making the target as big as possible. "Head shots work on freaks too, right?"

"You're insane," the second jock says, but his knuckles tighten around the baseball. A muted pang runs through me, somewhere beneath all this new fiery bravado. These kids are on the baseball team. They must know Paige's brother, which means he'll hear about this sooner or later. And if he tells Paige about her freak friend in the record shop—

"All talk and no action," I say, mostly to stop that line of thought in its tracks. "The life of disappointment your girl-friend must lead—"

He drills the ball, right into my chest, and I double over, the wind knocked out of me. But I'm electric now, hellfire still buzzing in my veins, so I catch myself on the record bin and smirk up into the jocks' scarlet-furious faces. "Not making a case for yourself, big boy."

"You *freak*—" His fist winds back again, ready to fly—

"*Hey.*"

I hadn't heard the clacking of beads as Jerry emerged from the back of the shop. He's standing there now, clattering strings swinging behind him. Jonathan hovers at his shoulder, a Smiths album clutched in both hands. He looks about two breaths away from sprinting across the shop to wrap his brother in a shock blanket or something.

"It'll take me five seconds to walk over to that phone." Jerry points to the chunky off-white phone on the front desk. "If you're not out of here by the time I get there, then you get to listen while I call the cops."

There's no countdown as he starts pacing toward the desk,

but he doesn't need one. The two jocks exchange clench-jawed looks before the second one shakes his head. "Whatever," he mutters. Then he's turning, heaving the door open with enough force to shake the wall. His friend follows a step behind, an acid glare at me his only goodbye.

I'm not sure if I was included in Jerry's threat, but I don't leave. I'm too busy trying to will air back into my lungs. And when Jerry reaches his stool, he just settles back down onto it with a groan, flipping his magazine open to some random page. He doesn't reach for the phone.

Jonathan, meanwhile, has swooped in on Will like a mother hen. "Are you okay?" he's asking, patting at his brother's hair, his shoulders, his arms.

"Fine."

"You sure?"

Will ignores his hovering. He's looking past his brother, toward me. "Thanks," he says.

I manage to haul myself back upright. Breathing is finally coming a little easier. "Those guys are assholes. They're not worth listening to."

"What were they saying?" Jonathan glares daggers toward the door. "Was it—"

"It's not just them!" It bursts out of Will, like it's been building up since forever. "It's everybody! They look at me like I'm a *freak*—"

"Hey," I say. *Jesus,* my side hurts. That baby jock had a better arm on him than I'd anticipated. "To hell with what they think."

Will's big eyes are shiny with tears. "But—"

"I mean it," I say. "They can call you whatever they want. That doesn't mean a single thing about you. It just means something about them. At the end of the day, you're the only person who knows who you are." I smirk. "Besides. Zombie Boy? As far as nicknames go, that one's metal as shit."

There's a line between Will's brows. He's chewing this over.

He'll be chewing it over for a while—it's not the kind of thing a person absorbs the first time around. Nobody knows that better than I do. And in the meantime—

"You play D and D?" I ask.

A tiny smile ticks up one corner of Will's mouth. "How could you tell?"

As though it's not written all over him. "When you get to high school, you should check out Hellfire Club. I think you might like it."

"Yeah?"

"I think you'll fit right in."

"We should get home," Jonathan cuts in. He's watching me warily, like he's trying to suss out an ulterior motive. "Mom's back from work soon." Wrapping an arm around his brother's shoulders, he starts to steer Will toward the door.

"It was nice to meet you!" Will says from beneath Jonathan's armpit.

"You too, Zombie Boy." And then, because there's no time to start a new business enterprise like the present, "Oh, Byers, hang on a second." Jonathan wheels back toward me, a questioning eyebrow raised. I drop my voice, glancing back to make sure Jerry's not paying attention. "You smoke?"

Jonathan looks too appalled for someone with that haircut. "No, dude, I don't touch that shit."

"Let me know if that changes."

He just shakes his head. A moment later, both Byers boys are hustling down the street outside. I watch them through the window until they're out of sight.

To hell with what they think. It had felt right coming out of my mouth. It feels right sitting in my chest now. *You're the only person who knows who you are.*

And for the first time in my life, I think I've got an idea of who that might be.

Chapter Thirty-Seven

"Mr. Munson." Janice's gaze is sharp behind the thick lenses of her tortoiseshell glasses. The chain hanging from the arms jingles as she looks up at me. Her long purple fingernails never stop scratching as she works through an endless stack of paperwork. "I thought you were no longer gracing our halls with your presence."

"That was the plan, Janice." I lean my elbow on the desk and give her my best Al Munson smile. "But the thought of going another day without a glimpse of your gorgeous face was simply too much to bear."

"Mhm." *Scritch-scritch* goes her pen on the paper. Her lips are stuck in an unimpressed pout.

"I knew you missed me too. Would you do us both a favor and order up your finest reenrollment paperwork?"

Janice doesn't say anything, and her pen, incredibly, does not even falter as she reaches into some unseen filing cabinet and whips out a sheaf of forms. I intercept them before she can smack them down on the desk.

"You're a doll," I say. "Now one last question—"

"I'm very busy."

"I can see that, which is why this is a quick one. Is Principal Higgins in?" She doesn't answer, but her eyes do flick to the side—in the direction of Higgins's office. And that's enough information for me. "*Swell.*" I sidle around her desk, sauntering in the direction of the principal's closed door.

"He's in a meeting—"

I can feel that electricity rising within me again, buzzing in my bones. "I'm sure he's got time for me," I say, not breaking stride. "After all, it would be rude for me to visit and not say hi."

YOUR PRINCIPAL, declares the sign taped smack-dab in the center of the door I'd come to hate so fiercely over the last four years. I give it a tap with my middle finger.

"Knock-knock," I singsong as I slide the door inward. "How's my favorite small-town tyrant doing this afternoon?"

Higgins's "meeting" has apparently pulled a disappearing act, because I catch him tossing some dubious-looking paperback mystery novel into the corner. "What the f—" he yelps, cutting himself off before he lets slip any interesting four-letter words. When he sees me, his ruddy face dips even further into scarlet. "*Munson.*"

"*Jeremy.*" I echo his gravelly, poisonous tone for the simple pleasure of increasing his blood pressure.

"I'm not sure if you're aware, but dropouts are not welcome on school grounds," Higgins says. "What you're doing right now counts as trespassing."

"Good thing I'm not a dropout, then." I wave the stack of paperwork and watch the fury take him even further under.

"No."

"Oh, yes."

"*No.* You're out. You're gone."

I wander toward him, sidling around to his side of the desk so that he has to look up at me. "Do you know something I don't?"

"We don't allow felons to enroll—"

"How many times do I have to tell you? I'm not a felon. You can ask Chief Hopper. My record is as squeaky-clean as they come."

"For *fuck's sake.*" Higgins lurches to his feet, and for a second I actually think he's going to come after me. "Don't you understand? Nobody wants you here."

I think about Gareth and the dejection in his eyes when he thought he didn't have Hellfire anymore. I think about little Will Byers, cowering between the record bins in Main Street Vinyl. I think about my uncle waiting for me, hat in hand, in the Hawkins police station.

"Maybe," I say. *Maybe not.*

"Then why the *hell* do you want to come back?"

"Lots of reasons. Top of the list? Hellfire Club."

Higgins's eyes narrow. "We had an understanding, Munson. It's not too late for me to send a concerned letter to the admissions department at NYU. Miss Ecker's place there is far from secure." The blatant threat to Ronnie's future sends a surge of white-hot anger coursing through me, but I batten it back behind my smile. "Not to mention," Higgins continues, "that even if this was of no concern to you and you wanted to carry on with your *club* anyway, there are no sponsors willing or available to take you on. *Hellfire is dead.*"

"We have a sponsor."

A cruel sneer twists Higgins's mouth. "Not on this campus, you don't."

"We have a sponsor," I repeat. "And it's someone you respect. Someone you admire." I lean back against his desk. "And I haven't had the chance to thank him yet. So *thank you*, Principal Higgins, for agreeing to sponsor Hellfire Club here at Hawkins High."

He gapes at me. "You've really lost it, if you think—"

"Ah, shit." I shake my head. "I was hoping to—what did you call it? Appeal to your better nature? But I can tell you're not following. Okay." I reach down and slide open the top drawer of his desk. "Let's try this in a language you'll understand."

Sure enough, just as it had when Higgins deployed Stan's letter on me all those weeks ago, a bright blue pill bottle rolls into view. I pick it up and hold it at eye level so that both Higgins and I can get a good, long look.

"What do you think all those concerned PTA busybodies would do," I say, calm and curious, "if they knew the high school principal was popping bennies just to get through the day?"

For once in his life, Higgins says nothing. He just stares, at me, at the pill bottle, his eyes huge in his pallid face. "You starting to catch my drift?" I ask. And the jerky nod he gives me in response fills me to the brim with pleasure. "Good," I say. "Because I don't want much. I'm not asking you to mess with my grades or my GPA or anything. Just sign off on Hellfire. And keep in mind that, if you don't?" I shake the bottle. "All those pearl-clutchers in the town hall meetings and the church pews are gonna learn about this. *Then* your supply is going to dry up. And I don't know about you, but that doesn't sound very fun to me, does it?"

Higgins's mouth is opening and closing like a beached fish. "This is blackmail," he manages to get out.

"It looked so fun when you did it," I say. "I wanted to give it a try." I slip the pill bottle back into the drawer and close it again. "You asked why I want to come back, *sir*. I want to come back because you didn't think I could." I give him a little wave. "Toodle-oo, sponsor. I'll see you in September."

He's still staring after me as I head back toward the front desk. "Thanks, Janice," I chirp as I pass her. She doesn't have a chance to reply, because there's a bellowed *"Janice!"* tearing from Higgins's open door, and she's on her feet, scrambling after him.

I laugh. I'm still laughing as I push out of the office and into the hallway. I laugh until the weight of what I have to do next settles in my chest and shuts me up. And then I just shove my hands into my jacket pockets and trudge through the last-day-of-school crush of Hawkins students, ignoring the whispers and glares that follow me as I go.

I head straight for Mrs. Debbs's first-floor social studies classroom, the last refuge for Hellfire at Hawkins. The door is shut when I arrive, but it doesn't take a keen ear to pick up Dougie's voice as it filters through the flimsy plywood.

"It, uh. Shoots you with its spikes. Three times!"

"Are you kidding?!" That's Jeff, sounding uncharacteristically pissed. "Dude, I'm, like, fifty feet away!"

"—and then it's gonna close in to *bite you*," Dougie plows on, talking even louder to be heard over Jeff's protests. "For—twenty-two points of damage. Well?"

"Well what? I'm down, man. I'm—"

I swing the door open. "Sounds like things are going well in here."

Five faces turn toward me, all wearing varying degrees of mistrust. They range from conditionally-happy-to-see-me (Jeff) to if-I-could-I-would-fireball-you-where-you-stand (Gareth).

Ronnie's face is impassive. There's not even a flicker of surprise in her eyes.

I clear my throat. "Long time, huh?"

"Good to see you, Eddie," Jeff says. It's cautious.

"Thought you'd be in California by now," Dougie glowers. "With your *girlfriend*."

"You don't get rid of me that easily. Nah," I wave my re-enrollment paperwork in the air, "I'm not finished with this place just yet."

The sight of the forms runs through the group like the ripples before a tsunami, the tide drawing back. "Are you gonna run Hellfire next year?" Jeff asks, then deflates as soon as he catches the edge of Dougie's acid glare. "Not that—I mean, Dougie's been great, but—"

"I . . . guess that's up to all of you." I force myself to meet each of their eyes in turn, but I save Ronnie's stony gaze for last. "I know I let you down. I—walked out on you, and I didn't even bother saying goodbye. At the time, I thought I was doing the right thing—" Ronnie's eyes narrow, just a millimeter, and it spurs me into "—but that doesn't matter, because I was wrong." I take a breath. "California . . . it's not happening."

"Because you shot a cop?" Jeff asks.

I blink. "What? Is that what people are saying?!"

"Yes," says Dougie.

"No," says Jeff.

"Some people *are* saying that," argues Dougie.

"Some people are saying it was your dad." That's Gareth. He's not looking at me, keeping his gaze pinned to the pad of paper in front of him, but his voice is clear and steady enough. "But the chief's been shutting it down pretty hard. It hasn't gotten a lot of traction."

"Okay, um. Cool." I'm gonna have to process that some other time. "What I wanted to say was: I'm sorry. I shouldn't have disappeared. I owe you all more than that. I owe Hellfire more than that."

"Easy to be sorry when it's all blown up in your face." It's the first thing Ronnie's said since I walked in the door, and I feel her words like a blast of Arctic wind.

"I know," I tell her. "I'm sorry anyway."

"Higgins says he's gonna shut this club down next year," says Gareth. His eyes flick up to me, and in that split second, I catch a glimpse of the rattled kid who'd thought his life would end right alongside Illian the Unvanquished's.

"He's had a surprising change of heart." And then, because cockiness alone can't take me across the finish line, I drop the grin. "No matter what happens, you are my party. My adventurers. And I hope you can forgive me. I—I want to make a promise. I will never, ever abandon this group or anybody in it, ever again." The next breath I take has a shake to it, one that I fight down. "So what do you say? You got room in your club for one more?"

There's a silent beat where everyone mostly just shoots significant looks at one another, long enough for me to start feeling my pulse throbbing in my teeth.

Jeff is the first one to break, a relieved grin spreading across his face like he's been trying to hold it back. "It's your club, man."

"It's not his club—" Dougie huffs.

"You're not even going to *be* here next year, Dougie," Jeff says. "I say yes. Eddie's back in."

"Fine," Dougie says. He flops back in his chair, arms crossed across his stomach, but I can see the smile pulling at the corners of his mouth.

I turn to Gareth. "Freshman?" I say, and then—"Gareth?"

He glances back down at the table—at the dwarf sketched in his notebook. "If you want to stay," he says slowly, "you should be able to stay."

Ronnie says nothing. She just nods, her chin dipping once. And that's enough for me, for now. It's got to be.

"Shit," Dougie hisses. "It's four-fifteen. Debbs wanted us out of here fifteen minutes ago."

Pretty short amount of time for a Hellfire session. Dougie must not have done a good enough job cleaning the chalkboards. But since truce has been so recently and delicately called, I don't say any of that out loud. I just stand back and take in the familiar sight of Hawkins High's resident freaks shoving their belongings away and filing out the door. And then—

It's just me and Ronnie.

I brace myself for another unending silence. But she takes pity on me, like she always has. "You've been staying with your uncle," she says, folding her arms over her stomach.

I nod. "Dad left."

"I'm surprised you didn't go with him."

I just shake my head. "I should have come by."

"Since you moved back into the trailer park?"

"Since before. I mean, I tried, but—shit. Ronnie, I'm sorry."

She tilts her head to the side. "You've been saying that a lot."

"I know," I say. Ten minutes ago, I was rubbing Principal Higgins's nose in my existence, and now all I want to do is curl up and disappear. "And you don't have to believe me, but I just needed to say it. I got so used to feeling like nobody was on my side, I forgot that somebody was. You believed I was worth something—me, Eddie Munson. Not some . . . rock star dream or Satanist demon. *Me.* And I'm probably really, really dumb for taking so long to put these pieces together, but I realize now—"

"Oh, God, don't say you're in love with me—"

I laugh. I can't help it. "I was gonna say—I realize how important it is to have that person in your life. Someone who's got your back, who'll let you know when you're screwing up. Who'll help you watch out for the big bad wolves."

"But I can't keep doing that, Eddie. You made it pretty clear you didn't want me to."

Not forgiven yet. "I'll always want you to. But you've been looking after me for long enough. It's my turn on wolf duty. My turn to watch over the lost little sheep."

"So you're just gonna go toe-to-toe with Higgins forever?"

"Let's not go overboard," I say. "He'll have to let me graduate sometime. And I'm not gonna get out of his face until he does." I fiddle with the hem of my jacket. "I can't let him be right about me. I'm not going to. No matter how long it takes."

Ronnie nods. *"Good."*

Her ferocity is bracing. Finally—*finally* I hazard a smile. "So," I say. "Do you . . . need a ride?"

There's still no answering smile from Ronnie. She just considers me for an excruciating moment, and I resist the impulse to squirm. After a long silence, she cocks her head. "Last time, right?"

It's the sadness in her eyes that punches the breath out of my lungs. "I—"

"Hey, freak!"

My head whips around at the shout. It came from the hallway behind me, and I'm striding over to peer out the open door before I realize what I'm doing. When I'd made my way to Mrs. Debbs's class, the halls had been crammed with kids sprinting for the front doors and the freedom of summer. Now there are only a few stragglers left, clearing out the unspeakable depths of their lockers or chatting in knots as they plan the first blow-out rager of the season.

My first instinct is to look around for Tommy H. But it's one of his goons I find instead, that guy who might be named Cooper or Colin or whatever, towering over a greasy-haired kid in jeans that are two inches too short for him.

"He's not in Hellfire," Ronnie mutters, somewhere behind me.

I shove my hands into my jacket pockets, to hide my clenched fists. "I know."

"You don't have to do anything."

"Yeah."

Ronnie clears her throat. "You know what? I actually biked today." I glance back at her, and finally catch a glimpse of her evasive smile. "I'm good on that ride."

"You sure?" I ask, but what I mean is, *Is this it?*

Her sad little smile deepens. "Gareth plays the drums. He's actually pretty good." But what she means is, *Goodbye.* She gives me a little punch to the shoulder in the same place she always does, and I realize that in the weeks since I decided to go it alone, the bruise has faded. "And Eddie—you don't have to be a clean-cut Clark Kent to be Superman, you know."

I catch her hand. Squeeze it once. Then—

"Hey there, fellas!" My sneakers squeak against the linoleum as I saunter into the hallway. "I heard you were looking for me!"

And maybe Chief Hopper's been doing a pretty good job at quashing those rumors after all, because only about half these guys take a nervous half step back at my approach. The rest of them—maybe-Colin included—just do what they do best and channel their confusion into angry glares. "Why the hell would I be looking for *you?*"

The greasy kid is smart enough to shuffle back as I step forward. Once he's past me, I hear the thump of his feet as he breaks into a sprint. And then it's just me and the big bad wolf, and my smile is wide enough to make Al Munson proud.

"Because you wanted a freak, sweetheart," I say. "Congratulations. You found the biggest one in Hawkins."

Acknowledgments

Thank you, thank you, from the bottom of my heart, to . . .

The team at Penguin Random House, and especially to Gabriella Muñoz, for guiding me through this whirlwind process and for always being ready to ask, "But wouldn't it hurt more if you did *this* . . . ?"

My agent, John Cusick, who helped open a door into publishing that I don't think I'll ever want to close.

The Fellowship (yeah, I said it): Matt, Ross, Curtis, Paul, and Kate. You all had some hand in Eddie's creation, and I count myself lucky to have been there in the room with you for it. And Matt and Ross—thanks all over again for letting me on this crazy ride.

The teams at Netflix and Upside Down Pictures, for giving me the chance to tell this story.

Joe Quinn, for breathing life into everybody's favorite misfit.

My family—Mom, Dad, Willa, and Nick, for being the reason I do what I do and being the reason I *get* to do what I do. I love you all.

And finally, thank you to everybody out there who has ever been an Eddie Munson, been saved by an Eddie Munson, or loved an Eddie Munson. You're not alone.

About the Author

CAITLIN SCHNEIDERHAN is a TV writer and novelist, whose work can be seen on Netflix's hit show *Stranger Things*. She hatched from a cocoon of Terry Pratchett novels when she was thirteen years old, and her love of fun, genre-focused storytelling runs deep. Originally hailing from Silver Spring, Maryland, Caitlin now resides in Los Angeles. She still has a full shelf of Terry Pratchett paperbacks.

—— About the Type ——

This book was set in Aster, a typeface designed in 1958 by Francesco Simoncini (d. 1967). Aster is a round, legible face of even weight and was planned by the designer for the text setting of newspapers and books.